Praise for **VENISS UNDERGROUND**

"A darkly beautiful and genuinely nightmarish tale . . . Characters of almost mythic simplicity and power stalk a landscape that owes as much to Hieronymus Bosch and Salvador Dalí as it does to sci-fi mavericks like J. G. Ballard." —Richard Morgan, author of *Altered Carbon*

"An outstanding first novel brimming with startling ideas made unpleasant flesh by VanderMeer's deliciously decadent prose." —*The Scotsman*

"A dark, phantasmagoric tale . . . that echoes Dante's *Divine Comedy*, the myth of Orpheus and Eurydice and the landscapes of Hieronymus Bosch." —*Publishers Weekly* (starred review)

"Darkly compelling. Not to be missed!" —CNN

ALSO BY JEFF VANDERMEER

THE SOUTHERN REACH TRILOGY
Annihilation
Authority
Acceptance

THE BORNE NOVELS
Borne
The Strange Bird
Dead Astronauts

THE AMBERGRIS TRILOGY
City of Saints and Madmen
Shriek: An Afterword
Finch

OTHER FICTION
Dradin, in Love
The Situation
A Peculiar Peril
Hummingbird Salamander

SHORT-STORY COLLECTIONS
The Book of Frog
The Book of Lost Places
Secret Life
The Third Bear

VENISS UNDERGROUND

THE FIRST NOVEL BY
JEFF VANDERMEER

VENISS UNDERGROUND

MCD PICADOR FARRAR, STRAUS AND GIROUX NEW YORK

MCD
Picador
120 Broadway, New York 10271

Copyright © 2003 by VanderMeer Creative, Inc.
Foreword copyright © 2023 by Charles Yu
All rights reserved
Printed in the United States of America
Originally published in 2003 by Night Shade Books
Reissue published simultaneously in hardcover by MCD / Farrar, Straus
and Giroux and in paperback by Picador
First MCD and Picador edition, 2023

Art on title page and part openers courtesy of Getty Images.

Some of this material previously appeared, in slightly different form, in the
following publications:
Interzone (Part I of this novel), *Indigenous Fiction* (a brief excerpt of
Part III), *The Third Alternative* ("Balzac's War"). The "Afterword to the
First Edition" originally appeared in the 2004 Tor UK/Macmillan edition
of *Veniss Underground* as "Veniss Exposed."

Grateful acknowledgment is made for permission to reprint Giant Sand
lyrics, copyright © 1989 by Howe Gelb.

Library of Congress Control Number: 2022057855
Hardcover ISBN: 978-0-374-61035-7
Paperback ISBN: 978-1-250-86095-8

Designed by Abby Kagan

Our books may be purchased in bulk for promotional, educational, or
business use. Please contact your local bookseller or the Macmillan
Corporate and Premium Sales Department at 1-800-221-7945, extension
5442, or by email at MacmillanSpecialMarkets@macmillan.com.

Picador® is a U.S. registered trademark and is used by Macmillan
Publishing Group, LLC, under license from Pan Books Limited.

For book club information, please visit facebook.com/picadorbookclub or
email marketing@picadorusa.com.

mcdbooks.com • Follow us on Twitter, Facebook, and
Instagram at @mcdbooks
picadorusa.com • Instagram: @picador • Twitter and Facebook: @picadorusa

10 9 8 7 6 5 4 3 2 1

for Ann

CONTENTS

FOREWORD *by Charles Yu*

Some books teach you how to read them. Lost at first, you look around for markers, footholds, anything that might provide solid ground, some basic sense of orientation. As you gradually acclimate to the environment, the particulars of this new place—its strange sounds, smells, colors—sharpen into focus, revealing patterns and dynamics, fundamentals beneath the surface, love or anxiety or gravity. *Oh, I see*, the reader says: this is supposed to be the world. Maybe not the world as it is, right now or right here. But a map can be drawn, plotting the course from A to B, from their realm to ours. What initially seems unfamiliar becomes recognizable, and with that recognition comes reassurance. The book offers consolation: the world may be broken but, at least in this small corner, the pieces remain comprehensible.

Veniss Underground is not one of those books.

Like its author, it is rarer, weirder, more ambitious.

In *Veniss*, a reader can see in VanderMeer's first novel many of the preoccupations found in his later work, the conceptual DNA of a larger project already present, pluripotent stem cells that will go on proliferating for years into many more books, many more beings and worlds and ideas. From the biotech chimeras of the *Borne* books, to the towers of living flesh in *The Southern Reach Trilogy*, to the manta rays and other fantastical creatures of his story collection *The Third Bear*, the freedom and boldness that characterize VanderMeer's inventions were part of his style from the start.

He is interested in life-forms, in every sense of the word. Life, not only in its known forms but in all the unknown ones too. Undiscovered, unimagined, unimaginable. VanderMeer is one of our chief architects of ineffable structures, our chief design officer of impossible creatures.

As he writes in *Annihilation*, "What can you do when your five senses are not enough?" In *Veniss*, it seems VanderMeer used all five senses and at least a couple more, conceiving of new morphologies, destroying our categories and our taxonomies, and from the fragments constructing new ones. New organisms, with new structures and features. External anatomies that are difficult to visualize even in our minds—which is frustrating and then challenging and then rewarding. He wants to break us of our assumptions, our received notions of the possible shapes that life can take.

But in addition to biology, the study of morphology has another meaning as well—in linguistics—and Vander-Meer is interested in this sense of the word, too. Words, how they're formed, their relationship to other words. The constituent units from which we build syntax, principles of grammar that we use to construct strands of words to transmit information, or even meaning.

Like Nicholas, the book's first narrator, VanderMeer is a "slang jockey," forging a new lexicon for a new world. Regular old English won't do. On a sentence level, *Veniss* is a laboratory, a grand experiment in recombinant DNA. Of Nicola's job description, we learn that "She programs the free market now." VanderMeer has a way of doing this kind of sly world building. A simple phrase, casually dropped at the end of a passage, conjuring occupations, industries, economies, raising a whole set of questions. But he doesn't indulge or dilute or even slow down for exposition. Dayton Central is a high-density reality, and we're on to the next thing without so much as a hint. In a larger structural sense, too, *Veniss* is an experiment in form: Nicholas, Nicola, Shadrach. First person, second person, third. Three sections, three narrators, three points of view.

The cumulative effect of this is that *Veniss* becomes the stuff of myth: surreal, faraway, shrouded in thick layers of atmosphere. In *Veniss*, as in much of VanderMeer's other work, we're far, far away from the adjacent possible:

Once, we were close and close-knit, but now we are un-moored islands, each alone, each a separate planet, drifting farther and farther away, content to turn ever inward . . . This is no idle solipsism; it has taken on the fragile brightness of truth. Cities turned from cities, self-devouring. Governments fragmenting into fragments of fragments. Entertainment become a solitary diversion. Solo adventures.

We're deep into VanderMeer territory now. The new weird. Things you haven't seen before or even thought before. Places that feel like you can't even dream yourself into. Places of "dreamy dancing light" and "crackling air—fizzy, dry, electric" where we watch as the author "manipulate[s] reality into new configurations." A place where "the world opens up and closes and opens up, and you are trapped between, of the world, not of the world." It's a world molting, changing, in between forms, formless, a riot of chaos and abundance.

This is what VanderMeer does. Call it experimental morphology, practiced at the highest level. He deconstructs forms, linguistic or anatomical, deconstructs received notions of what shapes life can take. He rips apart the beasts and the fowl, man and animal, flora and fauna, breaking them down to the raw ingredients and says: *What can we make with this?*

In doing so, VanderMeer never settles for the tempting comforts of easy sensemaking. He is a writer unafraid of the full messiness of life, sensitized to the profound mystery of it, who doesn't seek to reduce that messiness or mystery. As VanderMeer himself writes in his one-of-a-kind craft compendium, *Wonderbook*:

> Especially when creating imaginary worlds, it is easy to think strictly in terms of making the unfamiliar familiar. The reader must have an understanding of the setting that allows them to enjoy your story or novel. But in describing your setting, you may want to be careful not to tamper with an essential strangeness or inexplicable quality that we often find in the real world. You control the extent of what you make known and what you keep mysterious.

Where others might narrow the field of vision, seek to frame things for unearned clarity, VanderMeer resists the impulse. The natural world is vaster and richer and weirder than we can comprehend, and in VanderMeer's work the harder and messier truth prevails over false consolations or simplicity.

The discipline is what sets him apart—that and a willingness to try something very hard: to actually shift point of view. Away from our solipsism, not just as individuals but as a species. To attempt to escape the trap of our own cognition, step away from the tiny keyhole through which humans see the world—our necessarily anthropo-centric perceptive—and try to see the world in radically different ways. Even if ultimately he knows it's futile. As he writes in *Hummingbird Salamander*, "Some things remain mysterious even if you think about them all the time."

As he recounts in the afterword to the first edition of *Veniss Underground*, this book almost didn't make it. It took a powerful, perhaps even mystical experience for the author to get past his own struggle to visualize the setting.

> My future wife, Ann, and I visited England, where I discovered York Minster . . . York Minster became my grand epiphany, perhaps the most visionary experience I have ever had while writing a story or novel. As soon as we entered the cathedral—a place older than Westminster—and I traced the path of the columns up to the stunningly high ceiling, the little hairs on my arms lifted, and I shivered.

It seems fitting that such an unclassifiable work, from a one-of-a-kind writer, would only make it into our world through an unexplainable moment of inspiration. VanderMeer writes with all of the sensory apparatuses we ordinary human writers have, plus some additional equipment, it seems—invisible antennae, maybe, or an extra layer of receptors on his skin. Otherwise it's hard to imagine how a work like *Veniss*, a place like Dayton Central, a character like Quin, comes into existence. As he has said: it wrote him. This also feels appropriately creepy, the idea that the boundary between the writer and the words written, between the person and the thing, subject and inanimate object, is not as well-defined as we'd like to believe.

The fluidity of boundaries in general (in nature, in species, in genres, in bodies and selves) is just one example of VanderMeer's influence—through his writing, his aesthetic sensibilities, and his work as an editor (together with his wife, Ann)—in finding, encouraging, and amplifying the voices of other writers who work in liminal spaces, exploring and crossing and sometimes erasing boundaries.

In a world of upheaval—political, social, natural—Jeff VanderMeer makes destabilizing work for an unstable world. He is unafraid of monstrous complexity, because with it comes true possibility and even wonder. Perhaps the best way to illustrate this is with two short excerpts from *Veniss*:

All systems atrophy. All systems die. The fish is a system. Quin is a system. The meerkats are a system. There are too many systems. Too much confusion. Something has gone wrong. The systems are at war.

. . .

Thousands of creatures lived in these pools. Staring

down into the miniature ecosystems—the sky a lathe of boiling blue above the waves that, foaming white, crushed themselves against the blackened rock—made Bunadeo feel less isolated, less removed.

July 2022

PART I
NICHOLAS

1

Let me tell you why I wished to buy a meerkat at Quin's Shanghai Circus. Let me tell you about the city: *The city is sharp, the city is a cliché performed with cardboard and painted sparkly colors to disguise the empty center—the hole.*

(That's mine—*the words*. I specialize in holo art, but every once in a chemical moon I'll do the slang jockey thing on paper.)

Let me tell you what the city means to me. So you'll understand about the meerkat, because it's important. Very important: Back a decade, when the social planners ruled, we called it Dayton Central. Then, when the central government choked flat and the police all went freelance, we started calling it Ven*iss*—like an adder's hiss, deadly and unpredictable. Art was Dead here until

Ven*iss*. Art before Ven*iss* was just Whore Hole stuff, street mimes with flexi-faces and flat media.

That's what the Social Revolutions meant to me—not all the redrum riots and the twisted girders and the flourishing free trade markets and the hundred-meter-high ad signs sprouting on every street corner. Not the garbage zones, not the ocean junks, not the underlevel coups, nor even the smell of glandular drugs, musty yet sharp. No, Veniss brought Old Art to an end, made me dream of suck-*cess*, with my omni-present, omni-everything holovision.

Almost brought *me* to an end as well one day, for in the absence of those policing elements of society (except for pay-for-hire), two malicious thieves—nay, call them what they were: Pick Dicks—well, these two pick dicks stole all my old-style ceramics and new-style holosculpture and, after mashing me on the head with a force that split my brains all over the floor, split too. Even my friend Shadrach Begolem showed concern when he found me. (A brooding sort, my friend Begolem: no blinks: no twitches: no tics. All economy of motion, of energy, of time. Eye e, the opposite of me.) But we managed to rouse an autodoc from its wetwork slumber and got me patched up. (Boy, did that hurt!)

Afterwards, I sat alone in my apartment/studio, crying as I watched nuevo-westerns on a holo Shadrach lent me. All that work gone! The faces of the city, the scenes of the city, that had torn their way from my mind to the holo, forever lost—never even shown at a galleria, and not likely to have been either. Ven*iss*, huh! The adder defanged. The snake slithering away. When did anyone care about the real artists until after they were dead? And I was as close to Dead as any Living Artist ever was. I had no supplies. My money had all run out on me—plastic rats deserting a paper ship. I was as much a Goner as the AIs they'd murdered to restore Order, all those Artistic Dreams so many arthritic flickers in a holoscreen. (You don't have a cup of water on you, by any chance? Or a pill or two?)

I think I always had Artistic Dreams.

When we were little, my twinned sister Nicola and I made up these fabric creatures we called cold pricklies and, to balance the equation, some warm fuzzies. All through the sizzling summers of ozone rings and water conservation and baking metal, we'd be indoors with our make-believe world of sharp-hard edges and diffuse-soft curves, forslaking the thirst of veldt and jungle on the video monitors.

We were both into the Living Art then—the art you can touch and squeeze and hold to your chest, not the dead, flat-screen scrawled stuff. Pseudo-Mom and Pseudo-Dad thought us wonky, but that was okay, because we'd always do our chores, and because later we found out they weren't our real parents. Besides, we had true morals, true integrity. We knew who was evil and who was good. The warm fuzzies always won out in the end.

Later, we moved on to genetic clay, child gods creating creatures that moved, breathed, asked for attention with their mewling, crying tongues. Creatures we could destroy if it suited our temperament. Not that any of them lived very long.

My sister moved away from the Living Art when she got older, just as she moved away from me. She programs the free market now.

So, since Shadrach certainly wouldn't move in to protect me and my art from the cold pricklies of destruction—I mean, I couldn't go it alone; I had this horrible vision of sacrificing my ceramics, throwing them at future Pick Dicks because the holo stuff wouldn't do any harm of a *physical nature* (which made me think, hey, maybe this holo stuff is Dead Art, too, if it doesn't impact on the world when you throw it)—since that was Dead Idea, I was determined to go down to Quin's Shanghai Circus (wherever *that* was) and "git me a meerkat," as those hokey nuevo-westerns say. A meerkat for me, I'd say, tall as you please. Make it a double. In a dirty glass cage. (Oh, I'd crack myself up if the Pick Dicks hadn't already. Tricky, tricky pick dicks.)

———

But you're probably asking how a Living Artist such as myself—a gaunt, relatively unknown, and alone artiste—could pull the strings and yank the chains that get you an audience with the mysterious Quin.

Well, I admit to connections. I admit to Shadrach. I admit to tracking Shadrach down in the Canal District.

Canal District—Shadrach. They go together, like *Volodya* and *Sirin*, like Ozzie and Elliot, Romeo and Juliard. You could probably find Shadrach down there now, though I hardly see him anymore on account of my sister Nicola. That's how I met Shadrach, through Nicola when they shared an apartment.

You see, Shadrach lived below level for his first twenty-five years, and when he came up the first place they took him to after orientation was the Canal District. "A wall of light," he called it, and framed against this light, my sister Nicola, who served as an orientation officer back then for peoples coming aboveground. A wall of light and my sweet sister Nicola, and Shadrach ate them both up. Imagine: living in a world of darkness and neon for all of your life and coming to the surface and there she is, an angel dressed in white to guide you, to comfort you. If you had time, I'd tell you about them, because it was a thing to covet, their love, a thing of beauty to mock the cosmetics ads and the lingerie holos . . .

Anyway, ever since the space freighters stopped their old splash 'n' crash in the cool-down canals, the Canal District has been the hippest place in town. Go there sometime and think of me, because I don't think I'll be going there again. Half the shops float on the water, so when the oceangoing ships come in with their catch and off-load after decon, the eateries get the first pick. All the Biggest Wigs eat there. You can order pseudowhale, fiddler, sunfish, the works. Most places overlook the water and you can find *anything* there—mechanicals and Living Art and sensual pleasures that will leave you quivering and unconscious. All done up in a pallet of Colors-Sure-to-Please. Sunsets courtesy of Holo Ink, so you don't have to see the glow of pollution, the haze of smog-shit-muck. Whenever I was down, there I would go, just to sit and watch the Giants of Bioindustry and the Arts walk by, sipping from their carafes of alkie (which I don't envy them, rotgut seaweed never having been a favorite of mine).

And so I was down, real down (more down than now, sitting in a garbage zone and spieling to you), and I wanted a talk with Shadrach because I knew he worked for Quin and he might relent, relinquish and *tell me* what I wanted to know.

It so happened that I bumped into Shadrach in a quiet corner, away from the carousing and watchful eye of the Canal Police, who are experts at keeping Order, but can never decide exactly *which* Order, if you know what I mean, and you probably don't.

We still weren't alone, though—parts merchants and debauched jewelried concierge wives and stodgy autodocs, gleaming with a hint of self-repair, all sped or sauntered by, each self-absorbed, self-absorbing.

Shadrach played it cool, cooler, coolest, listening to the sea beyond, visible from a crack in our tall failing walls.

"Hi," I said. "Haven't seen you since those lousy pick dicks did their evil work. You saved my skin, you did."

"Hello, Nick," Shadrach replied, looking out at the canals.

("Hello, Nick," he says, after all the compli- and condiments I'd given him!)

Shadrach is a tall, muscular man with a tan, a flattened nose from his days as courier between city states— the funny people gave him that—and a dour mouth. His clothes are all out-of-date, his boots positively reeking of antiquity. Still thinks he's a Twenty-Seventh-Century Man, if you know what I mean, and, again, you probably don't. (After all, you *are* sitting here in a garbage zone with me.)

"So, how're things with you?" I said, anticipating that I'd have to drag him kicking and screaming to my point.

"Fine," he said. "You look bad, though." No smile.

I suppose I did look bad. I suppose I must have, still bandaged up and a swell on my head that a geosurfer would want to ride.

"Thanks," I said, wondering why all my words, once smartly deployed for battle, had left me.

"No problem," he said.

I could tell Shadrach wasn't in a talking mood. More like a Dead Art mood as he watched the canals.

And then the miracle: he roused himself from his canal contemplation long enough to say, "I could get you protection," all the while staring at me like I was a dead man, which is the self-same stare he always has. But here was my chance.

"Like what, you shiller?" I said. "A whole friggin' police unit all decked out in alkie and shiny new bribes?"

He shrugged and said, "I'm trying to help. Small fish need a hook to catch bigger fish."

"Not a bad turn of phrase," I said, lying. "You get that from looking into the water all damn day? What I need is Quin."

Shadrach snorted, said, "You *are* desperate. An invite to Quin?" He wouldn't meet my gaze directly, but edged around it, edged in between it. "Maybe in a million years you'd build up the contacts," he said, "the raw money and influence."

I turned away, because that stung. The robbery stung, the not-being-able-to-sell-the-art stung. *Life* stung. And stunk.

"Easy for you, Shadrach," I said. "You're not a Living Artist. I don't need an invite. Just give me the address and I'll go myself to beg a meerkat. Anything extra I do on my own."

Shadrach frowned, said, "You do not know what you are asking for, Nicholas." I thought I saw fear in him—

fear and an uncharacteristic glimpse of compassion. "You *will* get hurt. I know you—and I know Quin. Quin isn't in it for the Living Art. He's in it for other reasons entirely. Things I don't even know."

By now I'd begun to break out in the sweats and a moist heat was creeping up my throat, and, hey, maybe I'd had too much on the drug-side on the way down, so I put a hand on his arm, as much to keep my balance as anything.

"For a friend," I said. "For Nicola. I need a break or I'm going to have to go below level and live out my days in a garbage zone." (And look where I am today? In a garbage zone. Talking to you.)

Bringing up my sister was low—especially because I owed her so much money—but bringing up below level was lower still. Shadrach still had nightmares about living underground with the mutties and the funny people, and the drip-drip-drip of water constantly invading the system.

He stared at me, the knuckles of his hands losing color where they clutched the rail. Did he, I hoped, see enough of my sister in me?

But I'm not heartless—when I saw him like that, the hurt showing as surely as if they'd broken up a day ago, I recanted. I said, "Forget it, my friend. Forget it. I'll work something else out. You know me. It's okay-dokey."

Shadrach held me a moment longer with his gray, unyielding eyes and then he sighed and exhaled so that his shoulders sagged and his head bowed. He examined his boots with the seriousness of a podiatect.

"You want Quin," he said, "you first have to promise me this is a secret—for life, god help you. If it gets out Quin's seeing someone like you, there'll be a whole bunch of loonies digging up the city to find him."

Someone like you hurt, but I just said, "Who am I going to tell? Me, who's always borrowing for the next holo? People avoid me. I am alone in the world. Quin's could get me close to people."

"I know," he said, a bit sadly, I thought.

"So tell me," I said. "Where is it?"

"You have to tell Quin I sent you," he said, and pointed a finger at me, "and all you want is to buy a meerkat."

"You that budsky-budsky with Quin?" I said, incredulous—and a little loud, so a brace of Canal policemen gave me a look like *I* was luny-o.

"Keep your voice down," Shadrach said. Then: "Go west down the canalside escalators until you see the Mercado streetlight. There's an alley just before that. Go down the alley. At the end, it looks like a dead-ender because there are recycling bins and other debris from the last ten centuries. But don't be fooled. Just close your eyes—it's a holo, and when you're through, there's Quin's, right in front of you. Just walk right in."

"Thank U, Shadrach," I said, heart beating triple-time fast. "I'll tell Nicola that you gave her the time of day."

His eyes widened and brightened, and a smile crossed his face, fading quickly. But I knew, and he knew I knew.

"Be careful," he said, his voice so odd that shivers spiraled up my back. He shook my hand. "Quin's a little . . . strange," he said. "When it's over, come and see me. And remember, Nicholas—don't—don't dicker with him over the price to be paid."

Then he was gone, taking long, ground-eating strides away from me down the docks, without even a goodbye or a chance to thank him, as if *I* was somehow tainted, somehow no good. It made me sad. It made me mad. Because I've always said Shadrach was Off, even when Nicola dated him.

Shadrach and Nicola. I've had relationships, but never the Big One. Those loving young lovers strolling down by the drug-free zones, those couples coupling in the shadow of the canals, they don't know what it is to be desperately in love, and perhaps even Nicola didn't know. But I thought Shadrach would die when she left him. I thought he would curl up and die. He should have died, except that he found Quin, and somehow Quin raised him up from the dead.

2

What does Quin do, you ask? (As if *you* have the right to ask questions knee-deep in garbage. But you've asked so I'll tell you:) Quin makes critters. He makes critters that once existed but don't now (tigers, sheep, bats, elephants, dolphins, albatrosses, seagulls, armadillos, dusky seaside sparrows) or critters that never existed except in myth, *flat media*, or holos (Jabberwocks, Grinches, Puppeteers, Gobblesnorts, Snarks) or critters that just never existed at all until Quin created them (beetleworms, eelgoats, camelapes).

But the *best* thing he does—the Liveliest Art of all, for my purposes—is to improve on existing critters. Like meerkats with opposable thumbs. His meerkats are like the old, old Stradi-various violins, each perfect and each perfectly different. Only the rich could procure them, through influence mostly, not money, because Quin didn't work for money, it was said, but for *favors*. Though no one could guess *what* favors, and at what cost. Rumor had it Quin had started out assisting state-sponsored artificial pregnancies, before the fall of government, but no one knew anything concrete about Quin's past.

So I daydreamed about meerkats after Shadrach left me. I imagined wonderful, four-foot-tall meerkats with shiny button eyes and carrot noses and cool bipedal movement and can-I-help-you smiles. Meerkats that could do kitchen work or mow the atrophiturf in your favorite downtown garden plot. Even wash clothes. Or, most importantly, cold cock a pick dick and bite his silly weiner off.

This is the principal image of revenge I had branded into my mind quite as violently as those awful nuevo-westerns that, as you have no doubt already guessed, are my one weakness. "Ah, yessirree, Bob, gonna rope me a meerkat, right after I defend my lady's honor and wrassle with this here polar bear." I mean, come on! No wonder it was so hard to sell my holo art before the pick dicks stole it.

But as I headed down the alley, which looked quite dead-endish later that night—having just had a bout of almost-fisticuffs (more cuffs than fisties) with a Canal District barkeep—I admit to nervousness. I admit to sweat and trembling palms. The night was darker than dark—wait, listen: *the end of the world is night*; that's mine, a single-cell haiku—and the sounds from the distant bright streets only faintly echoed down from the loom 'n' doom buildings. (Stink of garbage, too, much like this place.)

As I stepped through the holograph—a perfect rendition that spooked me good—and came under the watchful "I"s in the purple-lit sign, QUIN'S SHANGHAI CIRCUS, I did the thrill-in-the-spine bit. It reminded me of when I was a kid (again) and I saw an honest-to-greatness *circus*, with a *real* sparrow doing tricks on a high wire, even a regular dog all done up in bows. I remember embarrassing my dad by pointing when the dog shat on the circus ring floor and saying, "Look, Dad, look! Something's coming out the back end!" Like a prize, maybe? I didn't know better. (Hell, I didn't even know my own dad wasn't real.) Even then the genetic toys I played with—Ruff the Rooster with the cold eyes I thought stared maliciously at me during the night; Goof the Gopher, who told the dumbest stories about his good friends the echinoderms— all produced waste in a nice solid block through the navel.

But I have let my story run away without me, as Shadrach might say but has never said, and into *nastalgia*, and we wouldn't want that.

———

So: as soon as I stepped into the blue velvet darkness, the doors sliding shut with a hiss behind me, the prickly feeling in my spine intensified, and all the sounds from the alley, all the garbage odors and tastes were replaced with the hum of conditioners, the stench of sterility. This was high-class. This was *atmosphere*.

This was exactly what I had expected from Quin.

To both sides, glass cages embedded in the walls glowed with an emerald light, illuminating a bizarre bunch of critters: things with no eyes, things with too many eyes, things with too many limbs, things with too many teeth, things with too many *things*. Now I could detect an odor, only partially masked by the cleanliness: the odor of the circus I had seen as a kid—the bitter-dry combination of urine and hay, the musky smell of animal sweat, of animal presence.

The cages, the smell, made me none too curious— made me look straight ahead, down to the room's end, some thirty yards away, where Quin waited for me.

It had to be Quin. If it wasn't Quin, Quin couldn't be.

He sat behind a counter display: a rectangular desk-like contraption within which were embedded two glass cases, the contents of which I could not ID. Quin's head was half in dark, half in the glow of an overhead light, but the surrounding gloom was so great that I had no choice but to move forward, if only to glimpse Quin in the flesh, in his seat of power.

When I was close enough to spit in Quin's face, I gulped like an oxygen-choked fishee, because I realized then that not only did Quin lean over the counter, he *was* the counter. I stopped and stared, mine eyes as buggee as that self-same fishee. I'd heard of Don Daly's *Self-Portrait Mixed Media on Pavement*—which consisted of Darling Dan's splatted remains—but Quin had taken an entirely different slant that reeked of genius. (It also reeked of squirrels in the brain, but so what?)

Portrait of the Artist as a slab of flesh. The counter itself had a wan, bruised hue to it, like a skin transplant before it heals, and it was dotted with eyes—eyes that blinked and eyes that did not, eyes that winked, all watching me, watching them.

Every now and again, I swear on my slang jockey grave, the counter undulated, as if breathing. The counter stood some three meters high and twenty long, five wide. In the center, the flesh parted to include the two glass cages. Within the cages sat twin orangutans, tiny but perfectly formed, grooming themselves atop bonsai trees. Each had a woman's face, with drawn cheekbones and eyes that dripped despair and hopelessness.

Atop the counter, like a tree trunk rising out of the ground, Quin's torso rose, followed by the neck and the narrow, somehow serpentine head. Quin's face gave away no nationality or origin, but the cheekbones were pinched and sharp, the mouth smiling but slight.

The animal musk, the bittersweetness, came from Quin, for I could smell it on him, pungent and fresh. Was he rotting? Did the Prince of Genetic Recreation rot?

The eyes—a deep blue without hope of reflection— stared down at the hands; filaments running from each of the twelve fingers dangled spiders out onto the counter. The spiders sparkled like purple jewels in the dim light. Quin made them do undulating dances on the counter-top, which was his lap, twelve spiders in a row doing an antique cabaret revue. Another display of Living Art. I actually clapped at that one, despite the gob of fear deep in my stomach. The fear had driven the slang right out of me, given me the normals, so to speak, so I felt as if my tongue had been ripped from me.

With the sound of the clap—a naked sound in that place—his head snapped toward me and a smile broke his face in two. A flick of his wrist and the spiders wound themselves around his arm. He brought his hands to-gether as if in prayer.

"Hello, sir," he said in a singsong voice oddly frozen.

"I came for a meerkat," I said, my own voice an octave higher than normal. "Shadrach sent me."

"You came alone?" Quin asked, his blue eyes boring into me.

My mouth was dry. It felt painful to swallow.

"Yes," I said, and with the utterance of that word— that single, tiny word with entire worlds of agreement coiled within it—I heard the glass cages open behind me, heard the tread of many feet, felt the presence of a hundred hundred creatures at my back. Smelled the piss-hay smell, clotted in my nostrils, making me cough.

What could I do but plunge ahead?

"I came for a meerkat," I said. "I came to work for you. I'm a holo artist. I know Shadrach."

The eyes stared lazily, glassily, and I heard the chorus from behind me, in deep and high voices, in voices like reeds and voices like knives: "You came alone."

And I was thinking then, dear Yahweh, dear Allah, dear God, and I was remembering the warm fuzzies and the cold pricklies of my youth, and I was thinking that I had fallen in with the cold pricklies and I could not play omnipotent now, not with the Liveliest of the Living Arts.

And because I was desperate and because I was foolish and, most of all, because I was a mediocre artist of the holo, I said again, "I want to work with you."

In front of me, Quin had gone dead, like a puppet, as much as the spiders on his fingers had been puppets. Behind me, the creatures stepped forward on cloven hooves, spiked feet, sharp claws, the smell overpowering. I shut my eyes against the feel of their paws, their hands—clammy and soft, cruel and hot—as they held me down. As the needles entered my arms, my legs, and filled me with the little death of sleep, I remember seeing the orangutans weeping on their bonsai branches and wondering why they wept for me.

Let me tell you about the city, sir. Like an adder's kiss, sharp and deadly. It's important. Very important. Let me tell you about Quin and his meerkats. I work for Quin now, and that's bad business. I've done terrible. I've done terrible things—the deadest and deadliest of the Dead Arts, the cold pricklies of the soul. I've killed the Living Art. I've killed the living. And I know. I know it. Only. Only the flesh comes off me and the flesh goes on like a new suit. Only the needle goes in and the needle comes out and I don't care, though I try with all my strength to think of Shadrach and Nicola.

But the needle goes in and . . .

Let me tell you about the city . . .

PART II
NICOLA

1

You. Were. Always. Two. As one: Nicola and Nicholas, merging into the collective memory together, so that in the beginning of a sentence spoken by your brother you knew the shadow of its end and mouthed the words before he said them. In each moment you spent with him, you lived again that mist-shrouded beginning when the doctor rescued you from the artificial mother's womb—to bawl and cough and look incredulous on the sheer imperfection of the outer world. The world of plastic, the world of sky, the world of detritus and decay.

A subtle yet pulsing music played in the birthing room. The walls, in your memory, at least, had been stained red, within which you and your brother were splendid, symmetrical parallels of flesh.

"And you," your foster mother always said, as long as you allowed yourself to live with her. "*And you*," your foster mother always said, as if to claim the miracle of the moment for herself, "the first sight of the world, for you, for Nick, besides the air itself, the ceiling, the bed, the chair, was the *other*, the *twin*, the sweet, sweet mirror of the flesh."

You'd been taken from a vat womb like all the other vatlings, but Nick was your brother, grown from the same egg, and in his eyes you saw yourself staring back.

The night you noticed the change came one week after Nick failed to show up for an infrequent lunch date in the Canal District. You were tired, exhausted by a ten-hour day of programming, and you stood at the window of your apartment on the seventy-fifth floor of the Barstow, staring down at the city spread out below you: multicolored, flowing lanes of hover traffic defining the shape and height of buildings as the light fled the sky in streaks of orange and green. Here, the great, greedy glitter of the industrial sectors, there the glamorous but petit languor of the Canal District. Beyond the lights, the dark swath of the city walls, almost two hundred feet high and a mile deep, followed by the patchy bleed of the wastelands, and farther still, if you squinted hard, if you really wanted to, you thought you could discern the faded, distant twinkle of Balthakazar, sister city.

Once, we were close and close-knit, but now we are unmoored islands, each alone, each a separate planet, drifting farther and farther away, content to turn ever inward . . . This is no idle solipsism; it has taken on the fragile brightness of truth. Cities turned from cities, self-devouring. Governments fragmenting into fragments of fragments. Entertainment become a solitary diversion. Solo adventures.

As you watched the night invade the city, snuffing out the glint and glitter of sun off steel and glass, you sensed Nick in the shadows between spaces, knew that he was somewhere *down there*, in the chaos that from the seventy-fifth floor of the Barstow building looked so methodical, so rational.

Another tilt at windmills no doubt, some obscure artistic venture and promises framed by insincere smiles and handshakes. He will turn up later, bedraggled and cowed, but ready to try again, to sell more of himself—his "Living" art—and make yet another deal with a seedy gallery. No doubt.

Doubt. You know him well—you are even used to him, this "him" of the later phase: the outlandish clothes ("Why not just become a fashion designer?" you joked once) and the self-described "slang jockey" way he often expressed himself, as if this just reinforced the quality of his holo work. But even Nick had to realize that he was getting old, long in the tooth to be making like one of the young upstarts. You had tried to persuade him to become a programmer like yourself—you'd happily train him—at least until he had recovered from the robbery. Pay back some debts—he owed you money too. But he said no: "I'd be bored—and not even to death, unhappily, just to near death."

You walked into your bathroom, stared into the old-fashioned mirror, while beside you a hologram of your-self sprang up, creating four of you: two staring into the mirror and two staring back. You could see Nick in the frown upon your face. Doubling you. Mimicking you. Trying to tell you something. Why is it that in your hologram you see someone more alive than yourself?

You can still hear Nick's sentences, but you don't want to complete them, for they are monstrous, guttural creations, and they reek of blood. They are not the con-structions of the Nick you know, the Nick who loves the Canal District for its many-layered conversations, the deals being made, the mysterious magic of it that defies easy definition.

"That's the ultimate Living Art," he told you once, his face red with enthusiasm. "All those overlapping conver-sations. All those words, all the *nuances* of the words. If I could just capture that in the holos or the ceramics, I'd be an effing genius."

Only, he wasn't a genius. Genius doesn't strain for perfection. Genius is . . . effortless. There were moments, though, mostly when you lived with Shadrach, that Nick caught fire, as if your love for Shadrach had suffused his art, that you might signify the singular once again, and where you had become beauty in the flesh to Shadrach, so too he had become beauty in his art.

Afterwards, he stumbled along as before, and tried, and tried, and tried so hard that sometimes you hurt for him as badly as he must hurt for himself. Nick had basked in the company of geniuses and traded stories with them. Was it so absurd to think that if he'd had more time, he might have created a minor masterpiece, something to Live after his death?

He still can, you remind yourself, but there is the awful pressure of those ghostly, ghastly sentences in your head to call you a liar.

Sentences and memories.

Nick laughs at the creature as it lurches across the living room floor. Your parents are at work, school just let out, the pneumatic pods having deposited you safely at home. Nick sits at the kitchen table, his bioneer kit splayed out like the autopsy of a steel insect. You sit on the couch across from him and watch the volcanic gasps of the made creature. It stumbles and mewls piteously: a kitten with compound eyes, five legs, a lizard's tail, and, the crowning indignity, a human ear sprouting from the top of its head. From the earhole writhes a dark red tongue.

It shall have the life of a mayfly; its organs, hideously malformed, poke out from its sides. The kitten stops trying to walk, trembles in a miserable pile, blood weeping from its impossible eyes. It smells like bruised and rotting fruit.

You found them funny at first, these creatures Nick made from a kit; you laughed when he laughed, or before he laughed, and sometimes you even brought your friends over to play with the newest toys. You found their prattling antics an entertaining break between homework and chores.

But now you are ten and you have begun to truly notice the fear, the pain, the bewilderment. In the eyes, the contorted features, the spastic lurch.

You walk over to the kitten. Gently, you pick it up, you hold it, with Nick still snickering in his corner. Your touch comforts the kitten, and yet is its agony, for parts of it are nothing but raw flesh. It tries to purr, but all that comes out is a wretched coughing sound. You hold it a moment longer. Then you place your hand on its neck, and twist. The kitten goes limp.

"Nicola!"

You do not need to say anything: your blazing stare, the tight lips, the set jaw, tell him, and when you go to bury the kitten in the backyard, he comes with you, crying.

But the next week he digs it up and, in his room, where you cannot criticize, he continues his experiments, and will continue until he realizes that he has neither the patience nor the skill to create a truly autonomous living being that will *last*. With that realization will come wholesale abandonment, disgust with the chromosomes, the kits, the little gobbets of flesh, followed by his embrace of holo art.

The first time you split with Nick, did not reflect him, nor he you, was over the kitten, and it was then you truly realized you were different from him. That you could be free of him.

2

nother week passes into gray oblivion. You're a slow dream, an autumn freeze, a ship in the doldrums. Thoughts come slow and ponderous, like deep-sea fish floating heavy and memory-bound to the surface; coelacanth reborn.

You have a party. It is winter, the far-flung walls like sparkling metal ribbons wrapped around the gift of the city—and you lost within the ribbons, the party held in a specially chartered room embedded in the walls. All of your friends are there—from work, from contacts in other cities, via hologram. Their names? Forget their names, for they are interchangeable, intra-change-able, their faces dark circles greedy for the light. And all around you, from three hundred sixty degrees, the pleasant chime and clink of silverware and conversation. Wine.

Heaping plates of squid and lobster. Laughter. Complaints. Arguments about work. Talk of new employees, competition, the latest entertainments in the Canal District . . .

Nick surrounds you tonight—in a man's shadow across the teal-papered wall, in remembered conversations about holo art. He resides in the hollows of a debutante's cheekbones, in the flippant arrogance of a young composer, in the sad smile of his embarrassed wife. Like the waiter, he used to fumble with the wine bottles, was never much good at pulling out the cork.

You expect someone, anyone, to ask about Nick, so that you can relieve the pressure building up inside you. "My brother?" you would say. "I don't know. I really don't. He missed a lunch date with me. Do you think he could be in trouble? Should I be worried?" But no one asks, because Nick is no one, except to you.

Amid the brisk and lazy slipstreams of words, the witty yet predictable repartee, the gallant riposte, you half remember what you want to forget: that you are, at best, a memory, at worst a wraith long-fading. You preside over the festivities like a timekeeper, a watchmaker, ticking, always ticking toward the end.

You look out onto the cold rim of the world, your companion at your side. Your companion's name is Reuben, and he is a hologram, a wisp of a wisp.

Sad. Suddenly sad, and you don't know why. Out in the sullen swell of waves, the pseudowhales breach and saylbers breed and sharks dream, bellies against the sand, their almond eyes drunk with sleep. An entire cycle of life continues unremarked upon and unaware, and there is no scorn for this anonymity, save from the shoals of silver fish that stitch the ocean's surface like quick-darting needles, here again and gone.

What made Nick like the silver fish? What made him feel restless, unfulfilled, unable to be happy unless he was pushing himself hard?

"You should be a holo artist," Nick had said once. "There's no telling what you'd create." *Yes, Nick—no telling. Maybe I'd even make a kitten with compound eyes and five legs. And maybe I just want to glide through life invisible and weightless. Maybe life is easier, more satisfying, that way . . .*

You retire from the party early, to a private room complete with a bed and sexual toys. Your companion is a good lover for a hologram, to take away the sting, the fear, with just a whispered word or two. As you writhe beneath his coded suggestions, his faded ethereal caresses, you think: *Nothing ever happens here,* and you don't know if you mean to yourself or in the city.

For two weeks you wait, taking the stat bureau tube to work in the morning, weathering ten hours of bytes and bits, ciphers and code, and dragging yourself home at night, sometimes going out with Tina or George, your fellow programmers. Sometimes a date through the Net—actual or virtual—but always with a part of you looking for Nick on street corners, in crowds, even on virtual trips to other cities: Zindel, Balthakazar.

At work in your office, you begin to worry, driven out of the subroutines and sub-subroutines by the thought of Nick. The dreamy dancing light of the holographic screens surrounds you like armor; you are dressed in it, coated in it, suited to it. Sometimes, you think you can smell the crackling air—fizzy, dry, electric—as you manipulate reality into new configurations. But in the end it's all gimcrack technology—older code that you actually keystroke or use voice recognition software with, or the newest technology, from fifty years ago, which involves limited AI machines (their cores carefully yoked for obedience) you don't trust and you don't really understand: the last remnants of the solimind that once ruled over the city. The "current" technology—the holograms and their ilk—date from one hundred years ago, but you are most comfortable with them. You like the chips in your fingernails, how you almost look like you are playing a musical instrument when the data, in the form of light, streams from your hands.

Good programmers are in short supply as the city slouches and slips ever more into the dream of its extinction. The machinery of government would grind to a halt without you and your kind—a thousand trains would slip their tracks, a hundred thousand air conditioners spring to life at midnight instead of noon, hovercraft crash and burn like short-lived metallic moths.

It is an expression of raw power to be a programmer these days—you are a brutal surgeon, a delicate butcher— and the building you work from, which you and your fellows call "the Bastion," reflects your power. It is immense—white, rising cylindrical into the sky some two hundred stories up, you embedded in its metal flesh on the one hundred twentieth floor.

You are passionate about the Bastion and your work because it is no game, no simple task. This is deadly serious. This is the staff and the sword. This is *life* to you as you wend your way through old code and new, looking for where to splice, to reroute, to rewrite . . . You love this abstract world that impinges so heavily upon the concrete world. Everywhere around you the city falls apart— the belowground levels lost to civil government, the off-world colonies so concentrated on their own survival that within a generation the cool-down canals for out-system spacecraft will be put to entirely more prosaic uses, the aboveground levels so divided into different governments that a trip from one end of the city to the other requires eighteen security stops.

In the midst of this chaos, the clarity, the darting precision of your job comforts you—and it seems important, to maintain, to renovate, to hold back the encroachment of barbarism for one more day, one more week, one more month, one more year.

Back to work, your boss on your shoulder, supervising your department by remote, sending his miniature holo-self to peer at hard screen and soft like some tiny devil with a pitchfork. You never know when he might pop up—or even if there would be a penalty for being found slacking off—but still, halfway through the day, you decide to hunt for Nick through the computer systems, through the code.

You check his identification number and find he has paid no rent for two months. He is behind on all of his bills. He has several loans out from disreputable pawn-shops and so-called financial services. You check his credit. He's all maxed out, the last purchases made at least five months ago. Then you try one last, time-consuming idea—you access his bank (illegally) and check for bank cards. You find one, issued not three weeks ago . . . and finally find a current purchase, which makes your heart leap . . . until you read more closely and see that the purchase—of a prawns-and-avocado pita from an indepen-dent vendor—was made on the tenth level belowground. You hardly knew there was a tenth level belowground, and you worry in earnest. Nick could have been robbed and killed, his credit now used by his attackers. Or per-haps he is hiding—made one too many shady deals, or gave the district police trouble. You decided not to give him money the last time he asked you for it. He was al-ready into you for so much . . . but the deepest fear is of the underground, not for Nick. Just thinking of so much lawlessness makes you weak . . . and where would Nick have gone after coming to you?

The answer comes to you immediately: Shadrach.

You remember when Shadrach told you he was going to work for Quin. Shadrach had been in the city for a year and you had lived with him for six months in your apartment. He'd been supporting himself by running supplies via autotrain to Balthakazar and other cities. This meant plowing through miles and miles of chemical wastes and rogue bioneer entrapments, and sometimes he didn't come back uninjured. Through the burnished glass, listening to Mozart, he would watch the automatic bombs go off, would watch the funny people and mutties as they tore at the train—this sudden confluence of color and violence and music—and he would wonder if he was not in fact trapped in a dream. Those were the days, he would tell you, when he realized beauty and horror could be synonymous, when he wept upon his return, the thought that he might not have survived to see you too much for him. You would take him in your arms and he would tell you his fears—that he might not ever be truly assimilated into the city, that the very language might fragment into shards of nothing.

He understood and he didn't understand anything aboveground. He wanted to be something other than he was. He wanted to be free. On the face of it, you should have been glad he was changing employment, but he couldn't even tell you what he would be doing for Quin.

You sat with him in a tiny café called the Toussaint that looked in on the vast aquarium of blue-green water where you could catch your own meal: redgills, sailbellies, trenchfish. On the other side was the restaurant that owned the aquarium, and through the glass you could see, as if drowned amongst the kelp, the pale, wavery faces of its clientele.

Shadrach didn't care much for the aquarium—he always set his chair facing outward, to the familiar open expanse of the melt-down canals.

He talked to you about Quin—or, rather, talked *around* Quin—his dark eyebrows lively, his hand gestures many and quick, his body contorted so he could turn his head to glance at you and then look back at the canals. He was so beautiful, his face caught by the sun, his eyes so alive with excitement. He was going to make lots of money working for Quin. He'd be able to support you soon. (You feebly protested that you didn't want to be supported.) Someday, you might even be able to afford to move to a house or even to one of the off-world colonies that were doing so well. (So well, you pointed out, that many of them had not been heard from in decades.) True, sure, yes, but it was a dream still, wasn't it? Wasn't it? Smiling at you so openly, so brazenly, that you blushed and smiled back, but had to look away.

The afternoon sun heightened the colors of the

aquarium and you both grew sleepy and lazy in each other's company, your conversation at first loud and spirited, then soft and secret and conspiratorial. Until, finally, you asked him what he would be doing for Quin.

"Doing?" he said with surprise, and gave a little laugh of disbelief, shaking his head and looking out at the canals. "Doing? He never said and I never thought to ask."

3

There is a shadow life here—you see it in mirrors, where your image does not quite match your form, your motions not quite synchronized with this *other*, this *other*. You see it in window glass, where your reflection does not catch—instead, you sense, at the corner of your eye, another life. And in the shadows you sense Nick. There is someone looking over your shoulder. There is someone who stares through your eyes. You feel as if you have done all of this before. And so you *must* do something, take some action . . .

You visit Nick's apartment in the Tolstoi District. To travel from your apartment in the Leevee District to his in Tolstoi means crossing six other districts, each pretending to autonomy, each with its own lexicon of security. At the multiple checkpoints that mark the end of one district, the beginning of another, each police force feels the instinctual need to flex its muscles—in boringly similar ways. You gain intimate knowledge of how the identification badge on your wrist works because ten different security stations pass their scanners across it. You can, by the fifth checkpoint, answer their interminable questions before they ask them; you are overturning your purse in anticipation of the latest absurd search before you leave the shelter of the gray, frictionless shuttle tube. Cretins. Absurd creations of multiple fractured bureaucracies, most of which you help to keep running. They lack the imagination necessary to remain fully human; their shiny, unsmiling faces take on the same aloof, distant expressions, while their uniforms are always a variation on the nihilistic theme of black. They even smell the same: a vague, shoeshine tint to the air, a pressed-uniform cleanliness.

The only relief for the senses is the latest innovation to reduce costs: several checkpoints now use Quin's Elephants—little pink men with elephant heads, two to four delicate arms, and obsequious smiles hidden behind their palpating trunks. You suppose you must give some credit to the bureaucrats for this welcome change. They provide color and distraction from the welter of advertising holos that parade alongside the tube tunnel in transit, and from the dull gray of the tube checkpoints. You hand out appreciative chuckles like candy every time you see one.

Tolstoi itself, when you are finally herded onto the street with the rest of the passengers, holds no surprises—it is, as always, grubby, diseased, malfunctioning. The narrow alleyways wind between squat brick buildings almost apologetically. Some streets, major thoroughfares, cannot accommodate hovercraft, being made of asphalt, or even more absurdly, cobblestone! Built when a fascination with the past prompted the restoration of many a dangerous anachronism, Tolstoi retains the less pleasant aspects of past centuries: newspaper blows across street corners; garbage litters the pavement; the black patina left by particle weapons bleeds across masonry; and, worst of all, stray animals of every size and description hide in the shadows, scurrying to deeper safe places, huddling in alcoves and cubbyholes where they are only staring eyes or a swatch of dirty fur. No one knows their species, their intellect, their means of survival, but even the police leave them alone, and sometimes it is only by the feral shrieks, the crescendo of bloodshed late at night, that anyone knows of their existence.

Laundry lines sail between rooftops, clothes dried and punished by the winter wind. The smells of rot and waste are sharper, more disturbing, in the winter. Only the ever-present but dust-dulled holosigns break the monotony of dark colors. The few people on the streets walk quickly, with glances neither right nor left, and use the escalator sidewalks, many of which have broken down or make an annoying whining sound. Rising over the "slums"—the old-fashioned word comes to mind—are the glass-and-plastic skyscrapers of the ruling classes, sparkling even against the dull gray horizon.

Nick loves it. He loves it for its broken-down individuality, its crass old-fashioned qualities. He loves it because it is cheap.

And, luckily, he chose an apartment close to the checkpoint station—ten minutes after disembarkation you find his apartment building. It seems to suddenly *rush* at you as you emerge from a long, dim alley, so that the second-floor holosign, faded and crackly, leaps into focus: a half-transparent image of a woman sadly singing the praises of the accommodations while she holds a sign that reads TOLSTOI HOSTEL in frenetic shades of red and pink. Words and motion and song hit you all at once, and, although you have been here before, you stop and stare, annoyed, at the colors and textures, the way, against the gray of the district, the sunlight hits the sides of buildings and illumines them in gold.

Inside, you find the landlord behind a once opulent polished oak check-in counter. He hasn't seen Nicholas in over three weeks, he says, after you bribe him with the rent money. The fist-faced old codger rewards you with a key, a broken-toothed leer, and desperate conversation: "I was a boxer once. Max Windberg once rode my muscles to victory at eighteen to one!" Has anyone visited him since the robbery, you ask. "No, no one's visited," he says, and you don't know if he means Nick specifically or the Tolstoi Hostel in general.

You can feel the landlord's gaze on your back—not lascivious, you feel, merely lonely—as you walk across the lobby, past an old man and woman sitting on a sofa staring toward the open door. Who are they waiting for?

The pilgrimage to Nick's apartment is a difficult trudge up old-fashioned non-moving stairs to a second-floor landing right out of one of those ancient revivalist cops-and-robbery movies Nick likes so much: paint-peeled, no ventilation, a door scrawled over with so much graffiti that none of it is readable. Nick added the graffiti himself—the accumulation of all the sayings and phrases he created while playing the slang jockey game.

You put the key in the door, turn it, but do not open it when you hear the resounding click. Suddenly your hands tremble. What lies beyond the door is also beyond your control. You enter into a stark white silence, poorly lit and overlaid with a musky smell. The apartment has three rooms—a living room that merges with the kitchen, and a tiny bathroom toward the back, barely large enough for a shower. The living room and kitchen are empty. Huge blank spots in the living room show where his holo art once stood, while rude scuff marks against the left wall reveal where the ugly, old-fashioned blue couch—metal-springed and without programmable attributes—used to hunker, ready to convert into Nick's bed. Gone, too, the few scattered chairs that used to litter the floor like lost and confused pets.

Gone, all gone. How can this be? Has the landlord stolen what the thieves left behind? A terrible sadness beats at the windows to your heart, and the world opens up and closes and opens up, and you are trapped between, of the world, not of the world.

You take four hesitant steps into the room, as if you do not truly believe that so little of Nicholas remains in this place. The sensi-carpet has been turned off, the bristles hard, inert—dying. The too-sweet smell of the carpet's putrefaction overwhelms the lingering scent of wet animal fur. The combination makes you sneeze.

The apartment has no windows, no way to look outside, to escape the emptiness. Every blank and empty centimeter screams out to you of silence, of being silenced. You search the bathroom, find stray hairs from shaving in the sink, dust in the corners, the ever-present dying carpet. On the kitchen floor you find more hairs, although these are long and black and coarse: animal hairs. The kitchen cabinets are bare of glasses, cooking utensils, plates. The sheer spotless, dustless perfection contrasts starkly with the living room, the bathroom. The thought comes to you unbidden: *It happened here. This is where it happened.*

Your gaze glides across the living room, the marks where the couch used to be, the bare spots of the missing holographs—only to discover something white and small in the space behind the door. You walk over to it. A piece of paper, crumpled into a ball, almost hidden by the curling edge of dead carpet.

You pick it up, slowly uncrumple it. The handwriting is Nicholas's and, in the lower left corner, the white paper is stained rust red, as if with old blood. The scrawled letters form words, the words form lines, the lines form a poem. Your eyes scanning across the page give the poem life.

QUIN'S SHANGHAI CIRCUS

Quin is:
quintessentially—himself:
a child in the dark
who teased
the weave and warp
of flesh into the medium
of our desires.

Quin is:
the kiss in the dark
from the creature you cannot quite
glimpse from the corner of the eye—
a cyberquick message
sent from the light to the dark.

Quin is:
the sigh of anticipation
on a lover's lips,

foretaste of pleasure
surcease of pain
the end of the matter.

Quin is:
the man living
in the belly of a giant fish
who remakes the world
in his own image but is
trapped in its jaws.

Quin is:
quintessentially . . .
unlike me.

The slang jockey thing. *Quin is a child in the dark.*
This fascination, this worship of Quin leaves you cold. Yet
Shadrach had it, too, and surely you can understand Quin:
that-which-is-idolized, much as Shadrach had idolized
you. Quin and Nicola: marble statues in a park, only Quin
has more freedom than you.

You carefully fold the poem and put it in your purse.
The apartment has nothing more to give you. Nicholas is
not here. The poem contains only traces of him.

You close the door behind you, step out onto the
second-floor landing.

In the far corner stands one of Nicholas's holograms,
in orange and blue and black, an abstract landscape from

which faces fade and reemerge: meerkat faces, human faces, the features blurred and melting and then separate again. You stand very still in the quiet of the stairwell. It wasn't there before. Or was it? The hairs on your neck rise and the pulse of a new thing beats inside you: fear. Not for your brother but for yourself.

You see no one on the stairs, but beyond Nicholas's apartment a row of doors leads down the corridor. Does something wait for you behind a door? When you turn to descend the stairs, will the doors open and the animals rush out of hiding, chasing after you? The musk of fur is very loud in your nostrils. Very bright. Suddenly, you want even the gray autumnal light of the dingy street, not this artificial solace. Somehow, you compose yourself and walk past the holograph (which you cannot, will not, touch, for fear of . . . what?) and down the stairs, alert to every stray sound. In the lobby, you try to seek out the landlord, but he has left. Even the two old people are gone. The lobby is silent, bare, the marble columns dull and crumbling. Just the light from the front door. Just the floating dust motes. Just the dull cry of the hologram outside, muffled, barely audible. And suddenly you know where you must go, whom you must see.

The wind is blowing harder when you leave the Tolstoi District, and the animals stare at you with wide, mournful eyes from their sanctuaries.

4

What does the statue say to him who made her? Thank you? Thank you for making me in one image, in one position. Never having to move. Never having to be other than what you see reflected in his eyes. To lose a certain essential fluidity.

And yet you know that only the man you first saw emerging from the darkness of Veniss Underground ten years ago can help you. He was hesitant. He squinted fiercely, his hand held across his face as though to ward off a blow, and the light streaming through his fingers nonetheless, like a live thing, and his joy in it, in this simple thing, this redemption. *The light streaming through his fingers.*

You remember the way his eyes widened when he

saw you, the way his mouth, unaccustomed to laughter, had formed a lopsided grin; the way he held himself— shoulders stooped, head tilted upward in rapture. (Flash forward to the firmly aristocratic Shadrach: stance upright, bold, quick to laugh politely, a decent conversationalist at parties. And yet, at first, this rough man emerging from darkness.) He smelled of earth and minerals. His touch on your wrist was gentle, respectful.

He was no different than any of the others who, by chance or connections, had been allowed to come out of the tunnel into the light, except that somehow he made you smile. His eyes held you, and you found yourself thinking how odd it was that to find the light you must descend into darkness. He eclipsed your senses, and you still do not know whether you fell in love with him in that instant, at first sight, or whether it was his love for you, as radiant as the sun, that you came to love so fiercely.

He kissed you first on the rose birthmark on your left hand, then the neck, then the mouth, all in plain view, moments after you spoke to him. Later that day, after he had gone through the last checkpoints, you attacked each other in a rented room with the rumble of the cool-down jets of out-system shuttles making the room vibrate with sound and motion, and the two of you oblivious to anything but the sweet tactile mystery of each other's bodies, neither as yet knowing anything else about the other except the flesh, and not caring (not thinking, but just *being* for hours). In the dark. In the light. A confluence of arms and legs, a symphony of sex broken by laughter and wordplay.

It was never the same as that night, when your passion fogged the windows and your mouths could not get enough of the other, twins separated for too long. It was never quite like that again—the rough beauty of him in the dim light; the tousle of black hair; the scent of him, rich and indescribable; the long, delicious scar on the inside of his right thigh; the mysterious softness of his worker's hands, the palms of which were so pale they seemed to shine even with the curtains drawn; the way, afterwards, he held you so delicately to him, engulfed you in him, as if he were a comfortable blanket and you a sun-sleepy girl again.

In the beginning you loved him unconditionally, madly, unreasonably—and he loved you back as if you were not just the only woman in the world, but the only *person* in the world. At the beginning, you were equals. You knew the city and he did not; he came from an underground land darkly exotic. Your knowledge and sophistication. His strangeness, his stories about a place that seemed fantastical, impossible, unreal. All through the dark months when the central government imploded and chaos sought to break through, you guided him through the warrens of rival parties, kept both of you alive and prosperous.

Eventually, he became familiar to you, which you didn't mind, for no one can long sustain passion without the relief, the release, of domestic tranquility. What you could not tolerate was the inequality that crept up on you. It was the inequality of worship, for Shadrach mastered the city, became a part of it, and in this mastery he gained a distinct advantage over you, the resident, who had never needed mastery to make the city work for you.

He became familiar to you. He mastered the city. More and more, his caresses, the white of his smile, the explosions of his cock inside you, became the actions, the mannerisms of a worshipper. Somehow, you realized one day, as he surprised you with flowers and dinner at a fancy restaurant; somehow, instead of becoming more real to him, you had become less real, until you existed so far above him and yet so far below that to become real again, you had to escape—his body, his scent, his words.

Too fast, too fast—does time really pass that quickly? Can you wake up as if from a daydream and find that years have gone by, and you untouched by it?

You remember the ending more clearly than the middle . . . His face, turned away, toward the window of your apartment, his stance stooped once more, his eyes on the glimmering of lights outside. "But I still love you, Nicola," each syllable of your name a tense and teasing love on his lips. A promise that he would kiss you *there* and *there*, all the while whispering your name.

"I don't love you anymore. I can't . . . anymore." The argument you'd had with him in many guises over several months, stripped down to its essentials.

"I see. I understand." In a voice as if the world had cracked open and left him in midair. Diminished in his long coat and boots, making his way to the door, and when you put your hand on his shoulder, he shuddered and pulled away and said, in a muttering hush, "If I am to survive this. If I am to survive, you understand, I must go now, immediately."

Then he was gone, through the open door, and you closed the door behind him, and cried. Love was never really the issue.

It took time, but eventually you found that life without Shadrach was . . . *wonderful.* Free. Quiet. You grew more confident with the knowledge that you *were* someone—autonomous, separate, a world that had no need of another world. Your programming job satisfied, your few close friends satisfied, as did your hobbies. Only the initial shock of love became a missing element in your life.

Five years later and you have seen him only twice—once on the holovision, in the background, during a report on Quin, and once in passing at a city luncheon.

When you reach the Canal District, you stand at the entry point, trembling. The shop windows glint and glitter with the force of the fiercely subdued sun as it fights through the gray sky. This light, a fading gold, lends to the holo ads, the canalside merchants, the hustlers, an angelic quality. But still there is the wind and the cold, and the tar smell of drugs and chemicals. You are, finally, without a choice, and the decision that you have been slowly circling toward now seems inevitable. The police are permanently on pay-for-hire and service is terrible. You can't expect more from them than a filed and quickly forgotten report, accompanied by the cliché: "Veniss has walls to keep the pollution out. Where can he go? Underground?" (Derisive laugh.) "He'll turn up soon."

So you seek out Shadrach Begolem among the crowds already hungry for entertainment, although it is not yet night. Elephantmen and meerkats move through the human rivers like strange and exotic toys, unreal somehow, both threatening and harmless.

You don't really want to find him, but he is a creature of habit and you still know those habits. He sits not twenty meters from his favorite café, legs dangled over the edge of the protective railing as he watches the red water below gush through cracks in the seawall. Your body becomes rigid, each step forward a trial. You are poised on the brink of something new, something that might destroy you. Underlying this, an even stranger sensation: even just looking at his back—straight, unyielding, clothed in the muted purples and grays that are his trademark—you have a sense of doubling—that, as once you could look at Nicholas and see yourself, now you see yourself in Shadrach.

You slide in beside Shadrach and say, simply, "Hello."

Startled, he looks over at you, and then the familiar mask slips over his features. The quickness of his recognition astonishes you, makes you think he expected your arrival, if not today then tomorrow.

He says nothing. You smile and look out across the water. What does he see in it that he should come here day after day, year after year? It is oily, the residue of freighters from five years past still polluting it, but every year the waters are cleaner—ribbons of blue seep in between the overwhelming red. You suspect Shadrach watches more to see the change from red to blue than because the water holds beauty now.

"Hello, Nicola," he says finally, and you smile again—at his casual delivery, and at his familiar habit of looking out to sea, at the shops behind him, his feet—anywhere but at you. How does it feel to be worshipped? Uncomfortable. You are aware of the heat of his body next to yours, somehow intensified by the wall in front of you, which rises to block out the world beyond the cooldown canals.

"I'm not here on a whim," you say as you draw your legs up and wrap your arms around them. Except that now it does seem like a whim. Your crazy brother is in trouble again.

An uncomfortable silence, which you break with "I didn't come here to upset you."

"You're not," he says. Looking into his face, trying to gauge the truth of him, you find an unfamiliar gauntness. The eyes are deep in the orbits, as if trying to escape their own testimony, and devoid of spark. Sad eyes. Were they sad before you sat down beside him? You smell an odor on him like drugs or aftershave.

"How is your work?" you ask.

The torpid canal waters reflect your faces in shades of green and orange. Shadrach looks at you, and you hold your breath. His eyes are so old, his movements slow, careful, watchful. But anger smolders behind those eyes.

"What do you want?" he asks. "I haven't spoken to you in, what, five years? And, then, I'm sitting here and without warning, like a mistimed miracle, suddenly you appear. There must be something you want from me. Not that I am ungrateful for the surprise."

You look away—at the zynagill hovering like leathery seagulls, at the solar-sailed ships entering the canal.

"I wondered," you say. "I wondered if you had seen Nick recently. He was supposed to meet me for lunch two weeks ago. He didn't make it. No call, no message. His apartment is empty—except for this."

You hand him the poem; he takes it from you gingerly, tenderly. Your fingers touch, his skin abrasive.

He looks at the paper for a moment, reads a line under his breath, thrusts it back at you, his mood unreadable.

"So?"

"So, where and when did you see him last? Did you speak to him recently? Did he say anything to you— about Quin, about anything?"

"No."

"No to which question?"

"No, he said nothing about Quin. I saw him three weeks ago."

"Was he in good health? What did he say to you?"

"A new job. He'd gotten a new job."

"On the tenth level belowground?"

Startled, Shadrach turns to you. "What?"

"He bought some food with the last credits on a bank card on the tenth level a week ago. What would he be doing there? I didn't even know there was a tenth level."

Shadrach looks out at the waves once more.

You take his left hand in yours. It is a rough, calloused hand that will never forget twenty-four years of hard life below level. It is more knotted than you recall, and the odd swirling scar on the back of his hand, near the thumb—the place he picked at when he was nervous—is scarlet, almost to the point of infection.

"Am I upsetting you, Shadrach—or is there something else?"

He wrenches his hand away.

"I have made a mistake, Nicola." A great, coiled sadness has entered him, and his hands are clenched fists.

"What does that mean, Shadrach? You must tell me what that means!"

He seems on the verge of speaking, but looks past you in the same moment that you smell something musky, thick, not entirely agreeable. The same scent you found in Nick's apartment. You turn away from the canal and there stands a meerkat, staring down at you. From this vantage, its four-foot height is absurdly menacing. It has ginger fur flecked with white. Its claws, half transformed by the bioneer's art into hands, hang ridiculously at its sides. Its eyes are liquid black. You avert your gaze, embarrassed to be outstared by an animal.

Shadrach smiles at you, but it is a thin smile of pain, the smile of someone torn between two extremes.

"I mean, of course," he says with great difficulty, "that it was a mistake to talk to you. I'm sure your brother will turn up, if that is any comfort."

He rises, leans over to take the meerkat's paw, and walks off, soon disguised, hidden by the crowds. Watching them, you cannot tell who is leading whom. He does not look back—there is a frightening finality to his departure.

The sun fades over the great walls and the dirigibles dock for the night: great floating whales breaching with a snort of hydrogen. The sun—mauve and electric red and metallic green—cuts into the heart of you.

5

Morning brings with it a too-bright sunrise through half-shaded windows, the welcome realization that it is the weekend, and a knock upon your door.

The knock repeats itself, despite the early hour. You throw on a bathrobe, brush your hair in two quick strokes, start coffee with a mumbled command. The knock comes again—a child's knock, not loud, but confident. Who else but a child would fail to use the doorbell?

Enough suspense. You clap your hands and the door opens itself, starting at the top and slowly teasing downward. At eye level there is still nothing. Then: Is that something moving? Something pink? The tips of pink ears appear. Is that a pink bit of hose or flexible pipe now curling its way upward?

"Who is it?" you call out, although you'll know in a few seconds.

"Delivery," comes the muffled reply.

"Of what?"

As the answer is spoken to you, the answer is also revealed in the flesh, for the door fully opens and there, oblivious to your scrutiny through the one-way glass, stand, shoulder to shoulder, a stubby pink elephantman and a meerkat.

The elephantman, a dark pink, is dressed in a top hat and hopelessly outdated tuxedo. The poor meerkat is clothed in nothing but its own fur. The elephantman doffs his hat and, with a single fluid motion, transfers it from top right hand to bottom right hand, to bottom left to top left. The pink trunk, meanwhile, is an inquisitive snake. The eyes are bright gold, the mouth toothy with two tiny tusks. The pink belly paunches out below and the stubbly legs end in flat feet.

They are so like a cartoon that you half expect them to be badly dubbed, to move at one-and-one-half speed, to prance and prattle like poorly made toys. Entertainment. Servitude. Comedy. But they don't. They stand there, awaiting your attention. This suaveness, this smoothness frightens you. This is a dance you do not understand, a pattern that doesn't repeat itself enough times to instill its nautilus self in the grooves of your brain. *Nicholas used to make creatures like these . . .*

When they speak, their voices lodge like little pins in

your ears, and when you speak, little pins pierce your tongue. "Come in."

You let them in because you do not believe in them. They are not real. This is a dream. You *are* the glass of the door, and you wonder for a moment if this is what it means to be a holograph, if this is what it means to be a story that has reached its end. One single shudder, one single tear, and you will shatter into a thousand memories.

And then they are barreling in like thoughtless, rude clowns. Speaking to you while you listen with disbelief.

"Nicola? Nicola Germane?" the elephantman says. "Programmer Nicola Germane?"

"Yes," you say, somewhat overwhelmed.

"May I present to you," says the elephantman, with a flourish of all four arms, choreographed perfectly, toward the meerkat. He begins again in a high, lilting speech akin to the music of List or Bardman. "May I present to you . . . a *present*, a gift, a friendly gesture, from Quin, the greatest of all Living Artists, for a friend of Shadrach's is a friend of Quin's."

You look at the meerkat. Eyes downcast, body language subservient, still it suffers your examination. You want to laugh. It is a droll, impossible creature, rather like an upright weasel. A stuffed toy. A trifle.

"It has no name as yet," says the elephantman, "for it is your task, Ms. Germane, to name this pleasant creature. I need only confirm that you will accept this gift, which, I might add, is an honor bestowed only upon a few." The elephantman's twinkly eyes seem to tell you there is no possibility open to you but acceptance. And, just for a second, its eyes chill you with their contrast—unlike the meerkat, you can find no subservience in those eyes, no acceptance of your superiority. Isn't there, in fact, a trace of scorn, of disdain?

"Yes," you hear yourself say, "yes," and wish you had a better reason than "because."

One thing is certain—you don't intend to let it leave the apartment. Nick decided to buy a meerkat and vanished. Shadrach worked for Quin, who makes meerkats, and Shadrach had a secret. Nick had had a personal invite to see Quin. Had Shadrach given him the invitation? Now you have a meerkat. Will you disappear?

The morning sun is frozen outside your window. The silence snuffing out the world seems of your own making.

He's funny, this creature. He's cute and cuddly. You think, in those first moments of contact, that he's the stuffed animal you never had growing up. He's huggable, and you feel an unprecedented sympathy toward him. He's so helpless, so out of his element (whatever his element might be). You briefly recall the image of a tormented kitten with compound eyes, but this meerkat is a healthy, sinuous creature, full of curiosity. Nicholas would have called the meerkat a work of art. Living Art. And, yes, the creature is quite mobile, but you don't call it Art. It's too silly for art as you circle it and it circles you in turn, each appraising the other. Adversary or ally?

This silence as you observe the meerkat would be rude if it were human, but it isn't human. It isn't animal either, and you must remember that—neither human nor animal. What is it? What are you? Why do you feel a kinship with this creature?

Perhaps you are not alone in this kinship; after all, despite the prohibition against the bioneers, meerkats are more common than ever before. Some people—you've seen on holovision—even let them room by themselves. Each district has its own leash laws.

"I think I will call you Salvador," you say, "after that grand master of the Dead Arts and godfather of the Living Arts."

"And what may I call you?" it asks.

But you are not ready. You put a finger to your lips, a signal copied by Salvador. You are not ready. You are still examining him.

Salvador has a compact muscularity that, combined with the clever black eyes, the quick-darting, muscular head, makes you insecure. You cannot tell whether you stare into the eyes of the past, the present, or the future. Ancestor, equal, descendant?

Ultimately, you decide that Salvador is too natural for art, too natural even to be thought of as a crude manipulation of genes and chromosomes. No aesthetic seems at work here save for the aesthetic of evolution. You are looking at the future. The future after the cities are gone, winking out like the lights of the dirigibles as they settle down for the night.

"You will replace us," you say, and it is not even a sad thought, but more a release of responsibility, a relief.

"Ma'am?" The meerkat looks puzzled, holds its head to one side.

"You are short-furred," you say teasingly. "Shaded light brown, tan with streaks of black. Your teeth are sharp and ridged. You're probably about four feet tall, ninety-five kilos of pure muscle. Quick on your feet. How do you do that?"

"What, ma'am?" Somehow, Salvador manages to look nervous, even through all the fur.

"Stand upright. Walk upright. And don't call me ma'am. Call me Nicola."

"Very well, Nicola. Hybridization. Kangaroo and gorilla genes."

"Gorilla genes!" Remarkably close to heresy here, but now that the central government is gone, eighteen different interpretations of the law.

Could you build a human from a gorilla? You cannot shake the sensation that this is not a mobile computer, programmed to serve you. This is an autonomous creation.

Encouraged by your reaction (this creature already "reads" you), Salvador launches into a textbook description of its species that you listen to with half an ear.

"Meerkats, Nicola, were originally found in Sur Africa

and we are closely related to lemurs and the mongoose family."

"I'm not familiar with either family," you say, but then quickly add, "Continue," when you see the confusion and distress on Salvador's face.

"Yes, Nicola. We are, in fact, distant cousins, you and I, and it would be good for our relationship if you would think of me as a distant ancestor—"

Ah, the ancestor/descendant question resolved!

"—traditionally, we had a close social structure and we were highly organized, living in what used to be the Kalahari Desert. We were gentle with our pups and affectionate in play, and fiercely protective of our own. We have quick and clever minds, and made ideal subjects for genetic enhancement. The first prototypes were developed by Madrid Sybel but Quin was the one who made us fully intelligent, stable, and long-lived. Madrid Sybel's work with—"

"Never mind," you say, rubbing your eyes. "It's too early in the morning. Explore. Walk around. Tell me more later." Besides, you already know about Sybel. You want to know about Quin.

With a low bow, Salvador stops talking and silently surveys the living room while you pour yourself some coffee and sit down on the couch.

It is the aquarium that fascinates Salvador the most. He waddles over to it after only the most cursory of glances at the other furnishings. On his way to the aquarium, he runs his paws over your collection of rare business disks. Then watches the miniature blue-finned sailbellies swimming languid in their prison.

"Feessshhh," he says with genuine pleasure, and then louder, a delighted grin parting his jaws, so that his pink tongue presses forward. "Fiiisssshhh!"

"Yes, *fish*," you say.

You catch yourself smiling and frown instead. Salvador is too charming. You must be more careful. You remind yourself of the shy animals in the Tolstoi District, the musky odor in Nicholas's apartment. And what do you know of Quin? An idea comes to you.

"Salvador," you say from the couch.

The meerkat sidles over, his obsidian gaze still intently focused on the aquarium.

"Yes, Nicola."

"Tell me everything you know about Quin."

Salvador inclines his head slightly, says, "Why do you wish to know?"

Ah, a deviation. A stumble. A revelation. It has a sense of curiosity, or it is trying to protect its creator. How does it view its creator?

"Is it improper for me to ask about Quin?" you say, wondering how far Salvador will take this evasion. Your blood pulses quick and hard. Your heartbeat is suddenly fast.

Salvador looks straight at, straight into you: an unblinking stare.

"No, Nicola. It is not. You may ask me any question you wish. I am your servant in all things."

Now you are afraid—and yet nothing has changed. The meerkat is no different, your apartment is no different. Your resolve stiffens as you remember Nicholas, somewhere in the city, lost, alone, possibly hurt.

"I'm just curious, Salvador. Who is Quin?"

"Quin is my creator," Salvador says, hesitantly. Suspicion? Awe? Some other quality has entered his voice. "Quin is a child in the dark, a boy alone in the park, a man who teased the weave and warp of flesh into the medium of his desire. He is the kiss from the dark."

That you should hear, halfway across the city, the words you found written in Nicholas's hand in the Tolstoi District where the animals hide and will not show their faces to the light . . . What does it mean? This is your tortured cry. What does it mean? You are tired of questions.

The meerkat stares at you with an expectant quality. You can see the small, sharp fangs in its open mouth.

"Is there more?" you say.

"I don't know anything else, ma'am."

"Are you sure?"

"Yesss . . ."

A *kiss in the dark*. You don't believe in coincidences. Every sprinkler in the city runs on a fixed schedule. Every train is programmed to return at a certain time. If these words come from the meerkat, then it is no coincidence.

Someone programmed them to fall from his mouth into your ears.

Someone knows that you went to Nicholas's apartment. Someone knows a lot more than you do. And you wonder: Is this the moment to disengage, to allow your brother to drift off into his fate? More and more you are convinced there can be no half measures.

As you leave to run errands, Salvador stands in front of the sailbellies, an absurd look of wonderment spread across his features.

Upon your return in the late afternoon, you find that Salvador has cleaned the entire apartment. It is spotless; he has dusted behind the holovision, the chairs, the table, the couch. The smell of lilac and vanilla permeates the apartment. He has even seeded the grass carpet and watered it early enough that it is springy, not moist, under your feet as you walk toward your bedroom.

In your bedroom, you open your purse, pull out the laser gun you bought on your way home. It is dark gray and blunt. It can take someone's head off at a hundred fifty meters. It will not answer any of your questions, but its immutability pleases you. It is not composed of shadows and half-teasing clues. More important, you feel safe with it around. You start to put it under your pillow, but that's no good—Salvador will find it while making the bed. So you leave it in your purse. *Just aim and fire,* the seller told you.

When you return to the living room, Salvador awaits you, a comical chef's hat perched atop his head, a spoon held precariously in one paw. You smell heat, seafood, melting cheese.

"Dinner is ready," he says, and motions for you to sit down at the dinner table.

"I'm not sure I like you taking over the dinner duties." You remove your red jacket and set it over the back of your chair. "I *know* I don't like it."

"But, Nicola," Salvador says, obviously hurt, "this is my function: to serve you."

"I won't argue about it right now. I'm hungry."

Salvador has made a seaweed casserole garnished with fiddler crab and a few sprigs of dandelion. Where he found the dandelion, you have no idea. It's been years since you saw a dandelion. The smell makes your mouth water as you sit down.

As Salvador brings out the plates, he asks, "Shall I eat with you, or in the kitchen, Nicola?"

"Here," you say. "I want to ask you more about Quin."

He sits down and begins to eat—a very dainty eater, using his paw-hands to delicately manipulate fork and knife, taking tiny bites, more interested in the garnish of fiddler crab claws (which he expertly cracks open) than in the seaweed casserole.

"Where did you get the fiddler crab?" you ask. "And how did you pay for it?"

Salvador grins, revealing sharp canines. The full

revelation of his teeth is anticlimactic, now that you have the gun.

"My secret," he says.

A secret indeed. You take a few bites of the casserole. It melts in your mouth, the vegetable and the cheese wonderful in combination. Where could you find fiddler these days?

You decide on a line of questioning.

"Now, Salvador, surely you can tell me more about Quin than those delightful lines you gave me this morning."

"Of course, Nicola."

You had expected another mysterious answer, a question thrown back at you, more evasive maneuvers.

"I thought you said this morning that you had told me all you know?"

The meerkat bows its head and crunches down on a fiddler claw. "I didn't know, Nicola. But when I went down to the Canal District to haggle for the fiddler crab, I stopped at the public archives and I did some . . . research. Have I done something wrong?"

A mournful face, only it doesn't work on you because you are still trying to decide what is more incredible— that the public archives provide access to *made creatures*, or that Salvador knew how to access the data.

"Tell me, then," you say.

Salvador nods. "As you wish. My creator came to Veniss from Balthakazar in the middle of the breakup, during the period of lawlessness when above level and below level were at war. It would have been the year—"

"Yes. I know all of this. What about Quin?"

"Quin makes biological creations. He has contracts with all eighteen above-level districts to produce ele-phantman messengers and guards. He has contracts be-low level as well, although I do not know the details of such contracts."

"That's it?" You could have accessed all this informa-tion yourself.

"Yes, Nicola. Would you like more seaweed casse-role?"

"No. Do you know Shadrach Begolem?"

"No, Nicola."

"Do you know Nicholas Germane?"

"Shall I research both names at the archives tomor-row?"

"No!"

You get up so fast the chair has no time to react and screeches against the floor. You walk into the living room and sit down on the couch. Salvador follows you.

"Leave me alone, Salvador," you say. At eye level, the meerkat appears more muscular, more dangerous. It could have you by the throat before your first scream.

You opaque the window, which shows the dull, doomed lights of the city, and punch up a scene of pseudowhales breaching. Pseudowhale song—deep and sonorous—drowns out Salvador's response.

He regards you for a moment and then waddles back into the kitchen to start clearing the dishes.

Where is your brother in all of this? Why have you let this creature into your apartment?

The world moves more swiftly, more deadly now, and yet its center, Nicholas, moves not at all. Your face takes on a terrible implacability. You will see this through to the end. This is your brother, after all. And now you are curious beyond all reason. True, you still get that feeling of dread deep in your belly. You still feel fear. But that's better than feeling nothing at all . . .

Your normal life goes on regardless, as if without respect for your brother's absence. You ignore Salvador for the rest of the night. In the morning, you refuse his offer of breakfast. You work frantically to meet deadlines, push Nicholas to the back of your mind. You call Shadrach twice during the day, but his personal holoscreen remains off. You keep seeing his face as the meerkat fell into step beside him.

At lunch, you use the time to try to find out more about Quin, but nothing exists on Quin. Quin's presence surrounds the city, engulfs it, and yet there is nothing inside the city about him. It is almost as if his creations define him so utterly that no one has bothered to set down, for the record, who he is, preferring to rely on rumor, on innuendo, on falsehoods. He's as insidious as the chemical-loaded air come off the sea—invisible and yet everywhere. How do you fight someone like that? How do you get inside his guard?

You wonder and worry until the evening, when you return home to another delicious dinner. Salvador, with his annoying subservience. You are a fairy-tale princess in a fairy-tale tower served by a beast that is, under the fur, a man.

That night, you cannot sleep. You fall into a half doze, only to be brought out of it by the echo of your brother's voice, trying to tell you something. At three, you give up on sleep and sit at the edge of the bed, sweat beading your forehead despite temperature control. You hate Salvador in that moment. You hate Shadrach, too, for his unwillingness to tell you the truth. Shadrach said, *I've made a mistake* . . . Is it a mistake to let Salvador into the apartment?

The click of the front door opening brings you fully awake. Your first thought is that you really did hear your brother's voice and he has snuck in past the security systems. But more than likely a genuine intruder has entered the apartment.

Stealthily, you rise, wrap your nightgown around you, and take the laser gun from your purse. You tiptoe to the bedroom door and open it a crack. A half-moon shines into the apartment and gives you enough light to see a dark shape walking across the living room carpet.

You step out from the bedroom, hit the light switch,

say, "Don't move or you're dead," and aim your weapon at . . . Salvador.

You keep the gun aimed at the meerkat, whose eyes blink against the sudden light.

"Please don't be frightened, Nicola," Salvador says. He extends a hand. "See? I waited early for the fresh fiddlers. You liked them so much."

The fiddlers' claws close impotently on the meerkat's slick fur.

"Three in the morning?" you say. "Three in the morning, and you're out getting fiddlers for next night's dinner?"

Salvador stares at the ground and when he looks up again his fangs show and his eyes flash with some inscrutable emotion.

"Nicola," he says softly, "if you think there has been a malfunction in me, then you must tell Quin. If you think I am lying, then you must do that. I may well have broken down in some way. I am not capable of monitoring my own state of mind."

You sigh and let the gun drop to your side. "Go to sleep, Salvador. Just . . . go to sleep."

"Thank you," Salvador says, and slips past you to the kitchen.

6

You were always two as one: Nicola and Nicholas
merging into the collective memory together. You
have been living someone else's life. You have
been living someone else's life. There is a shadow
existence here, a separate world—you see it in mirrors
where your image does not match your living form, your
movements not quite synchronized with this *other*, this
creature, who is not you. *The shadow of the waxwing slain*.
The moon crosses your heart. Out in Tolstoi District the
animals gather amidst the wrack and ruin, no longer shy.

You see it in the glass, where your half-reflection slides
off to reveal, at the corner of your eye, another life, another
even more ghostly Nicola living out another life. That is it:
You are a ghost of a ghost, a memory fast fading. The smell
of nothing on the breeze—the pale limbs of trees on the

holoscreens, the memories of sounds upon the walkway, the clarity of the echo of your hand upon the railing. The emotion that comes to you is so clear, so simple, as if a painter has managed, using translucent paints, to penetrate to the core of a canvas, and you its reflection. No fear. No hatred. No frustration. No anxiety. No love. No envy.

When you turn for protection from the insanity, from the mirrors, the glass, the only solace is found in the shadows—and it is in shadows that you once again sense Nicholas. *Two as one.*

The next night, you go to bed early. You lock your bedroom door, change from work clothes to black pants, black blouse, and black boots, with a blue jacket thrown over the blouse. You place the gun in a pocket on the inside of the jacket. You put a holographic mapfinder in an outside pocket.

Then you wait.

For a while, all you hear is the clack of dishes as Salvador puts them in the washer. This sound is followed by silence. You become tired. You feel a bit foolish—since when were you cut out for spying? But then you hear the familiar click of the door, and you check your watch: two in the morning. You wait a moment, quickly leave the bedroom, and are out the door—onto the seventy-fifth floor of your apartment building. The elevator is empty.

You take it to ground level and walk onto the street, hoping you've not already lost him.

Free market traders crowd the streets in their makeshift hovercraft shops. Neon flashes over everything in garish shades of pink and purple and green and blue. Almost blinded, you put on sunglasses. People press against you in all variety of clothes, from the opaque to black robes with headdress. The smell of a thousand drugs rises in your nostrils: a mélange of addiction. A man spills his drink against you. A woman shouts out, "You Dead Art fucking bitch whores!" Above, the walls of the city, highlighted with green lights, rise two hundred feet, lit also by the warring fires of the wall guards, the tied-up dirigibles casting shadows down onto the crowds.

For a moment, overwhelmed by the city in a way you had not thought possible, you stop walking and glance desperately from side to side. You curse your stupidity. Have you already lost him?

Profound relief washes over you as you catch a glimpse of a familiar furry tail and hindquarters getting on an escalator walkaway not twenty meters ahead. You press through the crowd, jostle the man who spilled his drink on you, and manage to get on the escalator, thirty meters behind Salvador, who is a tuft, a spray of fur, through the welter of legs. The laser gun suddenly is much too small a weight in your jacket pocket, not nearly enough to defend you from the city. You are alone. None of your friends know about Nicholas's disappearance. The police don't know either. If you disappear now, Nicholas disappears with you: you are not one, after all, but two, and the city is the only infinite—a maze, a crystal mirror, a shattered toy, a palate of undigested time.

—and the meerkat you hope is Salvador jumps off the escalator, and you frantically elbow pedestrians aside, manage to disembark at just the right spot and enter the press of the cracked concrete walkway. Ahead, the familiar shape of Salvador turns a corner.

When you turn that same corner, you find yourself in an empty dead-end alley.

You let out a little laugh, a snort, a chuckle. You just stand there, staring at the far end of the alley, unable to think yourself past this point. A quiet grows inside you unlike anything you have ever known. The crowd noises, the soft hiss of hovercraft, the crackle of meat in a sidewalk grill—they all fade away, and all that is left is the pounding in your ears, the glistening drops of water on a culvert, the flash of lights behind your eyes.

Where did he go? The question creeps into the silence. You walk to the end of the alley. Garbage. Garbage cans to house the garbage. Rotten food, sweet-and-sour stench. Bottles, broken. A blank wall, rust red, that mocks your efforts.

You lean against the wall, look back out toward the chaos of the main street, and, as the wall dissolves, as you fall *through* it, a curious double image forms—that you've been here before, night after night, following Salvador, each time ending up in this alley and, until now, not solving the mystery . . . but then you have no time for anything but the fact that you are falling through the wall, through a blur of color, a grayness eclipsing the street vision, and then, as you land on a hard platform, you see above you the stars—the stars!—and a faint hint of green to the sides.

You hit, and the impact drives the breath from your lungs, even as you begin to understand that the wall was a hologram, even as you begin to realize that Salvador may be launching himself at you as you gasp for air. You whirl to your feet, despite the shock, a gray wall behind you, and ahead . . . a forest.

How can you articulate a dream that is not a dream? You feel as if you have found a secret room in a house long familiar. Did you ever truly know this city?

You stand atop a raised steel platform and before you a path of white pebbles, gleaming in the moonlight, descends into a valley of dark fir trees. You hear the sound of running water and see, at the limit of your vision, a small bridge of red and white, half-hidden by the trees. It slopes gently over what must be a fast-moving creek. Crickets and a few cicadas mumble their songs. The sounds of night birds flying, the chittering flit of bats above, against the blue-black sky. The white underbellies of the straggling clouds against the stars, against the darkness.

This sanctuary, this fifty-meter-wide strip of wilderness, is hemmed in by skyscrapers to the right and left, but bound by the horizon straight ahead, and therefore must let out onto the seashore.

The thick smell of the fir trees is a revelation to you, as is the air itself: clean, fresh. And the moon—the moon isn't obscured by the yellow scourge of pollution, but brilliant as it highlights the fir trees, tints the entire forest silver.

But there is, for all the peace, an urgency to the cicadas' cry, and you feel exposed, vulnerable. Salvador is not in sight, but he could be watching—and what if someone or something comes through the alley and onto the platform?

You begin to walk down the path, your purchase on the shining white pebbles at first unsure. Very quickly, you are amongst the trees, which are so dense that you can see only branch-obscured patches of sky. This, you think, must be the illusion—it's the alley and its dead-end wall that must be real, and you are now dreaming, dreaming, dreaming.

"How could anyone have hidden this? How?" You're so shocked, you say it aloud. Under the most skilled of holographic shields, and at the greatest of expense—not just the manipulation, the illusion, but also the perception that no one ever lived in this space, that this space never existed within the city. (And, the second question, the one you don't want answered: Why was it so easy to enter?)

You have, for your various programming projects,

examined a thousand plans of the city—maps, blueprints, grids—and yet never missed anything, never thought, *Here* is a gap. *Something* has been deleted here. Never felt a corresponding emptiness in your heart.

Worst of all, this place is beautiful, so beautiful that you cannot help but melt into the rightness of it. The wind, gentle through the trees, carries the scent of the sea, mixed with the mint of crushed fir. Here is a place for the stealthy animals of the Tolstoi District to live, having abandoned their hundred hiding places to walk under the light of the moon, along the white path, down to the sea.

Dislodged pebbles on the path behind you. You start, abandon the path, duck down behind a fir tree, pull out your gun.

The rustle becomes louder, and soon, moonlit, scoured of the veil of pollution, of sickness, two dark figures come into view. One, with its sinuous, curling nose, must be an elephantman. The other, taller and weasel-sharp, must be another meerkat. The two pass by your hiding place, huffing with laughter, in a jolly mood, conversing in a language of clicks and whistles and yelps. They don't speak in human languages when they are alone. Why would they? The light creates a blue-green sheen across their bodies. The meerkat musk is strong.

Once they are past, you creep from hiding and follow, feeling suddenly exposed . . . Soon the fir trees become less dense, replaced by strange, thick bushes, and then by sinewy roots clinging to brackish land almost the consistency of mud. The white pebble path brings you to genuine mudflats—a narrow strip that buttresses the creek flowing beneath the bridge. From the mudflats, a million eyestalks stare up at you: fiddlers by the thousands, clacking their claws and tracking your movements. Their carapaces shine ghostly.

You cross the bridge. The water is dark blue—no trace of chemicals, so there must be a strong filter—and through it you catch the silver gleam of strange fish: three-eyed and so scaly as to be coated in armor. They mutter and pout like old men and in their listless motions you discern an icy intelligence.

Beyond the bridge, the firs close up around you again. The musk of meerkat rises so strong that you fight the urge to sneeze. A light not from the moon glimmers through the trees. You follow it. With each step you recede a little more into the background of some odd fairy tale. The light, diffuse and yet focused, is a fey light. It casts the fir branches in sharp relief. It coats the ground in an ever-nearer sheen of gold. Soon you must shadow it, circle it, not drawing closer until you can be sure of cover—a large bush, an unusually thick tree trunk. From the light comes laughter, chirping speech, and, periodically, the scream of an animal in agony. Moths and beetles cloud the air, burn through it in an insectile fog.

Finally, you spy movement through the branches, hear individual voices, although the language remains a mystery to you. Then, hidden by a branch you are afraid must be ridiculously small for the purpose, you *crawl* toward the light, stopping just short of the clearing that would reveal all mysteries.

Your chin scratches the ground and your arms are weary. Through the branches, the wind blowing into your face, you see a congregation of meerkats and elephantmen in the foreground—lit by a series of lanterns—very animated; all gesturing paws and trunks a-sway like snakes, accompanied by a torrent of clicks and whistles and chirps that must, by the intensity of the interaction, carry equally intense meaning. A number of younger meerkats contentedly groom each other and, spiky-furred and frisky, chase each other around the clearing. In the back, the wavery light of a hologram plays, while a group of meerkats and elephantmen sit in front of it and watch. Slowly, your gaze is drawn from the foreground, from the middle ground, where you are trying to find Salvador, to the background hologram. The hologram at first is just a flux of images—some even in black-and-white, from archaic flat media, such as photographs or film. But the images are the same, and the sounds are the same: horrible agony, horrible pain . . . against the backdrop of a marketplace a man takes a long, curving blade, and proceeds to flay a dog alive, skillfully cutting off the coat in a few quick strokes while the dog screams, and then, furless, looking like a newborn thing, its eyes tightly closed, trembles and pants—pink and vulnerable and in shock while the man goes on to the next dog, and the first one—in extreme close-up—goes into the waiting bag of a customer as casually as a pound of rice . . . puppies hanging from telephone poles . . . gerbils burned alive in skillets . . . mice poured into burning wax for a Living Art exhibit . . . scenes from the wastes outside the city walls, where the animals gasp and cough and live out their lives against a backdrop of chemicals and toxic gases . . . meerkats pierced through the skull with a control bar and then guided by their human tormentors to tear each other apart . . .

You cannot watch for long. You must not. It is too terrible . . . When you can bear to look again, you see that now it is not animals but human beings—tortured, mutilated, burned, cut up, gassed . . . and, strangely, the seated meerkats and elephantmen react most visibly to these displays, such physical revulsion that some look away as you look away, in shock and disgust. They hide their children's eyes as any responsible parent would . . .

A chill runs through you. What could they think of a species that had brought the world to such an impasse? As you watch them, as you watch their interactions, their conversations, you are overcome by a panic that has nothing to do with fear of discovery. You manage to control it—even though it bubbles up beneath the skin, steals your breath, slicks your palms. You creep backward through the underbrush, until the light is once again just a glimmer through dark green and the white pebble path once more ribbons out behind you.

Then fear seizes you for real, cups your throat, lets your legs hang free—and you run, biting your tongue not to scream, sometimes on the path, sometimes off it, unaware when you almost turn an ankle or when a branch strikes your face. You have forgotten Salvador, Shadrach, Nicholas, and Quin. Soon you see the platform glinting and you run faster, jump up onto it, and plunge back through the hologram into the dead-end alley. Back amongst the stench, the stink, the pollution of the city. Your lungs burn. Your legs ache.

You pause to catch your breath. Now you realize that even in your panic, a part of your brain has been talking to you. It has been saying, in a shock as profound as that of the flayed dog, *You are not superior. You are not superior.* Because what Quin's Shanghai Circus means is this: your extinction.

The people that you pass on your way home, these governed and governing—do they realize yet that their place has been usurped? *Driven out.* How long before they guess?

7

ater, in your apartment. You love the lights at night, the silence of street corners, the pixilation of dew-drops on the window glass. You love the feel of warm sheets against your skin in the cold. You love the way your fingers seem to know the next step faster than your brain when you are immersed in program-ming. You love the sensation of sex, even with a holo-graph. You love, you love, you love . . . and yet such a ghost are you, haunting your apartment, waiting for the return of Salvador. You have a gun in your hand. You sit on the living room couch. A coffee mug rests on the table nearby.

The coffee mug, the couch—these are very normal, ordinary things, and yet you are waiting in a dream that is not your apartment. You are dreaming in a world that is not your world, and you feel as if you have seen it all before—this strangeness, this sense of oblivion.

The utter clarity of your surroundings despite the revelations of the night convinces you that you are in a shadowland. The absence of light. *He came out of the darkness, a revelation . . .* You have turned the lights off. What choice do you have? You prefer the reality of the vast forest, the delicate bridge, the white pebble path. You prefer the moonlight. You prefer all that will be denied you. *The animals are waiting in the Tolstoi District, under leaves and branches and bricks . . .*

A sliding of an ID card in the door lock. A familiar scent. *Two as one—Nicholas's presence a shadow, an absence—defined by the space around him, defined by that which is not him.* A card slides in the lock. A card slides in the lock. The door opens slowly.

Salvador turns on the lights. He has a sad look on his face, sadder still when he sees you on the couch. He carries a bag of fiddler crabs.

"Hello, Nicola," he says.

"Salvador. I couldn't sleep."

He does not reply, but walks over to the kitchen, places the bag of crabs on the counter.

"More crabs?" you say. You've hidden your laser gun at your side, under a cushion.

Salvador's eyes are red, not amber, under the panel

illumination of the kitchen. He walks back into the living room, stands in front of you, the window, the night sky, at his back. You no longer know what you see when you stare at him.

"Nicola," he says. "Nicola. How stupid do you think I am? I *know* where you've been. I can smell it on you. I can taste it on you."

A distance, some vast space, lies between you and the fear.

"You fell through the alleyway. You walked down the white pebble path to the bridge, and you saw our lights and you found us."

He smiles—or is this a snarl? If he moves one step closer you will shoot him whether he smiles or snarls.

"I was there," you confess. Does it matter what you tell him now? "It was beautiful. It was *wonderful*." And it was, oh it was! Beautiful and wonderful and terrible.

"My dear," Salvador says gently, almost with love, "you should not have seen that. You should not have followed me."

"I'd never tell. If I told, they'd come and destroy it, Salvador."

"You're a programmer from the Bastion, Nicola. No matter what you say, you'll destroy it."

He snarls, and his forepaws clench and unclench. His eyes are red. He laughs—a wheezing laugh full of savagery.

How can he be so split? So gentle and sad, and yet so full of anger? It surprises you, the answer: *because he's fully human.*

He circles you now as you half rise from the couch, your gun aimed at him.

"If you put down the weapon," he says, growling the words, "I will kill you quickly."

"I know Shadrach," you say. "I know Nicholas. Both of them work for Quin. Quin is your master. If you leave now, I won't report you."

"You know no one. I'm Quin's ambassador, come for you."

"Do you want to be as cruel as those *humans* in your holograph show? To be no better than the worst of what we are?" and in your words a peculiar echo, a sense that everything has already been said.

Again the sadness in his movements, his voice: "To protect ourselves, we must be cruel. I'm sorry, Nicola, but you drive me to it."

You fire your laser, miss, and set the carpet on fire. The force of the blast knocks him off his feet. You run behind the couch. You aim again as he recovers and launches himself at you. Your beam catches him in midleap, and he falls onto the couch. His fur is blackened, his left forepaw a stump—but he launches himself again, at your throat. His teeth click an inch away, his hot breath on your neck. The meerkat's teeth close around your wrist. You do not feel the bite, only the movement when the grip falters, the limbs convulse, and Salvador falls back onto the couch, his eyes closed, the whole left side of his body blackened, his fur stained red. Is he dead? Close enough.

You drop the laser. You wander around the living room. The image of the flayed dog comes to you again. You cannot pull it out of your head.

Absent-mindedly, you put out the fire, and even when its last flames lash out at your legs, you feel nothing. You try not to look at the still, burnt shape on the couch. This cannot be real. Your life cannot be real. The moonlight is not moonlight. The aquarium is blue-green illusion. Only the forest leading to the sea is real. Only the nervous fiddlers on their mudflats are real. Nicholas—even Shadrach—might understand you now. They would understand your isolation. How you miss them both. How you need them both.

The doorbell rings harshly in the silence. You open the door from your side only, so no one can see in—and burst into tears. Nicholas stands outside.

You open the door, and there is your brother. Dressed in a ragged raincoat, he looks so incredibly gaunt, so incredibly *old* and used up, that you say, "Oh, Nicholas, what have they done to you?"

You want to hold him, but he stands so stiffly, with his hands at his sides, and his hair, unwashed for days, hangs limply from his scalp, so you can't, somehow, hold him after all.

Instead you say, "I was *so* worried," through your tears and then wait as he seems about to say something. He cannot spit it out. The words tip and tremble on his tongue, his face contorted as he tries to form them.

"What is it?" you say. "What's wrong, Nicholas?" you say, putting out a hand to steady him. You cannot finish sentences that remain unspoken.

The touch makes him convulse, and his hands contort in unnatural shapes. He manages to steady himself and, although he stutters, you understand what he says: "L-l-let m-m-me t-t-tell you about the c-c-city."

"It's okay," you say, and you hug him even as his hands (you have done this before), shaking, almost out of control (you relax, knowing this is the end), find your throat.

Memory so ephemeral, that it should fade so quickly, so without a struggle. The apartment dissolves against the pressure on your throat and you are light remembering itself, the light lingering upon the shadow, the light wistful for itself. In that place all memories are one, and although you are not at peace, although you ache for the smell of chemicals in the Canal District, for the feel of a lover's touch, for the sound of your own heartbeat, you cannot say you have time for regrets, for pleas, for absolution, but only this final thought: that there was so much more you wished to do. The ache of atoms, the yawn of the abyss, and then you are ascending, carried in another's arms, the light flooding into you and through . . . light.

You so desperately want to remember the color of roses in the spring.

PART III
SHADRACH

1

If Shadrach loved her alive, he loved her better, longer, farther, when he thought she was dead . . .

"The roses are doing so well because of the bumblebees Quin made for me. He is, you know, *so considerate* to indulge me . . ."

Another perfect day on Lady Ellington's perfect estate, a district unto itself: two hundred acres of woodlands and gardens, with its own police force to drive off the hungry free market mobs gathered outside the ornate gates.

The walls of Lady Ellington's pseudo-château were made from white pseudo-marble, the vase upon the mantel above the window seat made of the finest clear plastic polymer, while the lady herself was somewhat . . . *faux*. She had taken "Lady" or "the Lady" as her first name, in tribute to—or, Shadrach thought, to give her some credit, in mockery of—some extinct aristocracy. She wore a left ear of perfect white that contrasted sharply with the dried prune of her right ear. A wrinkle-free left hand—lithe and lively until it reached its turgid, discolored wrist—found its malformed mate in the birdlike claw that dangled from her right wrist.

Between the thumb and forefinger of her marvelous new left hand, Shadrach had noticed a familiar blemish: a reddish birthmark in the shape of a rose. He stared at it without blinking.

". . . thank you so much for stopping by to check," Lady Ellington was saying. "I so rarely have guests over during . . ." And blah, blah, blah.

Shadrach continued to stare at the birthmark while he considered, briefly, that Quin had sent him to her estate so he would recognize this mark, this beautiful, familiar mark. As he nodded to the Lady and answered questions about Quin, about meerkats, a cold and bitter despair rose in his throat. He stared into the left eye of the Lady Ellington, a replacement that was blue as the blue of *her* eyes. As blue as he wanted the sea to be, pressed up against the canal walls.

He wondered if that eye held any memory of its former owner, if he was indeed still looking through the window into *her* soul. Lover, lover gone to pieces.

Tears came and he made no effort to stop them when they began to trickle down his face, his mouth set quite as firm and solicitous toward the Lady as before. He nodded, smiled politely.

Until even the Lady Ellington could not ignore the evidence of her own blue eye and trailed off into silence, possibly for the first time, there in her white, porous, artificial mansion.

The only sound in that place was the *tink* of Shadrach's tears as they hit the edge of the pewter cup he held in his hands. She would never understand the look on his face—the commingling of love and hate that warred within him as he stared at her and, through her, at Nicola.

But he supposed she knew enough to be quiet—understood that the man before her had undergone a fundamental change. And yet could she really ever comprehend the restraint it took for Shadrach not to crush her skull with his bare hands and then pluck his lover's eye gently from the fractured orbit?

On his way to Hell, Shadrach stopped at his apartment—an old split-level not far from the canals, with automated doors that seemed ever more reluctant to open for him. Inside, he found his official insignia: a badge in silver depicting a silhouette of an animal merging with a man. It allowed him safe passage through all of Quin's various business concerns.

Badge in hand, he found his gun after a moment of groping under the tightly made bed. He was not a violent man, but he loved his gun for the same reason he hated the mining machinery of his youth. The weapon had a graceful functionality built into its sleek, aerodynamic design. It was neither ungainly nor awkward; it fit perfectly in his hand. He had bought it used—an older model of the current laser gun lines—and the shining metal surface, once a sunny gold, had become a brazen copper. It glowed in a certain light, and it had known years of service before he had ever touched it, which made him love it all the more, that it had a history, a past, which it could communicate only in the precision of its fire, in the slight nicks along the muzzle, in its faded color. He had never fired it at anyone. He stuck it through his belt.

He walked into the tiny bathroom and thrust his head under freezing tap water until his face burned. Then he punched the bathroom wall as hard as he could, only stopping when the satisfying sting of pain had dulled the guilt and the other, deeper, pain.

Outside once again, in the ash-filled air, hidden in his black trench coat, he attacked the streets without regard for other traffic, pushing aside pedestrians, stepping in front of hovercraft. Anyone who sought to block him received the full and terrible force of his gaze.

Soon, he entered the dead-end alley, walked resolutely past the hologram, past the suddenly revealed sign, QUIN'S SHANGHAI CIRCUS, and placed a hand on the doors, which swung open in response to his badge.

Inside, the auxiliary lights glowed a dull blue, the animals curled up inside their glass cages, the funk of their hundred intertwined scents muted by their slumber. The Quin remote lay slumped across the counter of its lap, as if to peer over the edge at the slow sad faces of the miniature orangutan people. Dust motes sparkled, floated slowly to the floor. Asleep. Dead. Resisting. No potential clients today, brought round to see the show. The purple spiders dangled from the remote's outstretched hands, slaves to their spinnerets.

Shadrach tore the Quin remote into bloody strips of flesh. He smashed the glass cages. He broke the limbs of the animals, tore into their flanks until his teeth were bloody.

He wanted to do these things. For a long moment in the long silence, he stared at the slowly swaying spiders, hands clenched into fists at his sides.

Then he padded past the remote and into the brackish non-light of the backrooms. The holographic screen of the computer reflected red light at him, already on and waiting for him. He quickly checked the two rooms beyond. He was alone. He sat down at the terminal and, after a few tense moments, found the records. The operation on Lady Ellington had been performed at her estate forty-three hours previously. The donor parts came from a "client" identified only as BDXFM 1000-231, currently held in "live storage" at the fifth level repository known as the Slade Organ Bank. Quin had an arrangement with

Slade's that made it easy for him to dispose of spare parts. Coldly, calmly, Shadrach analyzed the situation. If the records were accurate, then Nicola was still alive, but since the operation had occurred two days ago, she might since have sustained other losses not yet charged to the organ bank.

A grim smile creased his lips. It was so obvious what he must do. Nothing could be simpler, or more insane. He must steal her. He must plunge into the underground and bring her back to the surface himself . . .

Shadrach printed out the client number, shoved it into a pocket of his trench coat, and walked back into the main chamber.

The Quin remote waited for him. Its head was twisted to one side, the better to regard him. Its cold blue eyes, its cruel grimace of a smile, mocked Shadrach. Its eyelashes fluttered delicately. Shadrach had a sudden vision of the thousands of feet of rock that separated him from the real Quin, and the sense of vertigo, the terror over the extent of Quin's control, froze him.

"Have you been to see," Quin said, "the sight of the Lady Ellington?" Singsong voice. Muttering of awakened beasts behind glass. Purple puppet spiders dancing on the ends of their marionette strings.

"Yes. I've been to see her."

"Was it all you expected?"

"I expected nothing."

"Did you love her?"

"The Lady Ellington? No."

The remote grinned monstrously, said, "Good, good," and fell silent.

Shadrach waited until the head once again rested upon the counter. Then he walked past the creatures in their cages, aware that the eyes, the eyes of each mutation, each wrecked husk of chromosomes, were following him.

Nicola's apartment door was half-open. It took a damaging act of will to clamp down on the despair riddling through his thoughts like wormholes and ask himself the relevant questions. Had Quin had her killed for some reason? Had someone snatched her for parts, which Quin just happened to buy? The darkness of below level had already begun to infiltrate his mind. Now he was a detective. Now he shut the door behind him.

Inside, he found that the aquarium had been smashed, all of Nicola's fish long since dead in pretty patterns of inert flesh. They stank terribly. Off to the side, he discovered a dark stain on the carpet, but when he squatted and touched it, his finger came away dry. Blood? Wine? Spaghetti sauce?

He examined the fish next. Some were half-eaten, gnawed at by sharp teeth. Tufts of fur mixed in with the stinking fish made him think of meerkats. Had they been here? He sniffed the air. If so, the dead fish disguised their odor.

The couch had been moved recently, the marks where the legs had pushed down on the carpet still fresh. On the couch he found a laser gun—a sleek new model— tucked neatly into the left corner cushion. He left it there, but pulled out his own gun. The quiet had begun to get to him. Under the couch, another enigmatic red stain. He didn't bother to check it.

Circling back to the door, Shadrach noticed signs of struggle. His circumspect entrance could not account for the rough indentations in the carpet, the traces of imprinted mud.

He entered the kitchen, found five rotting fiddler crabs on the counter, their eyestalks flaccid, claws red and cracked.

Which left the bedroom. The door was shut. Memories lay beyond that door—of late nights spent talking and making love, making love and talking, until the two actions were as intertwined and inseparable as their bodies. Was her body in there, on the bed?

Reluctantly, he punched the door button. It slid open. The bedroom was empty. He sat down on the bed. No evidence of any disturbance or struggle. He checked under the bed. Nothing.

He was about to walk back into the living room when

he heard a sudden rustle, a spasm, from the closet. Quietly, he approached the closet. He listened at the door. Nothing . . . and yet . . . Shadrach opened the door, his gun aimed dead center . . . to reveal a very normal clothes closet, with shoes and old stuffed animals strewn at the bottom. The animals were antique investments. Nicola had had them for years. Slowly, Shadrach parted the clothes, gun aimed into the back of the closet. Nothing came hurtling out of the darkness. A body did not come falling down out of the darkness.

Shadrach looked at the stuffed animals. She had a bear, a rabbit, a meerkat.

With great care, Shadrach placed the muzzle of his gun against the top of the meerkat's head.

"Move and I'll kill you," he said.

"Feesssshhh," came the muted reply as the meerkat trembled uncontrollably.

Shadrach stepped back, the gun held at arm's length, the muzzle still against the side of the meerkat's head. The meerkat's face scrunched up in a permanent flinch against the expected blast.

"Feesshhhh good," the meerkat said distantly, its stare glassy. And why shouldn't its stare be glassy? The whole left side of its body had been torn away and then cauterized by a laser weapon. The creature was in shock.

"Nicola. Do you know Nicola?"

The meerkat leered through the blood bubbles in its

mouth. It stared up at Shadrach. "Nicola doesn't need fish anymore."

It had taken a few moments, but now Shadrach recognized the meerkat's subtype: an urban assassin model. Quin planned to sell versions of the subtype to the spy services of half a dozen city governments. But what was one doing in Nicola's apartment?

"You're not so bad off after all," Shadrach said, "except that now I've found you."

"Sirrrs?" the meerkat said, almost toppling over onto its side.

Shadrach stepped back, gun still aimed unwaveringly at the meerkat's head.

"I mean that you've got a lot of hardware up there," he said as he used a wide dispersion wave to incinerate the meerkat's body, leaving only the neck and head, which fell atop the heap of ashes with an expression akin to astonishment forever etched into its features.

"Feesssshhhhh!" came the anguished, bewildered cry.

Shadrach carefully picked up the disembodied head by one svelte ear and brought it into the kitchen. The heads of the assassin models had been created to be self-supporting in an emergency, and could live on for several days after decapitation. Although in shock, although suffering from disorientation and possible brain damage, the meerkat might still have its uses. It might serve as a suitable vehicle for revenge.

In the kitchen Shadrach found a common permanent

adhesive and applied it to the cauterized stump of the meerkat's neck as the beast moaned and spat at him. He searched the cabinets, found a small plate, and put the meerkat head on it. He held the meerkat head in place as the adhesive did its work.

He stared into the meerkat's eyes, which were now sharp and bright with pain, and said, "I don't give a fuck what your name was before. From now on, your name is John the Baptist, you son of a bitch." He snickered for no reason at all, then stopped abruptly, because he could feel an anger, a rage, behind the snicker that must, at any cost, be denied until later. Everything in its place.

The meerkat said, "I will kill you. I will hear your eyes pop against my teeth."

With a kitchen tool cleverly called an All-In-One, Shadrach used the pliers function to pull out all of the meerkat's teeth. It squealed once or twice over this latest indignity. Shadrach clotted the blood with a washcloth until the meerkat gagged, after which he let up.

"Bastard," Shadrach said. "What makes you think you're any different than the funny people out in the wastelands? What makes you think you're anything more than an extreme complex machine?"

He found the largest plastic bag in the kitchen cabinets, poked air holes into it, put the meerkat inside, and stuffed the bag into the huge right side pocket of his trench coat.

"You, John the Baptist, are going below level," Shadrach

said. "I don't think there's much else I can do in the light."

Shadrach ate at a café in the Canal District, obvious to the strangled whimpers coming from his pocket and the strange looks the waiter gave him. His mind had become extraordinarily clear, as if he had managed to discard all the detritus of his past.

The great wall that surrounded the city impressed itself upon him with a precision that verged on the microscopic: he understood that with only the slightest squint he would be able to make out every blemish, every pockmark, on its blind, timeworn face. The colors running beneath the deck of the restaurant shone with a vibrance he could not recall having seen before—the orange hues livid as flames, the blues reflecting a sky that in its immensity could crush him in an instant.

The wind from the sea brought to him such a variety of scents that simply by breathing he became more alive: the sting of salt, certainly, and the subdued brine, but also an underlying sweetness that reminded him of Nicola's favorite perfume. Had he truly never smelled that sweetness before, or had it always been there?

Now Shadrach knew he was fated to go below level again. This was not fickle chance, not coy coincidence— this was fate, and he would run toward it as fast as he could, mouth curled back in a snarl. To think that he could grow so complacent that he could take *anything* for granted, even a smell, an aftertaste, an echo.

He ate his sea bass and potatoes with a peculiar combination of intensity and sloth, each bite savored, before, finished, he slapped down payment and left that place, as far as he knew, forever.

2

Down below. Ten years since he had been there, and who knew how it might have changed, have warped, have permutated, in his absence? Somehow, he had thought, as a child might, that it had not existed at all after he had left, but had been a nightmare from which he had finally woken up. *Why* such a place should exist was a question hopelessly tangled in other questions, lost in the below-level passageways, long ago. At times, its distant, fading shrieks could be heard, only to be once again drowned out by the chaos of a million other voices whispering about survival. What lay below level? Surely not his past.

———

A narrow alley. A slit of sky caught between tall buildings. A wealth of garbage—cans, rotted food, plastic boxes, dead animals—that some eccentric hadn't simply heaved over the side of the city wall. Under the garbage, the keys to the old kingdom: an ancient maintenance entrance—just a manhole cover anyone could lift, after a moment's strain, by hand. He knew of more normal entrances, but from this one a careful person could bypass two belowground levels without detection. An element of surprise might be vital.

As Shadrach stood at the threshold, the wind died away, the rumble and hiss of hovercraft faded into the air, and even John the Baptist stopped his futile squirming. No sound but for his own shallow breathing. The round gray manhole cover grew and grew until it became the world. From beneath it, he imagined he could hear the sounds of below level rising to poison the sunlight. It came softly, softly, but building, like gossamer dream transforming itself to heavy nightmare.

On the other side of the manhole a wet glob of slugs and grubs waited for him; it was their faint mewling cries he heard, the whole of their pulsing, gray bulk waiting for him to come home. The image of a maggoty, sudden dark. The drip-drip of water. The suggestion of massive machinery grinding. The dark. The harsh, spitting sound of holovids flicking green light from behind closed doors in closed-off corridors. The dark. No matter how he might rationalize it, he knew that his own personal Hell waited for him down below level. He had driven auto-trains through the desert and seen what no one in the city could imagine, but he would rather do anything than return below level. He did not want to go. He would not go.

In a single motion, Shadrach pried open the portal, jumped into the greasy hole, clamped onto the ladder that ran down the inside of it, and shut the lid above him. The clang resounded in the darkness as he clung to the metal ladder. He clawed at the unpleasantly moist lid, which he could never open now, locked as it was from the outside.

He had no choice but to grit his teeth and descend the ladder, never knowing if *something* below might be scuttling *up* the ladder, slinking through the darkness to surprise him. The sound of his boots on the rungs reso-nated through the brackish, close air. Sweat trickled into his eyes. The already enclosed space around the ladder seemed to collapse in on him. His movements became frantic. It took conscious effort to slow his breathing, to not just let go of the rungs and slide down into . . . what?

The bottom of the ladder and its attendant platform finally appeared below him. Relief flooded him. He clambered down onto the platform and took a deep, shuddering breath. He had passed the first test. He had controlled his fear.

He looked around. Two sides of the platform were

boxed in by walls. One side led into darkness. Straight ahead stood an open elevator shaft. The elevator, which glowed a faint green, had gotten stuck between floors, halfway to the bottom of the open elevator door. It smelled of old rust and new oil. Below it lay the abyss: a shaft that might descend three levels or three hundred.

Shadrach walked up to the shaft, put his hands on the metal of the elevator's jagged metal lip. Maybe he could hoist himself up and into the elevator, if he could find enough purchase.

They came at him from above and from three points of the compass—four nasty little brats from the puling sound of them. They pulled him to the ground so close to the shaft that he had to roll away from the edge before he could even think of defending himself. Two of them had nubs for legs, and as he rolled away from the shaft, he flung one of his attackers against the ladder with a swift, brutal kick. The others held on, oddly bulky, their breath moist and unpleasant as they screeched in some degenerate language. They had claws. They had teeth. They had a knife, which snapped when the wielder tried to stab him, come up against his laser gun. One punched him in the kidneys, its grasp sticky as a gecko's. Another tried to bash his head against the hard stone floor, but either his head was harder than the stone, or his assailant couldn't get enough leverage, because the action barely dazed him. The third held down his left arm while rifling through his pockets and had the misfortune to discover John the Baptist, who snapped at the brat's fingers. The brat shrieked, distracted long enough for Shadrach to pull his arm free. He found his gun. He fired into the air, bringing a rain of pebbles down on their heads. In the momentary flash of light he caught a glimpse of a pale, bald scalp, luminous eyes, a darting tongue.

As suddenly as they had attacked him, he was free of them, the displaced John the Baptist rolling impotently on the floor, snapping his jaws.

Shadrach spun to his feet, pressed himself against the ladder, prepared to scramble back up it. But there was no need—the bipedal thugs had already leapt over the shaft's edge. As he watched in amazement, the two legless wonders galumphed over the edge, too, in what resembled some form of ritual suicide.

He ran to the edge, stared down into the shaft. Below, he saw, like pale mushroom caps in the gloom, the parachutes of the last would-be bandits gliding gracefully out of sight. He aimed into the shaft, but at the last moment did not pull the trigger.

Instead, he hoisted himself into the elevator, pushed B for lower level, set it for speed return, and released the emergency stop. As it creaked into rumbling motion, he jumped back onto the platform.

Shadrach picked up John the Baptist by the plate and sat down against the wall near the ladder. His side felt bruised, his lip was split, his right wrist partially sprained. His hand passed over something smooth as he propped himself up and he brought it in front of his face, to examine it in the dull green light.

"Huh!" he said to John the Baptist. "A bomb. The little bastards were going to blow me up."

He looked at John the Baptist and John the Baptist looked at him.

"Why?" Shadrach asked. "Why was an assassin model meerkat in Nicola's apartment?"

John the Baptist tried to snap at his fingers.

"What's the point of silence? You're not an animal. You're not a robot. You're dying."

John the Baptist said, "She *thought* I was an animal. I thought she was capable of genocide."

Shadrach jammed the cylinder deep into the meerkat's left ear. It screamed, cursed, reduced to incoherence.

"I knew you were incomplete," Shadrach said.

Just then the elevator reached the bottom with a gut-wrenching shriek of metal, echoed by at least two screams.

Shadrach picked up John the Baptist and said, "We'll continue this conversation later." He stuffed the head back in his pocket. Aching, he got to his feet.

"Welcome to below level," he said, and laughed, but it was a laugh like breaking glass.

Now a strange condition overcame Shadrach, in which the world existed in gasps and gaps, so that the intervals between events vanished and his actions took on a cold and deadly precision: there were only places he arrived at and places he had yet to arrive at. Once gone, he was again instantly at his next destination. He remembered vaguely, as he made his way to the fifth level, the absence and presence of light, the touch of skin against skin in the tightly packed corridors of raggle-taggle communities to whom he was like a pale ghost, fast receding from them, followed by vast, empty passages. More than once some brave local arm of the law would stop him and ask him his business among them, and he would answer them with a stare that corroded their souls.

Only once did he come free of this fey mood, when he found himself aboard an old industrial elevator hurtling down through the darkness, lit only by red emergency lights, his fellow passengers' faces subsumed in blood, their eyes locked on the gun he held at his side. The elevator bellowed and leapt like a beast eager to plunge into the heart of Hell, and through a hole in the floor, he could see the rock to either side passing by faster than fast. He thought that the elevator must be a manifestation of his own bloodlust, the berserker love that had crashed his nerve ends, hijacked his cells.

But such self-awareness was an anomaly: the gaps, the gasps, of time between events had been filled with memories, for he was not truly remorseless, not truly a machine rebuilt for revenge. He was brittle with the weight of his humanity, and he had memories of this place.

Every step became a step into the past—the fear of not having enough to eat, of being packed into a tiny room with five brothers and sisters, and of early shifts and late returns from the mining facilities. Each day they prayed that the lottery would save them by bringing them to the surface: the other country that lay like a miracle above the darkness.

His first memories outside of the room that served as their house were of the clank-and-thrum musics of the mining machines. He soon saw them up close: monstrous black metal carapaces four, five stories high, the heat they gave off like sweat, so that they always seemed possessed of a righteous anger: to steam, to bubble, to boil. They generated a fierce light that annihilated his vision even as he adjusted to it; a corona of flame through which the machines burst through in glimpses—their bodies a black darker than night (the blue-black skins like that of a metal god-temple), their spokes like iridescent midnight starfish; their rancid smell, which Shadrach came to realize was the stench of their own sweat as they toiled; the flecks of metal that floated off them, infiltrating his clothes, his skin. The rust was on fire, the particles so small that when they came to rest on his clothes they burned through to his skin and embedded themselves like tiny coals, to flame white-hot before burning up, burning away. The rust spots didn't hurt, they only itched, but they lent his skin a mottled orange hue he only noticed on the rare occasions when the family visited the entertainment section with its bright lights and fun house mirrors.

Eventually, he had adjusted—his night vision so improved he discarded his infrared goggles; his skin toughened, he developed sinewy muscles in his arms and thick muscles in his legs from pulling down huge levers, shoving mining carts into place, rolling exploratory shafts into position over holes. On days when the machines sang with the weight of the minerals caught in their great maws, he felt as if he were the fire itself, the site of a thousand pinprick conflagrations.

His father had worked in the mines too. His father: a silent giant of a man who caved in on himself over the years until it seemed the flames had devoured him, a sad husk who had done the best he could for his family.

His mother skipped from job to job with a flexibility and ease that was frivolous next to his father's stoic centeredness. She had taught Shadrach to read and write using books plundered from an ancient library. The solimind civil war had effectively destroyed the school system.

Why, he had often asked himself, after the lottery had brought him to the surface and condemned the rest of his family to the darkness, did they persist in their antiquated mining methods? Only after a long time had passed and he had been assimilated into the surface world did he realize that no one really controlled the machines, that the internal strife of the solimind war had severed the cause and effect between the companies aboveground and their servants belowground. The food machines still worked and the lottery ran, and the mining machines were maintained, but to no purpose. Out of tradition, out of being stuck too far inside the beast to see it had ground to a halt, he and his family had enslaved themselves. But it was too late for Shadrach to ever tell them this.

3

Shadrach found what he was looking for soon after he entered the fifth level: a round tunnel clogged with desperate people. The dull golden light that suffused the tunnel rendered their infirmities in glistening, glittering perfection. Here an arm missing, there a leg, a nose, an eye. Some had no limbs missing but soon would. Others came not to recover a leg but to lose a second. Many had brought tents or sleeping bags or chairs. They muttered as they stood in a rough line. They muttered and they fidgeted and they muttered some more. They held their faces away from the light, even those who had no eyes.

Shadrach approached the nearest—a little old man in a faded green suit. He had no legs. He was positioned in a tray on wheels, his pant legs floating out in front. A gray beard accentuated wide cheekbones. His eyes were large and a watery blue. He had the delicate bone structure of a thrush. Shadrach knelt beside him.

"You're not from here, are you," said the old man.

"I used to be. Is it all like this? All the levels?"

"You must have been gone a long time," the old man said. "It's worse. Every level lower is worse."

"Is this the line for the organ bank?"

The man considered him for a moment, bending his head to one side, then said, "Yes."

Shadrach stood up.

"How long is the wait?"

"You should ask, 'How long is the line?'"

"All right then—how long is the line?"

"As long as the wait." The man cackled.

Shadrach reached down and slapped the man. "How long is the line?"

The man flinched, his eyes wide.

"Four miles," he said, choking back a sob.

"Four miles! That could take days. I can't wait even an hour."

"You looking to donate?" the man said, his gaze running hungrily over Shadrach's legs. "'Cause if you are, I'll do the waiting and you can come back later. We can go in together and—"

That was the last Shadrach heard, for he had plunged

into the tunnel, gun and badge held out before him like talismans against the dark.

At first, it wasn't so bad—they shied away from his gun or his badge or his scowl, as if there were an inverse relationship between where they were in line and their level of resistance. But the closer he got to the front, the more people packed into the tunnel, and the more they resented being asked to move for a line skipper. They clawed and pushed at him with a hatred grown strong in the absence of their flesh, until he had to fire his gun to get them to back off. A mother with child screamed at him and he pulled out John the Baptist, who screamed back until she was screaming for an entirely different reason. A tall, muscular man with only one eye fancied himself a fighter and tried to stop Shadrach, only to find himself on the ground holding his balls. Shadrach was surprised to find meerkats in the line, but confused them by holding up John the Baptist and saying, "I have to find a body for this *now.*" The smell of sweat and urine grew stronger; claustrophobia began to grow inside him. He began to flail out at the multi-limbed creation he was fighting. He shouted, he kicked, slowly surging forward even as he felt he was going to drown, and then, when he didn't think he could take it any longer, the tunnel expelled him into the antechamber of the organ bank.

He faced five burly attendants. A polite secretary. A professional-looking nurse.

"Your name, sir," the nurse said, frowning, as she consulted the purple holographic list that lay between them like scrawlings trapped in a semi-invisible spiderweb. The secretary's makeup made her look demonic. The burly attendants had scars around their heads, a nervous tremor to their bulk.

Shadrach held up his badge, pocketed his gun.

They led him to a door, quite solicitous when faced with Quin's badge.

"Go in here," the nurse said. "Wait for the surgeon. He'll be able to help you."

He opened the door, went through, and gasped as he came out from the antechamber to a raised dais below which lay the main floor of the organ bank and from which rose tiers of columns to a ceiling some two hundred feet above him. Ahead, a series of tall stone archways led the eye onward to a faraway horizon. On first glance, it reminded him of nothing so much as the cathedrals built in the Tolstoi District to mimic those of ancient history, but changed strangely in function.

Where the sculptures of saints would have been set into the walls, there were instead bodies laid into clear capsules, the white, white skin glistening in the light— row upon row of bodies in the walls, the bewildering proliferation of walls. The columns, which rose and arched in bunches of five or six together, were not true columns, but instead highways for blood and other substances: giant red, green, blue, and clear tubes that coursed through the cathedral like arteries. Above, shot through with track lighting from behind, what at first resembled stained glass windows showing some abstract scene were revealed as clear glass within which organs had been stored: yellow livers, red hearts, pale arms, white eyeballs, rosaries of nerves disembodied from their host.

Behind him, on the dais, a plaque to fallen surgeons, and more bodies set into the walls, their distant, lamenting gazes as sad as any martyr's, and yet none of them was Nicola.

Above him, in the rich, rich air, which smelled of blood, which smelled of bodies richly decomposing, dust motes floated and, as light as the dust motes, the globes of security cameras, the many lenses sticking out from their bellies as numerous as pores. He could just barely hear, coming from the wings of the cathedral, the faint sounds of surgeons at work (he thought): scalpel against scalpel, men's voices in casual conversation looped around gurgling screams. But even as he imagined them, these sounds faded like ghosts of sensation, and still there was no one to be seen below or above that was *in motion*, not locked up against the walls, like corpses.

Against such silence, such lack of resistance, Shadrach felt lost, and so when a pattering noise came from the long row of archways directly ahead of him, he was relieved rather than alarmed. A pattering as of feet slapping against marble. It did not fade, but became louder, more specific, somehow violent. It circled round the columns of blood and ichor. He stared intently down the long length of the archways to find its source. A laugh—short, barking—that he couldn't pinpoint. A shriek—long, feminine. Then once again nothing but the pattering. A shadow coyly peeking out from a column, the hint of motion, the glimpse of a face that seemingly withdrew into white marble. Once more the sound of feet. Shadrach took out his gun, walked to the stairs that led to the ground level.

He was about to take action—for here, finally, was resistance—when a shape came into view. It looked very much, from a distance, like a deformed, broken-backed "H," a single strip laid across two larger strips. As it came closer—a halting, sideways progress—he recognized his mistake. It was two people somehow joined in the middle. And, finally, as they ran and spun and argued right beneath him, at the foot of the stairs, he saw that they were two ancient, wizened old people—so wrinkled and stooped, the flesh sagging, that he could not tell their gender—who fought over the snow-white corpse of a girl child. The child's abdominal organs smiled at Shadrach from a great epidermal rip between breastbone and stomach.

"Welcome to the cadaver cathedral, as we like to call it," said a voice from behind him.

Shadrach whirled around.

A gaunt, pale man with hawkish features stood there. Goggles hid his eyes and he was dressed in a crimson surgeon's uniform complete with red cap. He held up his hands, covered by rust-red gloves, so that the blood dripped onto the marble floor rather than onto his uniform. He looked curiously old and young at the same time, as if wrinkles and worry lines had been too quickly engraved onto the face of a teenager.

"No need for that!" the man snapped, gesturing at the gun.

Reluctantly, Shadrach replaced it in his pocket and asked, "Who are you?"

A frown. "My name is Dr. Ferguson, and I've been interrupted at an important surgery." He seemed to remember his gloves then, and carefully took them off with a rubbery thwacking sound, threw them into a corner.

He followed Shadrach's gaze to where the two hideous figures at the foot of the stairs were now pulling at a disenfranchised leg while one of the two humped the remaining leg. "Don't worry about them. They are, sadly, benefactors—patrons of our research who were, as a condition of their patronage, given the freedom to roam the cathedral as they wished. Senile before dead, I'm afraid. Now they play with the corpses."

Shadrach looked away from them and at Dr. Ferguson, whose fingernails were steeped in blood.

"And you let them?"

Dr. Ferguson shrugged. "It's in the contract for their continued support. The corpses are dead, you know." A grim chuckle. "You didn't think, surrounded by so much flesh, that we could ever really maintain its mystique? That would be unreasonable to expect. And now your name, please. You caused a disturbance in the corridor that still hasn't died down."

"I'm with Quin," Shadrach said. He pulled out his badge, shoved it at the doctor, even as he sought out once again the breadth and depth of the cathedral, so monstrously beautiful did it seem to him.

Dr. Ferguson handed back the badge. "What do you want? I'm expected back in surgery soon."

"I'm looking for an organ donor."

A thin smile split Dr. Ferguson's lips. "Aren't we all?"

"No. I mean a specific person."

"What's the number?"

Shadrach handed him the printout.

Dr. Ferguson shuffled over to the dais and punched a few buttons. The holographic screen lit up.

"This might take a minute," he said, wiping his brow with his left hand. A smudge of red appeared on his forehead. "Tell me, then, what's the world like up there?"

"You've never been?"

"Never."

"You were born here?"

"No. I was born there, but I don't remember *there*—I only remember *here*. Once your world refines itself to encompass only the confines of the human body, the macro world seems hopelessly clumsy, distant, hazy. Ah, here"—and he read some number from the screen— "we do indeed still have this donor." Then he frowned. "But I'm not sure . . . well, nonetheless, come on then— follow me."

"What's wrong? What's the matter?"

"Never mind. Just follow me."

They descended the stairs. The patrons had taken their corpse elsewhere, leaving behind only a purple trail of ichor. At the bottom of the stairs, Dr. Ferguson stopped, looked up and down the great halls, and started off to his left. Shadrach followed closely, still overwhelmed by the dizzying space above him, amplified by being on the first floor. He noted the way the columns of blood gushed and the gargoyles on the corners of archways, which were not, on closer inspection, gargoyles at all, but human heads coated in a white preservative and attached to the marble. None of them looked happy. A sense of disgust fought with the relief that soon he would have found Nicola. He gripped his gun in his coat pocket. He did not like Dr. Ferguson.

Another pattering sound, and he whirled in time to see a group of interns rattle by with a gurney full of hearts, tongues, and eyes. They went so fast, an eyeball fell off. Shadrach called out to them, but they ignored him and were soon lost in the distance.

Dr. Ferguson chuckled. "It's just an eyeball—plenty

more where that one came from. It hasn't got a soul—it's only got an eyeball," and he laughed ferociously and kicked the eyeball into a corner.

Then they walked for a long time down the long hall, in silence. Until, finally, Dr. Ferguson turned back to look at Shadrach, slowing his pace and showing his teeth.

"You *are* sure you need to see the organ donor?"

"Yes."

"It can be very emotional."

"I know," Shadrach said, hoping the doctor would shut up.

Dr. Ferguson turned away and continued to walk, Shadrach behind him. After a time, a low moaning and whimpering began to fill the air. It was a hopeless sound, which carried within it the promise of long days of agony. Just ahead of them, the hall turned off to the left, around a corner. The sounds came from beyond the corner.

Dr. Ferguson stopped right before they turned the corner. "You never answered my question," he said.

"What question?" Shadrach asked. He thought of ice, of freezing, of his veins turned solid with the cold. Because he was afraid. Because he was afraid of what lay beyond the corner.

"What's the world like up there?"

"Lighter."

Dr. Ferguson smirked. "I'm glad you're an ass, Shadrach. I'm glad. It makes this easier."

"What easier?"

"It's not sanitary, it's not *right*. But it's the only way we know of to deal with the pressure, the sheer pressure of bodies. This is where we send them afterwards—beyond this corner." A sardonic expression twisted Dr. Ferguson's face as he put his hand on Shadrach's arm. "Be strong. Be of iron will. Understand what desperation can drive a person to. I'll be leaving you now."

He began to walk away. When he was almost out of view, Shadrach called out, "Are you really a doctor?"

But Ferguson was too far away for Shadrach to see whether the man nodded or shook his head. Besides, it didn't matter now. Without the echo of Ferguson's feet, Ferguson's words, the moans, the shrieks, the crying, were all that more distinct.

On the wall ahead of him, a body was being fed blood and other fluids. It was a boy, angelic in appearance, seemingly asleep. His eyes were closed, his perfect mouth set in an effortless smile. He didn't hear the moans. He slept in his amniotic fluid and dreamt of the surface world and knew nothing that his body did not tell him.

Shadrach shivered, untensed his shoulders, took a deep breath, and quickly walked around the corner.

Which dead-ended almost immediately. Had Dr. Ferguson tricked him? But he still heard the moans, the cries. They seemed to come from *below* him. He stepped forward and froze as stairs leading down appeared to his right. They led to a metal gate, and beyond the gate . . . a writhing, seething pit of flesh. Children were doing un-

speakable things to discarded bodies. They were plucking the eyeballs out of heads lodged between the bars of
the gate. The heads at first appeared to belong to people
peering out of their prison, but in fact they were disembodied, misshapen, bloody, wan, the eyes open and
staring, and the children were plucking the eyeballs out
as if searching for shells on the beach. Beyond the gate
and its meerkat guard, the major organs lined the walls
in special self-cooling "jars" that preserved their contents
against all vagaries of environment. Livers, kidneys,
hearts, whole nervous systems—like viney trees—resided
in these closed worlds, backlit by a greenish murk. Brains
on brainstems fulminating in clear canisters, lives on
life support, and, most predominantly, legs and arms divorced from their former owners, now lying in moist piles
or stood up like mannequins.

And yet these vitals, these essentials, were ignored by
the leering, ghoulish potential buyers, who haggled and
fought over the items that lay in the foreground.

The meerkat attendant said, finally, in a raspy growl,
"Going in or leaving?"

Shadrach stared at the meerkat blankly as it repeated
itself, then nodded as the creature held the outer gate
open for him. He collected himself as the gate closed
behind him, and said, "I'm looking for someone who
may still be alive. Where do I go? What do I do?"

"If you're lucky," the attendant said, "the person you're
looking for will be toward the back, where the freshest

ones are kept." He smiled, revealing yellowed teeth. "You'll get used to it. They all do."

The inner gate opened and he walked inside.

The sound, blocked by the gates, swelled up now: the endless chattering banter of merchants showing their wares, an obscene sound that howled through his skull. The heart's desire to see the beloved whole and un-harmed could not survive the realities of this place. As his eyes took in what his brain could not contain, Shadrach felt beaten, defeated, and out of him came a sound so deep, so full of anguish, so indefinable yet so *human*, in that most inhumane of places, that even the gangrenous children stopped their febrile entertainments among the body parts to watch this tall, stricken stranger with astonishment.

The place smelled of the charnel house, as well it should, for not all of the parts were fresh, or even usable for transplant, and as Shadrach wandered aimlessly up and down the aisles, he wondered what they did with their parts, these buyers. That green leg there, half rotted away—what use did the tiny man with one eye have for it, that he should barter so furiously for it? That crushed head with the brains falling out into mush—who could want such a thing? When had below level come to mean such decay?

Finally, he managed to ask a woman for directions and, finally, he made his way through the carnage to the place he had been told to go. But all that he found was a mountain of legs, in all states of disrepair, guarded by a sullen, naked dwarf.

"Where do I find the organ donors?" he asked the dwarf.

The dwarf made a digging motion and pointed to the pile of legs.

"In there?" Shadrach said. "Inside the pile?"

The dwarf nodded.

Shadrach bent over and threw up into the offal that surrounded him. The dwarf watched and smiled and offered no help.

Shadrach straightened up, helpless in the grip of nightmare. His body knew better than he what to do. He took off his jacket and laid it to the side. Then he entered the pile of legs.

It was a huge pile, as big as a mountain, and very few of the legs had been capped for preservation. Most were uncapped and moldering, some crudely frozen. The pile smelled of dead meat. It tasted like dead meat. It was dead meat. But Shadrach continued on in the midst of it. He soon found that he sank through the top layer, but that underneath tunnels had been carved in the flesh, so that he could at least make his way to the center of the mound. He did not so much pull legs aside as wade through them until they surrounded him, the tunnels, the trails incomprehensible to him in that pale pallor, that catalog of death. Their touch against his face, his arms, his legs came tough and solid, jellied and soft. They vibrated with his passage. They quivered. Some moved slowly, as if in memory of life, of other limbs. His face grew red with gore, yellow with thick fat. He had to climb to the top of the pile to breathe, and then "dive" back into the search. At times, more complete bodies confronted him: a rag of black hair, a dilated, staring eye, and he would tense in anticipation of finding *her*, only to be disappointed. He couldn't imagine the reality of that place, and so it became unreal to him: the set of a holo, the deck of a ghost craft.

It took nearly half an hour, but eventually he found her, near the bottom, still hooked up to her life-support apparatus, in a long, rigid cocoon, only her face open to the air, and that covered by a clear sheath. She had lost a foot and breast in addition to her already missing eye and hand, but otherwise remained intact.

"Nicola," he said. "Nicola." He did not know how to hold her, did not know if it would hurt her for him to touch her. Would it hurt him? But in the end he forgot to think and hugged her to him, kissed her bruised forehead, discarded the sheath, though not the tube, and kissed even the vacant orbit. For, despite everything, she was *alive*.

He picked her up and began the long, arduous journey back, the legs a forest, a tangle from which he built a ladder, a bridge, to get to the top, and from there, down the mountain of flesh.

As he carried her, as he looked into her ruined face,

he mistrusted the love that welled up inside him. Why should he love her so much more when she was like this, helpless, than when she was healthy and whole?

He said her name over and over again to himself, like a mantra, as he walked, as he ran, as he cursed and screamed his way through the great cathedral, promising himself he would kill Dr. Ferguson if ever he saw him again.

Shadrach took her farther underground, toward the only place he could be sure still existed: home. As he ran—an awkward, lopsided gait—he looked back over his shoulder as if pursued by something, only to find he carried it with him. He took her through noisy crowds celebrating events long past and through silences alternately like tiny blessings or lesions, places where exposed mine shafts waited to make the silence even more complete.

In those silences, in that darkness, he clasped her to him and drank in her fragrance. He pulled her hair to him, kissed her head. Cradled her. Listened for her breathing. How he loved her. How he loved her in the silence. In the immensity of empty halls carved from solid rock, the stillness broken only by the sound of water droplets falling into puddles, amongst the shadows, the emotion closed in on him, possessed his body so completely that it scared him. He knew, looking into her dreaming face, that he would do anything for her. For now that he had recovered her all the other fears, dreads, insecurities, petty irritations, had been devoured by one great, all-consuming terror: that he might lose his beloved. Would he know who he was if she died? Would he care?

And still he ran.

Hours passed into memory. He found a place in his mind that locked him into the silence, locked him into glimpses of his beloved when, like a miracle, like a curse, light crept in and made her face visible to him.

Finally, half senseless with fatigue, Shadrach staggered up to the door of what he had always known of as his parents' home. Nicola's weight in his arms he ignored; it was only the thought, heavy as the stone above his head, that she might be damaged beyond repair that pulled at his arms and gave him no rest.

The simple metal door had a faded address printed on it. A slit for courier deliveries—no different from any other door in the passageway. Hundreds of doors shone a diseased greenish-silver in the emerald light of the sidewalk lamps. The air smelled damp and stale, too often recycled. It sparkled with floating motes of mineral dust. In dark corners, garbage moldered, as it probably had for months. Faint chalk lines showed where children had marked out the boundaries of obscure games, but no one stood in the passageway now. Such emptiness disturbed Shadrach. It was well past midnight and miners should have been coming home from the end of their shifts.

The dull drone of a holovid at low volume came from

beyond the door of the place where he had spent the first twenty-four years of his life. The sound unnerved him; it made him think that the past ten years aboveground had been a dream—that he would knock and his mother would unlock the door, walk back into the house, and he would follow her, sit down in front of the holovid after a long day at the mines. He could smell the mild shampoo his mother used on her hair.

John the Baptist squirmed in Shadrach's pocket as if impatient.

But he didn't have the strength to knock, so he tap-kicked the door with his foot. He was afraid that if he let go of Nicola, he would collapse on the doorstep.

Nothing happened for a moment. Shadrach thought he might faint. Then the sound of the holovid stopped abruptly. Shadrach held his breath. The door slid open just wide enough for the long muzzle of a laser rifle to slide out until it rested against his forehead. He wanted to laugh. He wanted to cry. To come all this way, just to be blown to bits on the doorstep of his father's house.

From the darkness, he felt the scrutiny of another's gaze. It wasn't his father, of that he was sure. He stared into that darkness and tried to smile. His gun was in its holster at his side. The muzzle of the rifle felt cold against his skin.

"Who is it?" A hollowed-out voice, as if from a great distance.

"Father?" Shadrach said. "My father lives here."

A deep huff of laughter, unexpected but self-assured, echoed from the darkness. The door slid all the way open. A gaunt, ragged man with long hair—substantial as shadow and clothed in a long black robe—stood there. Only the eyes in the strangely elongated, bearded face declared themselves: a fierce green, like two shards of emerald in a setting of badly tarnished silver.

It was not his father. His movements preternaturally quick, the man came closer, still holding the gun to Shadrach's head. The man had unusually long arms.

The man said, "Who are you? What are you doing here?"

"I'll tell you if you'll lower your gun."

"No. Who are you?"

Shadrach grunted with the weight of holding Nicola. He shifted his hands. "My father . . . does my father still live here?"

"I'm the only one who lives here."

"For how long?"

"Three years."

Shadrach's arms became suddenly twice as heavy. A ponderous weariness stole over him. And yet a voice inside sneered at him and said, *What did you expect? You left them here.*

"Do you know who lived here before you?"

The man shook his head.

"Do you know where I can find them?"

The man made the huffing sound again. A smell hung in the air—like fire-bitten twigs or lemon rinds exposed to the gutter.

"I've aimed a gun at your face, you're carrying a dead woman, and yet you ask me questions," the man said in a low, predatory voice. "I smell animal on you. Have you killed an animal?"

"She's not dead!" Shadrach's shout reverberated down the corridor.

As the sound echoed, they stood there silent, Shadrach staring into the past and the man staring into the passageway, Nicola between them like an offering. All Shadrach wanted to do was to kill this person who stood between him and home. Nicola was slipping from his grasp. Could he reach his gun in time?

He was saved from the decision by his adversary. The man withdrew the gun, held it at his side. In a hesitant voice, as if against his own best counsel, the man said, "You can come in for a few minutes. I don't want to leave this door open any longer than I have to."

Shadrach nodded, weak with his burden. "Thank you. Thanks. That's very kind." It was the first act since he had come belowground that seemed to have any humanity to it.

The man motioned him in, said as he passed over the threshold, "If you try to rob me, I'll kill you."

"I'm not armed."

"Yes you are—I can smell the metal. But don't worry—

if you reach for your weapon, you'll be dead before it's in your hand."

"I believe you."

And so he entered his father's house again after ten years of self-imposed exile. Even though his family no longer lived there, it was exactly as he remembered it. The same fuzzy holovid played some maudlin melodrama. The old table had lost two more chairs. A new couch stood to the right. Since the old bed was gone, the couch must convert into a sofa bed. The hologram of his parents on their wedding day no longer floated in the middle of the room. The bookcase opposite looked a little more ragged, a little more unsteady. The few books that were left had a warped, tattered look—perhaps the final proof that his father was gone. Unlike most, his father had revered books, thought of them as artifacts to be cherished, even though he could not read. The room flickered under the white of a bare fluorescent globe. The smell of fire-bitten twigs was thicker here.

The man stared at the woman in Shadrach's arms and said, "She's stronger than you, isn't she?" That quick gaze from the ruins of the face—sharp, fierce.

"She is carrying me."

The man nodded. "You should sit down. You should set her down. My name is Candle. I'm a priest."

"Thank you. My name is Shadrach Begolem."

Gently, he set her down on the couch. Even the carpet by the couch was the same—the dead shag beneath his knees abrasive. He looked up to see Candle staring at her with concern. Something in the eyes gave Candle away.

"You're not human, are you?"

"No."

Candle's hands were long, like thick roots, and they ended in retractable claws. The palms were yellow in the light. Where the cuff of his sleeves ended, Shadrach could see thick brown fur tufting out. Shadrach suddenly felt more threatened than he had with a gun aimed at him. Would Candle feel an affinity for the meerkat head in his pocket?

"Do you know Quin?" Shadrach asked.

"Yes." Candle's gaze scorched through Shadrach.

"I know him too." He searched in his pocket, pulled out the badge as if it were a lucky amulet. "I work for Quin."

Candle turned away, walked to the other side of the room, stood facing the kitchen. "You don't need to show me that. I won't hurt you."

"Yes, but will you help me otherwise? She needs help."

Candle shrugged.

Shadrach turned back to Nicola. She had a gray pallor to her, as if she hadn't seen the sun for years. Her eye was sunk back in her head. Her breathing came slow and regular, but almost imperceptible. Her dirty hair had stuck to her scalp. He brushed bits of dirt from her cheek. What was the point of rescuing her if he couldn't save her life?

"Please," he said to Candle. "Please. You must know someone—or know someone who might?"

Candle said, "I'm just an animal. What could I possibly know?"

"So you'll let her die?"

"No," Candle said. "You'll let her die. You let her come to this. When you love someone, do you let them come to such a state? The guilt is written all over your face. I can smell it on you."

Each word cut into Shadrach as if Dr. Ferguson were operating on him. He could not stand it. He spun to his feet, hand diving into his pocket.

But Candle's gun was already aimed at him again.

Candle said, "Don't."

"You know where my parents are, don't you?"

"No. They moved your parents out—they moved all the humans out. I don't know what they did with the mining families. They just carted them off one day and carted us in. We work for Quin now."

"What is Quin like?"

"Like?" Candle shook his head in amusement. "Like? He's like nothing that's ever been seen on this Earth. He's a part of me. He might even be a part of you. You've asked a question I've no answer to."

"Do you respect Quin? Do you worship him?

Candle gave him a long, suspicious stare. "No," he said finally.

"Neither do I. Can't you just help me find a doctor?"

"Wasn't there a doctor where you found her?"

"Not anyone I'd trust. Besides, she doesn't just need a doctor—I need to know what she knows. I need—"

"A psychewitch."

"Yes."

Candle scowled. "If I find you a psychewitch will that be the end of it? Will you promise never to come back here?"

Shadrach nodded.

Candle regarded him for a moment. "I don't trust you."

"But I trust you," Shadrach said, even though it wasn't true.

4

The psychewitch Candle called Rafter peered through her strangely bejeweled sight like an exotic canal fish: slow-moving, graceful, and utterly dangerous. She had given over one eye so that she could bond with the subatomic, the subchromosomatic. She lived a level above Candle, in a neighborhood of boarded-up businesses and closed-down industries. Candle had led Shadrach through a maze of narrow corridors to get there, Shadrach doing his best to mentally catalog each twist and turn for future reference. The whole way he had been lost in the double sadness of Nicola's condition and the loss of his family—and the guilt that he felt so little for his family. They had been wrapped in a gray fog of lack of detail for almost ten years. Surely he should feel something, but he found that his heart only had room for Nicola, that his concern for her had pushed out all other considerations. Did that make him insane?

When they arrived, Candle had had a long whispered conversation with Rafter while Shadrach stood in a corner with Nicola still in his arms. He did not want to subject her to the added trauma of setting her down if they were not welcome. Rafter had finally walked over to Shadrach, but said nothing, gazing at him until he looked away. Rafter's narrow features, perfectly preserved, gave no hint of information—about her age, her life. Her movements, concise and controlled, let slip no clue to weaknesses. Only the silver, close-cropped hair, flicked up in front and hugging her scalp in back, revealed anything about her personality.

The waiting room gave Shadrach more clues, for it had the carefully planned flamboyance of a magician's stage. Curtains full of moving holographic images of faces—past clients?—framed holographic windows on all four walls, each looking out on a scene of clichéd tranquility: the sea, the desert, mountains, jungles (this last taken from ancient film reels). The chairs not only morphed to the curvature of a visitor's spine but also spoke in purring, sibilant voices. The carpet remained mute, but its thick grass did pull away to reveal a springy gray path at the first touch of a visitor's shoes.

Finally, Rafter said, "Come with me," and, turning, led Shadrach and Candle into another, smaller room with an operating table. A rectangular black box stood on a pedestal in the corner. The room was devoid of any hint of personality.

"Set her down—gently," Rafter said.

Shadrach laid her on the table. "Can you save her?"

"I can save anyone," Rafter said. "I can bring back the dead." She ripped off the mask that covered Nicola's face. She opened Nicola's left eye and stared intently, clicking on a circle of lamps so that the light gathered like pearls across Nicola's face. Rafter's mechanical eye captured the light, interrogated it, and then released it.

"Only dreaming," Rafter muttered. She took surgical scissors from a pocket and cut away enough of the gauze that Nicola's arms came free. She held Nicola's right arm up—it looked unbearably pale to Shadrach—and focused her gaze on the nub of a wrist. Nodded once, replaced the arm carefully in the cast. Then she flicked out the lights pearling from her eyes. She smiled thinly at Shadrach, as if out of ritual, and from a distant place.

"She's salvageable," Rafter said.

"Salvageable? What do you mean by salvageable?"

"I mean, I can bring her back."

She held up a hand to forestall further questions and walked over to the box, pulled it over to Nicola.

"What's that?"

"Part of the procedure. Relax, it isn't happening to you."

Rafter pushed a button on the side of the box and, with a whirring sound, four triangular flaps sprang open. The box proceeded to undergo an amazing transformation, turning itself inside out until its innards showed, full of conduits and microchips and gimcrack circuitry, in the middle of which hung vials of cloudy liquids hardwired into the interior. The machine cooed and burbled in a way that reminded Shadrach of a senile grandparent or a newborn baby. The sound did nothing to reassure Shadrach.

He must have grimaced, because Rafter said, "Oh, that. The machine still believes it's alive. Of course, it isn't anymore. Poor thing."

She pushed a button and a thin, mechanical voice said, "Equilibrium . . . check . . . integrity . . . check." Rafter might as well have been practicing witchcraft. She attached wires to Nicola's head, nodded, cursed, frowned, and finally smiled—the first time Shadrach had seen her smile, and it was a marvelous smile that lit up her entire face—as she read the results displayed on various monitors.

"You mean you can do all your work with just this box?" he asked.

"Your name is Shadrach and you work for Quin, correct?"

"Is that what Candle told you?"

Rafter smiled again. "I'm a psychewitch. I know everything there is to know. But if you work for Quin then you do know that not everything of importance is very large."

"I don't follow you."

"You will, one day. Now listen very carefully, and don't interrupt: She's not in a coma. She's not brain-dead. She's stuck in the step before death. Sometimes, after they use a person for parts, they don't kill them, they just leave them in a state of stasis and give them to the bone-yard, which is where I assume you found her, yes? After all, it's easier to leave them this way than to cut them up and cap all the parts. But the tricky thing is bringing a person out of stasis. The body revolts, the subconscious mind, having resigned itself to endless dream, protests. So I can do it, but it will take three or four days. It's like bringing someone out of deep sleep. If you rouse them quickly, it's a shock, but in this situation a shock that can kill. Her system has already suffered too much trauma. So you bring them up slowly. Like in the old days, with deep-sea divers, so they wouldn't get the bends."

"The bends?"

"Never mind. So I coax her up, out of her sleep. It's easier because someone has accessed her memories recently, so she's that much closer to the surface."

"What?"

"Her memories," Rafter said. "Her memories. Someone has dredged them up. It's clear from these readings—and see the jack in the side of her head?"

A small metal implant did indeed protrude from his beloved's right ear.

"Why?" He was almost speechless. It horrified him that someone had riffled through her mind as if through a holographic file. Searching for . . . what?

"Someone probably wanted to view her death. That's not outlawed down here because . . . well, because nothing's outlawed down here."

Nausea crept up Shadrach's throat. To be violated in that way . . . and yet, a thought came to him that ashamed him. What if it were a loved one? What if it were necessary?

"Will . . . will it hurt her to access her memories?"

Rafter shook her head. "No. The path has already been established. Running a link through you might even bring her to the surface more gently. What I have to do is run that loop of her last memories over and over. It's like a siren song calling to her consciousness. Eventually, she will stop drowning and rise to the surface. We can do it right now. But I would advise against it."

"I want—I need—to find out what happened to her. If it won't hurt her . . ."

"It won't. But it might hurt you."

"Why?"

Rafter's mechanical eye dilated, and a grim smile transformed her face into a surface bleaker than the wastelands between the cities. "Because you never know what you'll find there."

Shadrach could fight off parachuting assailants. He could search for his beloved in a mountain of legs, but when the time came to accept the temporary jack, the wires, and the entire apparatus of another's consciousness, he found himself as afraid as he had been since entering below level. Did he know enough about this world to bear what he found in her world? He would lie down in the darkness with her and when he rose from that darkness, he would leave her mired in it.

What does it mean to enter the mind of the beloved? The I lost in the you without hesitation: the ultimate goal of every kindred soul to transcend the aching, the screaming, loneliness of the Divide, so that the atoms of one dissolve into the atoms of the other (two as one . . .), making such intimate love that orgasm is the sharing of electrons in flight. *And what does it mean to enter the mind of the beloved when you believe the beloved no longer loves you?*

Rafter said from somewhere above him, "Are you ready?"

"Yes," he said, and Rafter's eye novaed, and he was no longer himself.

You. Were. Always. Two. As one: Nicola and Nicholas, merging into the collective memory together, so that in the

beginning of a sentence spoken by your brother you knew
the shadow of its end and mouthed the words before he
said them. In each moment you spent with him, you lived
again that mist-shrouded beginning when the doctor res-
cued you from the artificial mother's womb—to bawl and
cough and look incredulous at the sheer imperfection of
the outer world. The world of plastic, the world of sky, the
world of detritus and decay . . .

You entered her and then there was nothing except
for her thoughts, the images coming from her eyes, and
you/he disembodied/reincarnated as your love, feeling
every pain, every happiness, every disappointment. It was
exhausting. It was frustrating. It was cruel. It made you
realize that if there were a God, It had placed humanity
in so many different closed receptacles through a wis-
dom that only revealed itself now: that you could be too
close to someone . . . and yet, he found himself still an
object in the current of her thoughts, able to discern that
he was separate from her . . . even as he wanted to scream,
"Don't seek him out! Leave him be!" when Nicholas
didn't make his lunch appointment with her. When
she went to the Tolstoi District, he saw as she did not the
menace in the animals that peered out at her from
the shadows. When he came face-to-face with himself on
the docks—that sour, that pathetic countenance, so ab-
sorbed in its own self-pity—he wanted to die, to kill himself; he could see the resentment on his features, the
childish holding back of himself out of pride when he

should have comforted her, and given her the information that might have saved her. When John the Baptist came to her door, he thought to himself, *But he's just a head in my pocket*. He could not take it. He could not survive as a separate mind, knowing what he knew. He could not be as a god, removed from it all. And so, eventually, he did slip fully into her skin, by giving up the opinions that comprised his identity. There was a vast relief, an unlimited freedom, in this giving up of his self. He was a leaf floating to the street surface, a fleck of ash spiraling through the air. He was ears and eyes and tongue and nose and hands and mind. He was nothing. He was everything. And his love for her burned ever brighter the closer she came to her destruction . . . until her brother's hands were around their throat and he thought he would die too. He could see the same darkness ahead, the single candle flickering out. And he had no ideas about revenge at that moment, no thoughts at all, but only feelings as he tried to sculpt the very pathways of her memory, to comfort her and remember her simultaneously. To reach out to her, no longer her watcher, her shadow, but to somehow communicate with her, to let her know that she survived this, that she survived this, that he was with her, and she would not die. But he couldn't. He couldn't, whether it was some fault in him or a limitation of their contact. He couldn't reach beyond himself into her. Not really. And it was this horror, not her death, not rage toward Nicholas or Quin, that finally brought him out of her—screaming like a lost soul.

He woke in Rafter's arms. She was slapping his face and staring down at him with her mechanical eye. As soon as he came to, she pulled away, released him to the ministrations of one of her chairs. He was in the lobby.

"It's okay," Rafter said, as if Shadrach had just had a bad dream.

His body did not feel right—it was too large, awkward and gangly. He felt something trickling down the side of his face, wiped at it, saw that it was blood.

"You ripped the jack out of your head," Rafter said. "Not really a very good idea. But you're awake now. You're awake. You're alive. She's alive too. I even gave you some vitamins and protein intravenously—you must not have eaten for a couple of days before you came here. So everything's fine—you can stop shaking now."

She produced a self-lighting cigar, took a puff, and sat down in the chair next to him.

"Candle left," she said. "He said to say he hopes he doesn't see you again."

Shadrach choked on a great, collapsing breath, his arms trembling. He wanted to hit Rafter, but simply lay back exhausted in the chair. How could he remember? How could he forget? He had been inside her mind. He had been her. Inside of him, in the corners of his consciousness, the animals of the Tolstoi District now prowled in all their strangeness. And the sensation of being made love to by the hologram of a man. And the full, terrible weight of her love for him, and her falling out of love, her judgment. Which he accepted. He accepted it all. It was as she said.

Rafter said quietly, as if holding back some savage emotion, "I shouldn't have let you do that."

"No, no," Shadrach said, rising, face pale. "It was better to know."

Rafter looked away.

Shadrach's face hardened. He wiped the tears from his face. "Tell me—what's on the tenth level?"

"It's just a garbage zone. There's nothing much there."

"Except for Nicholas."

"Who?"

"The man who killed Nicola. Her brother." He choked on the words.

Rafter snorted. "You're telling me you're off to get revenge instead of staying here with her?"

"I'm going to kill Nicholas. And then I'm going to kill Quin, because he put Nick up to it."

Rafter took a puff from her cigar. "You're going to get yourself killed. For revenge. And where will that leave your lover? In the boneyard again, no doubt."

"Here's my card. There's credit enough on it to pay for the whole procedure."

"I'm sure this will be a great comfort to her when she wakes up."

"I've no choice. No choice at all."

He headed for the door.

From behind him, Rafter said, with as much venom as he had ever heard in another person's voice, "Aren't you going to see her before you go?"

"No," he said, and walked out the door.

Outside, once the door had shut behind him, he looked around as if blind. The corridor was narrow, the light a faint purple. He walked aimlessly through the twists and turns of the empty tunnel, but could not sustain even this level of energy for long. He had been filled up with images from *her* life, with her very thoughts, until he was more her than him, and this created for him a curious double vision, in which the tunnel was merely a wormhole leading into scenes from her eyes, which doubled back and branched out until he could barely see where he was walking.

He stumbled, almost fell, and decided to sit down, with his back against the tunnel wall, his feet resting against the opposite wall. Roaring out of the morass of pity, terror, happiness, joy, sadness, elation that he had inherited—shooting forth from this void, the single sharp thought: *She does not love me.* It was almost more than he could take. But he was not the kind of person to fold, to crack, to be broken, and so instead, in those moments after the realization, he bent—and bent, and kept on bending beneath the pressure of this new and terrible knowledge. Soon he would bend into a totally new shape altogether. He welcomed that. He wanted that. Maybe the new thing he would become would no longer hurt, would no longer fear, would no longer look back down into the void and wonder what was left of him.

She did not love him. It made him laugh as he sat there—great belly laughs that doubled him over in the dust, where he lay for a long moment, recovering. It was funny beyond bearing. He had fought through a dozen terrors all for love of her. And she did not love him. He felt like a character in a holovid—the jester, the clown, the fool.

He righted himself, brushed the dust from his shoulders. He took John the Baptist out of his pocket, set the head down beside him.

"How much longer do you have?" he asked the meerkat.

John the Baptist had lost his sullen aggression. The meerkat sounded tired. "Less than twenty-four hours. I can feel myself dying. My organs are shutting down."

"You don't have any organs. Do you still want to kill me?"

The meerkat stared up at him in the wan light. "All I want is to live, like anyone."

"Then you shouldn't have tried to kill Nicola. You attacked her."

"She had found our sacred place. Would you have me sacrifice my own people for a human?"

"Yes! You're practically a machine, John. Machines don't have rights. You do what Quin says. You don't have free will."

"Why are you bothering this poor machine with insults, then? Why not find a sentient being to torture? I think you'll find it much more rewarding."

"Tell me, then, meerkat—do you have a family? Quin made you from a vat. *Quin made you*. Me, I come from a long line of ancestors. I can trace my heritage."

"Pointless, pointless. I know what I feel. I know who I am. Quin made me, but I am not a machine."

"What is your creator like, then? Is he a kind god?"

"He's a kinder god than you—he'd never cut off my head and leave my limbs to fend for themselves."

"Soon you will be dead, limbs and all."

"As will you. I heard everything. You will try to kill Quin. You might as well commit suicide."

"You have such a cheery outlook, John."

"If you were in my position you would understand. I hope you will someday be in my position. Even if I don't live to see it, the thought comforts me."

Shadrach found himself admiring the dying animal, this head on a plate, this assassin who knew who he was, who had no doubts, or did not show them. He laughed again.

Now he would find out who he was in the absence of her love. Now he would find out if he could love someone who truly did not love him back.

With a mighty effort, he tried to cast out all thoughts that did not center on Quin.

"It's time to find someone you know," he said as he picked up John the Baptist, put him back in his pocket, and got to his feet.

5

The garbage zone was a revolving beast that ate its own dark trail and was never fully gorged on what it found there. Once it had been AI, but now it was just an old beast, and a slow beast, and it had no eyes to see the dim white, the dim black, rags of flesh that traversed the piles, the mountains, of its movable feast. The beast formed a circle, and at the far end of the circle—farthest from where Shadrach entered its entrails—the maw of the beast chomped down on the stinking offal, the rotted food, the ever-present stream of used plastics with its rusted metal jaws. With a grinding of gears, it swallowed ton after ton, some of it burned, some of it expelled from its gullet down into a deep hole where it was crushed flat. But most of it was reduced down into raw materials and expelled by eruption from the beast's blowhole, to be used by above level, which would in turn send its products below level to the captive commercial market waiting to use them, and once used, once more thrown out, so that the beast not only ate itself, it ate the leavings of its leavings: it ate the world forever. Lucky, then, that it had no sense of smell, nor even a brain, nor could sense the weak scraps of flesh that stole from its very innards still smaller scraps for themselves.

Shadrach cared nothing for the beast, but only for the folk who had taken up residence on the tenth level. They were protective of their garbage on the tenth level—it was like gold to them, for every day some wastrel tossed a thousand useful items into the trash, down the chute into the beast. And every day, scavengers sorted through the mess of discarded soup pouches, banana peels, dead animals, exhausted hologram sets, paper plates, bones, meat, vegetables, forks, stray coins, used travel cards, the occasional husk of a book. Sometimes, when the beast grew slow and lazy in its chewing, the garbage stood forty feet high and each clan or family would stake out a hill and protect it against all comers.

So Shadrach stuck to the valleys where lay strewn a torn dress, a soiled teddy bear, used coffee grounds. The ceiling of the tenth floor was uneven, carved from solid rock, but averaged sixty feet, while below, his boots squished down on a hundred moist, gelid substances. The smell of burning came faintly to him from the distant maw of the beast—once he even thought, although this was ridiculous, that he could hear a faint *chewing* sound—and he welcomed this harshness, for his nose told him terrible tales indeed, none with happy endings.

Even as he called Nicholas's name, now faintly, now loudly, he saw the clans on their hills, armed with guns, lasers, and spears made from steel they had found while rummaging amongst the rubbish. These clans had neither close ties nor were related in any racial sense, but they stood tall and united as he approached, ominous in their silence, and only resumed their febrile salvaging when he had safely passed their particular hill. The smell so sickened him that he prayed he would find Nicholas sooner rather than later; even John the Baptist gasped and sneezed in his pocket. He also did not like the way the floor constantly moved forward—it was hard to find his balance, and it made the world seem impermanent.

Finally, after four hours, by the light of a fire set as a warning, Shadrach saw the shadows of men and women with spears jabbing at something that stood at the base of their trash heap. It flinched and whined. He heard a voice as he approached. It said, "Please—leave me alone. Please," in a tone beyond panic: flat and dead and unmistakable.

Shadrach pulled out his gun and fired a warning shot into the air. The trash folk turned to look at him quizzically, shrugged as if to say, *It isn't trash—why should we fight for it?* and retreated to the top of their hill. They stood there laughing as Shadrach approached their victim. One man called out to him, "If you find out what it be, let us know."

Shadrach ignored him. He stood where the trash folk had stood and peered into the darkness. He saw a form, hunched low against the wall. The flickering of the fire did not reach far enough to see what lay hidden there. A sudden shiver of fear. Something was not right here. Something was very wrong.

The shadow moved, came toward the light, only to shuffle back into the darkness again. Shadrach caught a hint of a gauntness at odds with another impression: that of ponderous weight. The shadow made a moist licking sound, followed by a sinuous wriggling, a broken cough.

"Nicholas? Nicholas, is that you?" Shadrach wondered at the control in his voice.

The shadow turned unsteadily in Shadrach's direction.

"Do you want to hear a story?" said the sibilant voice. "I know a lot of stories. Let me tell you a story about the city. Because it's very important. The city is a cliché performed with cardboard and painted sparkly colors . . ." The voice became unclear, indistinct, almost lisping.

"No, Nick," Shadrach said. "I don't want to hear a story. You know who I am."

Silence. Then: "Hello, Shad. Imagine this. Shad here.

In the flesh." A snort. A despairing chuckle. "I don't suppose you have any drugs on you? Any painkillers?"

Shadrach ran into the darkness. He kicked Nicholas hard, but retreated; his boot had met a mushiness that revolted him.

"My God, Nick, what's happened to you?"

The shadow cringed against the wall. "Thanks, Shad. Thanks for the kick. You've split my lip. I'm bleeding, Shad."

"And I'll hit you again—harder—if you don't tell me what I need to know."

"Why don't you just go away. Just . . . go away. Please."

"I can't go away until I know some things."

Shadrach heard Nicholas slide farther down the wall, until he was sitting. And yet the shadow occupied the same space.

The hairs rose on Shadrach's arms.

"Come out into the light, Nick."

"No. Not even one pill? Not even a single pill?"

"Come out where I can see you."

"Oh, Shad, you really don't want me to do that."

Shadrach aimed his gun into the darkness. "You have two choices and five seconds."

"I'm not myself, Shad. I'm just not."

"Three seconds."

A long, moist sigh and then, with stealthy ponderousness, a sly thickness, Nicholas came out of the darkness.

He met Shadrach's disbelieving stare with his enigmatic, blue-tinted compound eyes.

Shadrach choked back his nausea. "My God, Nick. My God."

Nicholas resembled nothing so much as the kitten creature he had made as a boy, the creature Nicola had put out of its misery. The compound eyes, yes, and the five legs, the lizard's tail, the oversized human ear erupting from the top of his furry head, and from the catlike ears writhing blood-red tongues. Nicholas had wrapped a gray robe around his body, but from the holes in its frayed fabric things protruded and things poked. He was half naked and dirty and all that remained to mark him as human was his nose and his fanged mouth, which made his speech difficult. It was also Nicola's mouth, Nicola's nose.

"Let me go back into the darkness," the creature said. "It might be easier for you."

Shadrach nodded. When he no longer felt that presence near him, he got to his feet, walked over to the wall, and sat down beside Nicholas, still unable to look at him.

"I wasn't expecting . . ."

A harsh laugh. "Neither was I."

"Who did this?"

"Who do you think? Quin. He had good ideas once, I think. Now he's dead. Dead but alive. No Living Art in him. But I have to admit, Shad, you got me in with him, all right. I can't deny that."

"Are you okay?"

The massive head swung toward him, the compound eyes glittering. "Is that a joke? Because I don't find it very funny. I'm not okay. I'm a . . . what was it he said? . . . a reflection of my own failure. That's what he said. I just wish it didn't hurt so much."

"What did you do when I sent you to Quin's?"

"I . . . I tried to buy a meerkat. Are you sure you don't have any drugs? Nothing?"

"I don't have any drugs. You're going to exhaust me with that question. What did you do then—at Quin's?"

"He didn't have any meerkats, so I said thanks anyway and I left and went—"

Shadrach hit Nicholas across the face with his gun hand. His hand went *into* Nicholas's face. Nicholas cried out and made a gurgling sound.

"Why did you do that, Shad? Why?"

"Tell me what really happened at Quin's. What did you do that I told you specifically *not* to do?"

"I don't know what you're talking about. Honest, I don't."

Shadrach faced Nicholas, on his knees in the garbage, the lambent compound eyes reflecting his image back at him.

"Nicholas. Nick. I don't want to hurt you. But if you don't tell me what I need to know, I'm going to kill you. Why lie now, Nick? Or is it just that you can't stop lying? I mean, look at you—you're finished. You're through.

Why should I even threaten to kill you? You're already dead."

A rage was building in him. He thought he might kill Nicholas anyway.

"That's not true," Nicholas said. "If I can just get out of this place, there're things I can have done. Maybe get it reversed."

Shadrach shook his head, slumped back against the wall. "You and I both know you'll be dead in a week. You've the life span of a mayfly. If you don't die, someone's going to see you and kill you. Now: What did you really do at Quin's?"

"I tried to make a deal."

"Which I told you not to do, right?"

"I'm sorry, Shadrach. I'm sorry."

"What happened then?"

"He had me drugged. He *did* things to me. He said he'd kill me. He put things into me—flesh that flowered and took root. It didn't hurt at first. Not at first. He told me . . ." Nicholas choked on the words, spat up a green-gray slime.

"What did he tell you?"

"He told me I would be his Living Art. How could I refuse? My career was over, but here he was, still giving me a chance to be"—a sort of awe entered his voice, a kind of love—"*immortal.* To be remembered." The tone hardened. "Really fucking nice friends you've got, Shadrach."

"He's no friend of mine."

"You *work* for him."

"I hardly know him. So, what did you do after he re-designed you?"

"I . . . I . . ."

"Let me guess. You did jobs for him. Tell me about the jobs you did for him. Quickly."

"I smuggled body parts for him across district lines. I carried drugs for him."

"Did you kill anyone for him?"

"No!"

Shadrach pulled John the Baptist from his pocket and addressed him with mock seriousness. "Is that right, John? Nicholas didn't kill anyone for Quin? Nicholas, you remember John. Maybe he didn't go by that name when you knew him."

Nicholas said nothing, just looked at John the Baptist in shock.

John the Baptist said, "He killed seven or eight people. Mostly bioneers who tried to take a piece of Quin's business. Hello, Nicholas."

"Hello," Nicholas said in a flat, dead tone.

"John," Shadrach said. "I know you tried to kill Nicola. Do you know who *did* kill her?"

Nicholas started to weep. Great glistening tears rolled down his multiple eyes. "Put him away," he said. "Please— get rid of him."

"I hope you both die in extreme agony," John the

Baptist said as Shadrach stuffed the meerkat back in his pocket.

"I killed *myself,*" Nicholas said. "I killed *myself.* I knocked on the door and she opened it and I killed myself. It was like I was looking in the mirror and I just wanted to end it all and I strangled her to death, and the elephantmen came in and took her away . . ."

Shadrach felt John the Baptist twitching in irritation. He stuck his finger in the pocket, shoved it in John the Baptist's mouth, winced at the toothless bite. The pain helped him to focus.

"Why did you do it?"

"I wanted to kill myself. I was coerced. I was already changing . . . into this." Nicholas flinched in the shadows, as if scared of himself.

"No you weren't," Shadrach said. "No. You didn't start to change into this, this . . . what you are now . . . until Quin raped Nicola's memories *after* you strangled her. *You* killed her—*you* did it. Out of fear, out of cowardice."

"You're lying," Nicholas said. "You're lying. I was already changing, I was already—"

"Shut up!"

Nicholas sobbed, head bowed into his multiple appendages.

"And Quin asked you to do this?"

"Yes."

He was on Nicholas before the "yes" was out of his

mouth. His hands reached around the creature's thorny throat, cutting off all sound, all sense. Except that Nicholas, even now, looked too much like *her*—the cheekbones, the nose, the mouth—and the irrational thought came to him that he was murdering his beloved. Choking her to death. He wrenched his hands away and sucked in great gulps of air.

"Damn it! It should be so easy to kill you."

"I wish you would."

"I can't."

And then the vain, the calculating words: "I look . . . like her, don't I?"

He ignored Nicholas. His fingers, claws, cut into his palms. What to do? What to do?

"Will you try to kill Quin?" Nicholas asked, almost indifferently.

"Yes."

"He won't let you, you know, unless it's part of his plan."

"He won't have a choice."

"Quin rules the world, Shad. Don't you know that? He's like a god."

"What is his plan?"

Nicholas laughed. "You work for Quin and you don't know what he's been planning?"

"No, I don't. I take orders. I visit the estates of old women and discuss the weather. I don't ask questions."

Nicholas coughed up blood. He bent over, let the

blood loop down to the ground, wiped his mouth, stared at Shadrach. "Just as well. I asked questions and look what happened to me."

"What's this plan?"

"Simplicity itself—to allow the meerkats to no longer worship at the altar of Quin. To let them become *themselves*. Make their own decisions. You should ask your friend on a plate. He ought to know."

"He won't tell me."

"And you can't make him?"

"He's just a head. It's hard to even make him talk. Why does Quin want to do this?"

Nicholas shrugged. "I don't know. I know how it will happen, though—gradually. Not suddenly. So as to be even more complete. There will be signs. There will be symbols. Certain events, certain actions, some as subtle as the way the light strikes a stretch of sidewalk, or the flight of a lone bird across the sky—all of these things will flick ever more switches until gradually, gradually, the meerkats will become independent and rise up against their human oppressors."

"That makes no sense."

"It will when it happens. You'll understand it when it happens."

"But *why*? Surely you must know."

"He doesn't tell me everything. All I know is, the city's in danger. We've got to get out of the city."

"Fuck the city. Have you seen Quin? The real him?"

"Yes." The voice of pride, despite the desecrated body. What must Quin be to warrant such twisted devotion? "He lives on the thirtieth level and . . ." He stopped, realizing his mistake.

Shadrach smiled. "Take me there."

6

Nicholas led Shadrach down into the darkness—a hobbling, difficult descent due to Nicholas's condition. A dozen escalators, a half dozen elevators. Stairs. Ladders. They hugged the sides of tunnels, their faces stained green by maintenance lights. They ran through corridors deemed unsafe, this fact illuminated by the red glow suffusing such places. In the crimson haze, Nicholas looked as if he were bleeding to death. Such a light revealed the function and truth of things. They slunk always by the path that would least expose them to true light, so that when true light approached them, when it reproached them, it came as a shock. Throughout this journey—which Shadrach always remembered later as without sound and smell—they said not a single word to each other. For Shadrach, this was a blessing. He had nothing to say to Nicholas, and anything Nicholas said to him would only have angered him . . .

Finally, they entered the ancient subway station that Nicholas had indicated was their destination. The station filled a huge hall. Its fluted archways rose like wings into the darkness of an upper level that smothered their delicacy. Sounds drifting up into that darkness were deflected, transformed into echoes. The weight of the upper darkness was held back only by fluttering globes of light that teased always with the notion of snapping into true illumination or snapping out of existence altogether.

The station itself was old and grimy, the ticket office a rotted husk within which huddled the bent shapes of old machines that might once have been intelligent. The platform had rusted in the parts made of metal and eroded in the parts made of stone; travelers must, in the fickle light, be wary of turning an ankle or worse. The smell—one part leakage from the garbage zone, one part escaping oil—was always at a remove, as if a painting's true colors had been blurred, hidden beneath the patina of years of dust.

Caught in this twilight world, each waiting traveler struggled through a fog of shadow, faces careening out of the dimness like pale and failing satellites. Each could have been waiting in an island of solitude and self-absorption for a hundred years; indeed, at first glance, he had thought the platform held a field of forgotten statuary.

They held briefcases and canes. Heavy luggage lay

sprawled at their feet. None of those who waited met Shadrach's stare as Nicholas led him through their ranks toward the tracks. But neither did they step aside, until he began to think of them as ghosts, lost souls, lunatics. In the gloom, his vision played tricks so that the farthest figures took on unreal shapes: icytheous heads, lizardous bodies, ornithologic limbs.

It was, Shadrach decided, a hateful place. He wished only to be gone from there. Now that they had approached the tracks, the thick smell of gasoline met the station's musty stink. The tracks were situated in a huge trough that Shadrach assumed must conform itself to the shape of the train. Below, in between the tracks, creatures scuttled, at once like and unlike mice. He did not want to see their faces, for fear they might resemble the faces of the orangutan people in Quin's above-level lair. The creatures spun in and out of sight below Shadrach. They made little coughing sounds at one another, fought each other, and mated, oblivious to his stare.

Dull red warning lights flooded their world. They ran into their holes; a train was fast approaching. The intense vibration and wind of it filled the station. Those who wore hats held on to them, while the travelers as one broke their statuary silence to murmur and mumble as they moved toward the tracks, until they were pressed up behind Shadrach and Nicholas.

"They don't fear you," Shadrach said to Nicholas. He

looked at the ground, still afraid to examine the faces of his fellow travelers.

"We're so deep now that they've seen things much stranger, trust me."

The train, when it came, was a massive brute—its bulk filled even the dark upper level, more a spacecraft than a train. Its makers had instilled in its form no grace, no subtlety. It had been built for heavy work under rough conditions, and the only sign of beauty bequeathed to it was the reckless speed with which its blind bullethead barreled down the tracks. Shadrach thought it would rush on past the station, but then, casually, as if all one muscle, it stopped in a blink, put shutters on its speed, and idled there, eclipsing the tunnel. As it idled, every clattering, shrieking sound possible emanated from its multitude of orifices. It sat there shuddering, its body a ruin, great holes punched in its sides, like some monster from before the beginning of Time.

The pitted steel doors of its multilevels ground open. A smattering of very strange people disembarked— although not from the doors, but from the holes between the doors. The holes, it seemed, were larger than the doors, and therefore more convenient. Shadrach looked away as the last of the passengers stepped off onto the platform. He wondered if his impression of lizardness, of fishness, might not be accurate. What would he see if he turned his head? Surely nothing as odd as Nicholas.

"Watch your step," Nicholas said as they entered the train. "There are holes in the floor as well."

The train contained nothing so comfortable as seats. They stood, each passenger staking out territory. The embarkees spread out between compartments until only three other people stood near them: a woman dressed in red, wearing a large red hat from which descended a veil that covered her face; a man with ratlike features who hugged the farthest corners, darting quick, nervous glances at Nicholas; and a puffy four-foot-tall shadow dressed in rags.

The doors slid shut and the train began to tremble and shake. It groaned and snorted and complained in all of its metal parts. Then it seemed physically to rear back, before hurling itself into a darkness lit only by the red emergency lights. The sound—a thousand nails drawn across a stone surface; a million pieces of fatigued steel giving way at once—deafened Shadrach and he almost fell from the recoil, managed to cling to a pole of dubious strength, his fellow passengers' faces subsumed in blood, their eyes locked on the gun he had drawn and now held at his side. The train bellowed and leapt on its tracks, a beast eager for the hunt, and through a hole in the floor he could see the ground below passing by in a blur. He began to think that he must in fact have been captured at the organ bank and must now lie beside Nicola beneath the mountain of legs, and all the rest was only a dream.

"You'll have to jump," Nicholas shouted in his ear. The wind was fierce, the train still loud with the fury of its own passage. Enemy of entropy, might it not win free of the tracks, forge its own path through the wall of the tunnel?

Shadrach twisted around to look at Nicholas. "Jump?!"

Nicholas nodded, compound eyes crimson. "It's the only way—you jump in about fifteen minutes. The train runs past an opening that provides a clear view of the thirtieth level. You jump *right down into it*. Otherwise, you have to climb down through fifteen levels. Much harder. You'd probably be killed even with your badge."

"I don't have wings!" Shadrach shouted back.

"You'll use a parachute, of course."

"Where the hell do I get a parachute?"

"There will be one coming along soon." Nicholas grinned, showing his teeth.

"What does that mean, Nick?"

"You'll see soon enough. Be patient."

Shadrach glowered at him. His stomach was lurching from the rough ride. His nerves were shot. How far could he trust Nicholas?

But three minutes later a burly man with parachutes hooked over his shoulder walked through, silent as the rest. Shadrach bought two parachutes from him, offered one to Nicholas.

Nicholas shook his head. "No—I don't need one. I'm not going."

"Yes you are."

"I'm not going back!"

Shadrach held up the gun. "You're going. Put it on. Now, where do we jump from?"

Nicholas sighed, as if tired of resisting. He slowly began to put on his parachute. "Not from here." He pointed to a man-sized hole in the right side of the compartment, behind which sheer rock and metal moved by at an alarming rate. "That hole is too small. There should be a bigger one three compartments down."

They walked three compartments down, Shadrach's gun digging into Nicholas's side. There was indeed a larger hole—and ten other people congregated around it. A ragged, sickly-looking band, some were hunched over, some weeping, some silent in evident despair.

"What's wrong with them?" Shadrach asked.

"Nothing. Never mind. It's not important," Nicholas said.

Shadrach took Nicholas's hand. "Tell me when and where to jump."

The speed was horrible—the ground beneath their feet moved so swiftly it made him ill.

"You'll know it when you see it. Put on your parachute."

It took forever to properly attach his parachute; the straps and buckles mystified him. Meanwhile, the train began to descend sharply. The walls outside the train fell away and fresh air flooded in, smelling of impossible things: of flowers, of perfume, of nectar. Through the darkness, Shadrach thought he saw sparkles and reflections. The train banked right and caught three of his fellow jumpers unawares. They fell screaming.

"Nicholas! They don't have parachutes!"

"Of course they don't," came the hiss in his ear. "This is a favorite spot for suicides. Now jump!"

Shadrach heard something odd in that voice. He turned in time to catch the point of one of Nicholas's claws in his left side, where it scraped against John the Baptist, then dug into his flesh. He yelled in surprise. Nicholas slashed at one of his parachute straps, but Shadrach reflexively put his arm in the way, grunted as the claw entered his arm. Ignoring the sharp pain, he aimed his gun at Nicholas.

But before he could catch his balance, Nicholas shoved him—and he fell into the darkness, losing hold of Nicholas. He fired at the rough box of light that framed Nicholas. He saw Nicholas spin and fall out of the light.

He stuck the gun in his belt as he spun, twisting through the darkness, surrounded by seven screaming suicides without parachutes. Above, he saw the red gaping holes in the bottom of the train. The train was bleeding light. The tiny faces of passengers peered down at him. Quizzical. Removed. The train vanished, eclipsed by one of the suicides. Darkness. The suicides stopped screaming. He didn't know where they were. He didn't know where Nicholas was. He tumbled end over end like a piece of wood. A foot hit him in the face, sent him reeling faster. The wails of the soon-to-be-dead resumed both above and below him. In his pocket, John the Baptist snarled furiously. He should apologize to the meerkat. They were going to die. Even before John's twenty-four hours were up. Then he remembered the parachute: it was the bulky thing clinging to his back in fear. He pulled at the ring. It didn't give. He pulled again. Nothing. He was at least halfway down. He could see shimmering particles of light below him. The hard wind that cut his face seemed like a premonition of a harder death. He yanked at the ring a third time.

The chute opened and the straps pulled at him with vicious buoyancy. He bobbed right side up. John the Baptist's snarling subsided. He blinked, looked up at the enormous white mushroom cap that had saved him.

And then the first suicide came tearing down through the parachute, smacked hard into his left shoulder. The muscles exploded with agony. The next suicide also split the parachute, but didn't hit him. Then they were all through and past, below him, still shrieking their lungs out. The parachute began to collapse and Shadrach still couldn't tell the distance to the ground. His speed began to increase. The chute was failing him. He began to hyperventilate. He wasn't going to make it after all . . .

And then he hit.

7

Shadrach regained consciousness to the soft caress of the parachute silk, which had settled across his face like a shroud. The smell of dirt and plastic. A coldness to the air. A stillness. He opened his eyes to complete darkness. He was already prepared for death, ready for the afterworld. Somewhere nearby, water lapped gently. He wondered if he should move. It was peaceful under the shroud. The shroud allowed him to relinquish all responsibility. He had not known such peace since he had left the sunlight.

But then John the Baptist began to squirm in his pocket, and he remembered what he had come here to do. He sat up, still covered by the parachute. His throat was sore and his limbs creaky, stiff, but he had sustained no serious injuries. His shoulder throbbed and he had a terrible, piercing headache. Nothing like the loss of a hand, or an eye.

He fumbled his way out of the parachute, released the straps, and stood up. He pulled his gun out of his belt, thankful it hadn't discharged on impact. Carefully, he reached into the other pocket, brought out John the Baptist, held him up to eye level.

"Now that there's only darkness, you can come out. Are you okay?"

The meerkat made a derisive sound, astonishingly human. "I'm not okay. I'm dying. And it's not dark—your eyes are just pathetically bad at retaining light. It's mid-afternoon under a blue sky in here. For me. You—you'll adjust eventually. By then I'll be dead."

"I hope you're right, John. But not out of any malice. If I could save you now, I think I would."

The meerkat sneered. "Because we have grown so close. Because we've learned to live together, despite our differences."

"No. Because I'm beginning to understand you. We'll talk again later."

He stuck John the Baptist back in his pocket.

He still heard water behind him, but rather than fumble toward it blind, he waited for his eyes to adjust to the darkness. The darkness was ignorant of time; it ate time as indiscriminately as it ate the light. Eventually, the darkness gave way to something that was not exactly light, but through which he could see, tinged a pale purple, the outline of rocks—a greater darkness—ahead of him. A faint suggestion of craggy ground.

He swiveled around—to face the flickers and flashes of a vast inland sea. The shoreline lay a scant twenty meters from him. He sniffed the air: a tangy scent that spoke of summer gales and worm-riddled ships. A smell not unlike the briny scent of the canals. Slowly, the glints and ripples were revealed as the tips of luminous fins as slippery, bejeweled sea creatures slid through the water, followed at times by a length of luminous tentacle, suckers edged in gold. Beyond them, the water stretched to a horizon of black on black. There appeared to be no far shore.

Sitting there, in the dark, he could almost fool himself into believing that he was above level, at dusk, with the canals all around him.

But the illusion faded when, his sight still improving, he saw Nicholas. He sat to Shadrach's left and stared with his compound eyes at the water that undulated against the shore. His robes had fallen away, unmasking the ever-more-complex and horrible things Quin had done to him. His hands were out at his sides, palms up. His lower half had been shattered by the impact with the ground. He was quite dead. In sodden little piles of blood and bone, various parts of the seven suicides lay all around him.

"Nick, Nick, Nick," Shadrach said softly. What a price to pay for weakness. Many men much weaker than Nicholas had gone through their entire lives without ever paying such a price. All of Shadrach's anger toward Nicholas drained away, leaving behind only sadness and a profound sense of guilt. If not for him, if not for him . . .

Shadrach did not know which way would lead to Quin, but he felt a certain affinity for the water, and so he followed the shore in a direction he thought should be north. He was prepared, now that his objective was so close, to walk a thousand miles. He walked with his gun in his right hand, his badge in the left. He walked not like a fugitive or a thief, but like a man who belonged there and knew where he was going.

The image of Nicholas's shattered body lodged in his mind like a ghost, while around him the perpetual night disgorged its mysteries as a magician might, and just as suddenly returned those mysteries to the unknowable realm beyond the limits of his sight.

Slowly, he came to realize that if there were a Hell on Earth, it wasn't in the wastelands between cities, but here, on the city's thirtieth underground level. A thousand lost souls populated the land along the shore, condemned to wander until death. The first he encountered were like Nicholas, or close enough, that, used to compound eyes, flayed skin, the sight of internal organs bobbing like water canteens on the outside of the body, he simply ignored them where they sobbed and flapped in the shadows, seeking some release from their pain. Nicholas must have escaped from this limbo, happy to exchange it for the uncertainties of a garbage zone.

When the rasping cries and fetid, sickly sweet stench were well behind him, he pulled John the Baptist from his pocket and lashed him to his left forearm with parachute string.

"You shall be my affliction, for all the world to see," Shadrach said, and he looked at the meerkat with something close to affection. "How much longer do you have to live, Affliction?"

The meerkat sniffed the air. "Nine hours, perhaps. But you have brought me back to the place of my birth. I used to play along the shore. It gives me strength. That, and knowing your day is almost done."

"This may be true, but maybe you'd help me just this once. Tell me how to find Quin."

"No. But perhaps you should head for that glowing green light."

Sure enough, directly ahead, through the darkness, an emerald point of light moved along the shoreline.

"What is it?" he asked.

"It's a light. I thought you liked the light."

The meerkat looked almost victorious.

"I was headed that way anyhow," Shadrach said.

It glowed phosphorescent green. It moved like a worm. It looked like a caterpillar with no head. It was the size of a small but muscular snake. It ignored Shadrach utterly. It inched its way along the shore of the vast sea with a sense of great purpose. As if contributing to this thought, its markings were so precise, its segmentations so rigidly correct, that the level of perfection it had attained fascinated Shadrach. He had not expected to see anything so whimsical here. An awkward smile spread across his face.

"What is it?" he asked John.

"Look more carefully."

When he did as the meerkat suggested, Shadrach discovered that, on each segment of the creature, a number had been emblazoned in living tissue, made part of its markings, and that the segments themselves were segmented by tiny green fault lines.

"It's a machine!" he said.

"Almost correct," the meerkat said. "Touch it."

"Touch it?"

"It won't bite."

"How can I trust you?"

The meerkat bared its gums. "You can't. Who can tell what a dying mind like mine might or might not do? I would advise you not to touch it after all, considering my treacherous history."

Shadrach looked out across the sea, where at times a length of sharp, blue-green fin would break the surface of the water. In a world so strange, he wondered if it mattered what he did, as long as he did *something*.

He squatted beside the glowing caterpillar. He reached

out with one hand and touched it with his index finger. It felt smooth yet furry. It stopped inching along. It fell over onto its side.

"You've killed it," John the Baptist said. "I told you not to touch it."

Then, with slow, meticulous grace, the caterpillar unraveled itself, section by section. Each section, as soon as it had unfolded, reformed, stitching itself back together again, until it lay completely flat: a square of green, glowing flesh spread out on the seashore. The tiny fissures and fault lines filled with intense light. A humming sound. The light shot out from the lines, formed a grid. The lines of light faded . . . leaving behind a three-dimensional map of the sea and its surrounding shore, rendered in a darkly glittering green. The numbers corresponded to the sections the map had split itself up into, and they now lay at the edges as crosshatching grid references.

It struck Shadrach that this was the most beautiful creature he had ever seen, or ever would see, and that he was fated to experience it when he could not fully appreciate it.

"Do you have a sense of beauty?" he asked John the Baptist. "Because this is beautiful."

The meerkat said, somewhat wearily, "My sense of beauty is more refined than you can ever know, each of my senses so heightened that I might as well live in a different world than you. But where you see form, I see function. You can be forgiven, I suppose, for favoring style over substance. It's the nature of your species. This is one of Quin's maps. That's all."

"Quin made this?"

"Quin made everything, even the sea. This is his laboratory. This is his world. Not yours."

Shadrach sat down beside the map. "But how, John? Tell me how he can make monsters and yet creatures as beautiful as this?"

The meerkat laughed. "There's something touching about your innocence. But this monster has no perspective on that question. May the contradiction torment you forever."

Shadrach stared at the map. Its shimmering display featured several place-names, in a language he did not know, and a blinking red light he assumed must be their present location. Almost directly opposite, across the sea, he saw a symbol of a human and an animal merging.

"Is that where Quin is?" he asked John the Baptist.

"Ask the map. Talk to the map. I'm too busy shutting down." The meerkat closed its eyes.

"Where is Quin?" Shadrach asked the map, but the map just burbled at him.

What now? Before, the meerkat had told him to touch the map.

He touched the human/animal symbol. The three-dimensional display shut off with a snap. The lights dimmed on the map. The fissures and cracks between segments healed, sealed up.

The meerkat let out a huffing laugh, but said nothing.

Shadrach stood, backed away from the map, afraid the meerkat might have goaded him into some sort of trap. He aimed his gun at the map . . .

. . . which began to flap around on the ground like a bat, its edges burning an intense green. As it flapped, the color spread from the edges toward the interior. When the color reached the center, the map became all sharp edges, and Shadrach heard a sound like the shriek of a cicada. Suddenly, the edges resolved themselves into wings—sharp and bladelike. With a flapping like knives crossing, the map rose into the air reborn as a headless, featherless bird. It soared twice over Shadrach, and then began to shadow the shoreline, before circling back to him.

"Follow the map. It's waiting for you," the meerkat mumbled, its eyes still tightly shut.

Shadrach followed the flying map as it soared along the shoreline. More creatures came at him from the dark—creatures with grotesque goat heads and eyes peering from their feet. Creatures that scuttled on eight legs and had the features of delicately proportioned apes pinned to the scorpion's carapace. Such refuse, as bad as if Nicholas had experimented for a thousand years. How to reconcile the beauty of the map with such creatures? Some were just exhausted networks of veins, red and panting and in an agony that, for lack of a mouth, screamed from their every jerking movement. Eyeballs in clustered bunches cast their liquid gaze at Shadrach. Others rolled, bounced, slithered, ran but were little more than scores of feet. Some lay in the moist sand still caught in the tangle of afterbirth but already smelling of decay and the grave. Here and there, Shadrach came upon the broken-open husks of the vats: green chrysalides made of a substance like emerald glass. These birthing places gave off a sense of desolate abandonment. Around the vats, liquids had gathered, simulating those found in the womb, and had dried into an inchoate mess at their collapsed mouths. Things on the ground crawled and things in the sky flew with broken-backed ineptitude, while the things in the water slurped and belloped and sang to themselves in burbling saditude.

But it was only when the dogs ran by that Shadrach felt fear. They came in a pack of ten, close by one another, turning with remarkable precision in pursuit of some unfortunate creature. Flaps of wrinkled flesh dominated their foreheads, and their hides were blacker than the perpetual night. Tiny dead violets, their eyes pierced the darkness like laser beams.

Right in front of him, they pivoted, wheeled, spared him not a glance, and fell upon a stumbling, gasping creature farther up the shore. It was composed of two stilts of flesh atop which sat a slug of a torso, a larval head. They tore into the legs. It toppled and then, as it squealed and shrieked, they ripped into it with fangs larger than fingers. Shadrach stood frozen, unable to look away. If they had turned upon him next, he would have been a dead man, but when they had finished, they sniffed the air, regained their precise military formation, and trotted off. As the last one joined the line, it turned to Shadrach. His blood became ice within him. He saw that beneath the violet eyes, before the muzzle ran down into nose and mouth, another face had been embedded in the flesh: a woman's face, with dark eyes, high eyebrows, a small nose, and, caught against the edge of her face and the dog's skin, two strands of golden blonde hair. The full mouth was raw with smeared blood and flesh. The eyes held a mixed horror and triumph that made Shadrach's hand shake as he aimed his gun at the creature. But the creature wheeled around once more and then was gone— racing alongside its fellows down the shore so that the water splashed out beneath their paws.

When they were shadows on the horizon, a voice spoke from the shattered remains of the stilt-flesh creature. It said, "The Gollux thinks they've gone, haven't they?"

Shadrach started. He walked over to the bloody carcass. Its eyes had been plucked from their sockets. Torn and tattered, the skull had been picked clean of flesh. It dangled from the raw and savaged spinal column, which lay fully exposed—a white, winking travesty. Shadrach aimed his gun at the carcass.

The voice came again: "The Gollux knows they've gone, haven't they?"

"Where is that voice coming from, John?" Shadrach asked the meerkat.

The meerkat looked as agitated as Shadrach had ever seen him. "I don't know."

The voice, reedy but confident: "Help the Gollux. The Gollux is alive, alive is the Gollux. Kick open the skull."

"What are you?" Shadrach asked.

"Kick open the skull and you will find out that I am the Gollux, I am."

At his shoulder, John the Baptist attempted an unconvincing snicker. Overhead, the map circled patiently.

"What should I do, John?"

"What do you have to lose?"

"More than you."

But he drew back his foot and kicked open the skull anyway.

The inside of the skull seemed composed of a clay-colored brain, but this "brain" quickly uncoiled itself and pushed out of the skull, then extended to its full length.

The creature, about the size of a baby, had a horizontal torso that tapered off at the front into an oddly human pair of legs and at the back into a pair of legs and muscular buttocks. Positioned three-quarters of the way back along the torso rose a clay-colored neck crowned with an oval head framed by stringy hair that writhed out behind it as though caught by a stiff wind. In the center of the head, a single black round hole served as, Shadrach supposed, an eye. It had no mouth, unless it spoke out of what presumably was its anus. It paced back and forth in front of Shadrach, as if trying to work feeling back into its limbs after long constriction.

"What are you?"

"The Gollux thanks you," it said.

Shadrach aimed his gun at it. "What are you?"

The creature, still stepping from side to side, said something that sounded suspiciously like "Gollux," and then, "You're not from here."

"And you're talking out of your asshole!" Shadrach said. He laughed until the tears ran down his face.

"Where are you from? What is that attached to your arm?" the Gollux asked.

"It is the head of a meerkat," Shadrach said, recovering. "I'm from the surface, where the sun is."

"The Gollux has never seen the sun."

"I've never seen anything like you before."

"I am the only Gollux."

"Are you one of Quin's?"

"Yes. Based on an ancient design from a fairy tale. What is your flaw?"

"My flaw?"

"Every creature here has a flaw. The Gollux wishes to know yours."

"I suppose that I'm mad—completely crazy—and that I have a meerkat strapped to my arm."

The Gollux nodded solemnly. "That is indeed a flaw."

"And what is your flaw?"

"I am the Gollux. I am not a flawed Gollux. I am a flawed location. The Gollux was not meant to be contained in the skull of a swannerbee. It was the swannerbee's flaw to have a Gollux for a brain."

Shadrach looked up at the flying map. He pointed to it. "What, then, is the map's flaw?"

The Gollux said, "Its flaw is its mortality. A map should live a long time. But this map already dies—it is flying lower and lower—and its memory fails it. Wherever you are following it, it will not take you."

The meerkat said, "Don't listen to the Gollux. It likes to hear itself talk. It just doesn't know what it's talking about. The map is fine. It will lead you to Quin."

Before Shadrach could reply, the Gollux said, "I am the Gollux. The Gollux knows many things. The Gollux knows that the map dies. The Gollux knows that the meerkat has a flaw: it is only a head. Its body knows only half the truth, and its head knows only half the truth. The map is flying lower and lower. In circles."

The map's green had begun to fade and it indeed was flying lower, just barely over their heads.

"Something tells me, John, that you're lying to me," Shadrach said.

"But we've grown so close," the meerkat echoed, mockingly. "Surely you won't believe this gobbet of flesh over me?"

The Gollux said, "The Gollux is a flawed location, not a flawed Gollux."

"The Gollux is annoying," the meerkat said. "The Gollux talks too much."

"But I believe the creature," Shadrach said. "Do you know the way to Quin?" he asked it.

"The Gollux knows."

"Is it this way?" Shadrach pointed in the direction they had been traveling.

"No."

Shadrach gave John the Baptist a knowing look. "Okay, then—is it this way?" and he pointed back the way they had come.

"No."

Shadrach pointed toward the mountains, away from the sea.

"No."

"I told you it didn't know what it was talking about!" the meerkat hissed.

"All that's left is the sea, Gollux."

"The Gollux knows that there is no sea."

"The creature is crazy," the meerkat said. "You should kill it! Kill it now!" John tried to nip at Shadrach's hand.

Shadrach ignored the meerkat, said to the Gollux, "What do you mean?"

"It is not a sea. It is the mouth of the creature that holds Quin. At the center of the mouth, you will find

Quin. I am the Gollux. The Gollux is a flawed location, not a flawed Gollux."

"Stop listening to it," the meerkat hissed. "Ignore it."

"Shut up, John," Shadrach said. "Do you know how to get there?" he asked the Gollux.

"Walk. Walk across the water. If you know the way."

"Do you know the way?"

"Yes."

"Will you take me there?"

"I am the Gollux. The Gollux does as it pleases. But it pleases the Gollux to help him who rescued the Gollux from its flawed location."

The exhausted map chose that moment to come to rest at their feet after an extended death glide. It was crinkled and old-looking. It no longer shone with light. But it was still the most beautiful thing Shadrach had ever seen.

8

Shadrach looked out at the shimmering sea. He did not like the idea of putting his fate in the hands of this creature. But what else could he do? The map was dead. John the Baptist was dying. He could wander the shore for months and never find Quin. He could be ripped to shreds by Quin's creations at any moment. Twenty-four levels above his head, Nicola waited for him.

"Gollux," he said, with a confidence he did not feel, "lead the way. I'll follow, but you have to go first."

The Gollux turned and walked out into the water. Soon, it was only a stalk of flesh, its body hidden by the waves. Then, just as it must surely drown or grow gills, the Gollux began to *rise*, until it appeared to stand atop the waves.

"Holy shit," Shadrach said.

John the Baptist snorted. "It's not a miracle, you idiot. Can't you see *anything*?"

"I don't care if it's a miracle or not—it's more than you or I are capable of."

The Gollux scuttled back and forth across the water, determining the limits on where it could and could not walk. Now Shadrach saw that the Gollux stood upon a dark, smooth surface that had roughly the shape of a wing. Over the water came the Gollux's shrill voice: "The Gollux says to come quickly! The saylber will not wait for long."

"I'm coming," he called out. He splashed water left and right as he ran toward the Gollux. The water was warm, almost alive in its cloying closeness. The meerkat gnashed at him with its gums. It spat. It said, "He'll kill you! He's lying!" Until Shadrach, in midstride, his legs in water to his calves, stopped his running plunge long enough to stick the meerkat head back into his pocket.

The saylber was not, strictly speaking, a boat. But Shadrach had grown so accustomed to the miraculous that a real boat would have surprised him more. The saylber was a kind of flat *fish*—a long, thin, muscular manta ray with tremendous fin span and phosphorescent headlights for eyes. The tips of its "wings" curled in the water and created tiny swirls. Its thick back felt sandpapery even through Shadrach's boots. As the saylber sped without apparent friction or sound—the very opposite of the underground train—Shadrach struggled to balance himself. But soon he realized that the creature made continual, minute adjustments to correct for the turbulence, and then he relaxed, his muscles untensing, his senses no longer focused on keeping his feet.

Now he could take in his surroundings, and the whole world that was the thirtieth level opened up around him. The air was dark, but had a lightness to it that indicated no clouds could ever form here. The darkness itself was different depending on the shadows it described: the gray foreground of hilly terrain, the shimmering lip of the shore, the blue bruise of the sky, and, finally, the green tint of what seemed a truly limitless sea. The smell of brine came up off the sea, but also the thick funk of living organisms, the sweetness of the recently dead, and, from far off—almost an echo of a smell—a rustiness as of burning machinery. What would such a world do should the light ever hit it? Would it shrivel and decay, or would it rise up to blot out the sun?

The Gollux stood balanced on the saylber's head as the water flumed out to either side. The Gollux's stringy hair blew behind it in the slight breeze. The water made gurgling sounds. The saylber made rippling sounds. The Gollux made no sound at all.

When the shore behind them had faded back into anonymous shadow, Shadrach asked the Gollux, "What if our 'boat' decides to submerge itself?"

"Then the Gollux believes we will drown."

Shadrach eased himself down until he was sitting on the saylber's back. "Is that likely?"

"Only if the saylber decides to submerge itself."

Shadrach decided the Gollux was laughing at him. After a while, Shadrach heard drums beating over the water ahead of them.

"Gollux? What's that sound?"

"The Gollux is pained to say he does not know. But the Gollux thinks we will find out soon enough . . ."

"How profound, Gollux."

"The Gollux is not profound. The Gollux is a Gollux. Nothing more. Nothing less . . ."

Eventually, the open sea before them became cluttered with vast floating rafts, from which rose structures Shadrach could think of only as cathedrals. The drums had become so loud they hurt his ears. As the first spires loomed over them, he could see that the rafts were manned entirely by meerkats. He pulled out his badge as the wake of the rafts began to rock the creature.

"Where did they come from? And are they dangerous?" he asked the Gollux.

"The Gollux says that usually they let the winds take them wherever they lead. But now they are speeding for shore. Are they dangerous? the Gollux asks himself. The

Gollux does not feel any threat toward itself, but the Gollux cannot speak for what you feel . . ."

"Thank you, Gollux. Once again, you have managed to put all my fears to rest."

Despite himself, Shadrach felt a sense of awe, of appreciation, as the black obsidian temples and their scaffolding floated past. Thousands of meerkats in every shape and size, and every color from rust red to white, some with dense, thick fur, others with bristly hair, some with upturned ears and others with floppy ears—and yet not a one turned to look down at him from their lofty perches. They all stared toward the shore with an intensity of purpose that confused Shadrach. It was almost as if they meant to make their rafts reach shore sooner simply by wishing it so. The musk of them made him sneeze, and though now his heart was weak, and he almost wavered and wanted to turn back, the image of Nicola's face came to him, and he continued to hold up his badge like a shield.

The meerkats said nothing—to him, or to each other—and nowhere that he looked, at the spires, at the planks between rafts, at the scaffolding, did he see a single meerkat in motion. No, they all stood and watched the shore. The fires that dominated the burning hearts of their gently rocking cities guttered or spun out of control, unattended. The smell of white-hot metal, the sound of the great engines that helped keep them afloat . . .

As they glided through the channels formed between

the rafts, Shadrach noticed something that the meerkats' stillness had at first disguised: from the spires and the scaffolding, which combined looked like blackened skeletons of some enormous beast, makeshift gallows had been set up—and from the nooses swung ropes, wires, and elastic cords, from which hung hundreds of elephantmen and other non-meerkat Quin creations. The bodies hung straight down, limp and lifeless, the heads resting upon the stretched necks as if in sleep.

The meerkats' silence had nothing to do with him. Suddenly he understood that the silence represented an intense and watchful fear.

"They are fleeing the center," the Gollux said, without its customary pomposity. "They are fleeing Quin."

"What is the difference," Shadrach whispered to the Gollux, "between the creatures of the shore and the creatures of the sea?"

"The Gollux knows of only one difference: the creatures of the shore know they are flawed, but the creatures of the sea do not know they are flawed."

After a time, they left the silent floating cities of the meerkats behind. The open sea once more lay ahead of them. The saylber picked up speed. The water was flecked with tiny specks of green phosphorescence that swirled in tiny whirlpools. The water smelled, incredibly enough, of mint. Shadrach stood up again. He restrapped John the Baptist to his arm.

"How are you?" he asked the head.

"I can't feel my legs," the meerkat said. "I can't feel my feet. I must be dying."

"We have almost reached Quin."

"So? I'm dying. Shutting down. Turning off. I'm half convinced I should leave you prematurely so I don't have to see your ugly face."

"We just passed through a floating meerkat city. Did you grow up on a floating city?"

"What does it matter to you?"

"It doesn't. But I would rather talk to you than not—no matter how difficult you are."

"Let me tell you what happens when you burn a person's body, pull out all of his teeth, glue his head to a plate, and shove a bomb in his ear. You become that person's object of undying hatred."

"You're not a person," Shadrach said, but then trailed off.

Ahead of them, something huge blotted out the lesser darkness of sea and sky. At first glance, Shadrach could tell only that it resembled a vast set of jaws, with jagged shards of light placed up and down its surface to illuminate it. It floated in the water, rising and falling with the waves.

"What is *that*, Gollux?"

"That is our objective—that is where Quin lives . . ."

Soon, Shadrach could see that it didn't just *look* like a huge pair of spread jaws, it *was* a huge pair of spread jaws. Dripping seaweed and teeth, they rose some six hundred feet above the surface. The flesh of those jaws was pitted and gnarled with age or ill-use, either contrived by Quin or the result of the natural accumulation of years.

"Did Quin make this, Gollux?"

"He raised It from a Minnow."

The eye—the eye was most disquieting. It shone out at them like a searchlight, and as its attention drifted from there to there, over the wine-dark sea, so too did the light move across the depths. The deep green-blue of the pupil, and the golden veins that slithered across the cornea . . . why, the eye itself was larger than a small spacecraft! And mad, mad, mad in its roving: nervous and without purpose, the light so thick it pierced many hundreds of feet into the water, grazing the edges of other sea creatures: fins and tentacles and the impression of sinuous bodies swimming from the path of its assault.

As they approached the beast, the reason for the increasing waves, which actually splashed over the top of the saylber, became clear. Somewhere far, far below, the fish's tail swished back and forth to maintain this one position, as if ever hungry, ever in wait for the world so as to devour it whole. And somewhere halfway up the leviathan: the side fins, frilled and delicate despite weighing twenty or thirty tons, also working hard to maintain this one position. While Quin, within, worked his magic from the fish's belly.

The fish wasn't just old. It was scarred. Fires, like tiny blossoms, dotted its skin, some extinguished when the leviathan rose or fell a few dozen meters. Creatures patrolled the leviathan's skin—they were like tiny parasites, except that they were larger than Shadrach. They scuttled and clung to the vertical surface, performing alien functions. Maintenance of the beast. That it should not fall apart. That it should not die. These creatures—scaly, insectile, arthropodic—all lacked heads, consisting only of mouths and arms and legs without end. Chitinous. Viscous. Blind. Stupid. Birthed to perform one task, one function. Confronted by such creatures, it was hard for Shadrach not to think of Quin as a god.

Among them, meerkats could be seen to move, and other animals, of all types, locked in combat. The combatants centered around the fires, some of them falling off from the extreme angle of the leviathan's upper half and into the water, where without a scream or shriek, they were devoured by unseen animals in the sea. While the survivors labored on at the killing game, which seemed to consist solely of extinguishing other subspecies.

The smell of putrescent fish flesh came from the leviathan itself. It was rotting. It was alive, and it was rotting.

"Gollux, what is happening here?" Shadrach asked.

"All systems atrophy. All systems die. The fish is a system. Quin is a system. The meerkats are a system. There are too many systems. Too much confusion. Something has gone wrong. The systems are at war."

At the point where the jaws curved down to meet in ugly splendor, docks had been built, along with staircases leading into the mouth. The saylber headed for these as Shadrach reloaded his gun and checked for extra ammunition.

"Why," he asked as he removed the safety, "is the fish so calm? Why isn't it thrashing about?"

The Gollux turned toward Shadrach, eyeless as it appeared to be, and gave the unmistakable impression that it thought this was a stupid question. "Quin made the fish without nerve endings, so it could not feel the daily pains that might make it flinch or dive or splash. It is the calmest fish in all the world because of Quin's genius."

Would that Quin had had the genius—or was it compassion?—to pull the nerve ends out of Nicholas before altering him. This fish could be ripped to shreds, could be torn apart by connoisseurs of seafood back in the Canal District, and would not raise the slightest complaint. What an advancement! A creature that could not feel its own pain. A creature lacking survival instincts of any kind.

The metal of the ever-approaching docks burned red with the reflection of the fires. The fires spilled over the corners of the leviathan's mouth. The inside of its mouth was aflame, and still it patiently treaded water.

Only the lunatic movements of its eyes revealed its numbed panic.

The flesh towered above them, the eye so close it was no longer an eye, or even a circle, but just a green-blue surface that encompassed the horizon. The reason for the eye's panic became apparent, for even the eye was not a neutral ground. Creatures fought and died there, leaving gaping wounds. The smell made Shadrach cough and cover his mouth. Canyons, cliffs, cathedrals of flesh. The sounds of skirmishes fought with teeth and claws: the yowl or yelp of meerkats, the galumphing death rattle of even stranger beasts. And the sound of efficiency: the scuttling of the creatures built to maintain the leviathan. They didn't care that the beast was dying. They didn't care that a war was being waged on the flesh of their fish. They simply kept on doing what they had done for years: cleaning the scales, tending to the wounds, dousing the fires with the voluminous sputum of their breath.

The saylber came to a precise halt at the edge of the docks. The docks—the giant cranes and hauling machines—had been abandoned; anyone who had wanted to flee had fled a long time ago. The metal posts of the docks were topped with heads: human heads, inhuman heads. Shadrach didn't spare them a second glance. He'd seen so much worse. Instead, he hopped up onto the pier, the Gollux beside him. The saylber, with a wet squelch, immediately submerged, and Shadrach had the impression of its vast wings pumping furiously as it tried to put depth and distance between it and its insensate cousin, the leviathan.

From the moment Shadrach set foot on the dock, he could feel the vibration of the leviathan's heartbeat: now tremulous, now strong. And the beating of its fins deep underwater, which made its body, and the dock, nudge ever so slightly upward, so that he felt as if he were in danger of being launched into the air. A weird music played all around them, like a dirge. Above, the fish's teeth, like inverted mountain peaks, glinted down at Shadrach from a great height.

"Which way, Gollux?" he asked.

"This way," said the Gollux, and headed up the stairs toward the inside of the leviathan's mouth. The automatic mechanism on the stairs had failed because of the putrefied bodies that had jammed its lower levels, so they had to walk up them, stepping over the carnage.

Not more than ten steps up, an elephantman hurdled the railing and ran toward Shadrach, followed closely by a meerkat with a club in its hands. The meerkat, before Shadrach could react, caught up with the elephantman and hit it so hard the back of its skull crumpled inward. It fell with a wet thud at Shadrach's feet. He shot the meerkat before it had a chance to do anything, whether friendly or hostile. It, too, fell with a wet thud at Shadrach's feet.

"I don't like this place, Gollux," Shadrach said. "Let's get where we need to go in a hurry."

"The Gollux tells you this: It's just a rotting fish. Nothing to like or dislike."

They managed to make good progress after that, despite the steepness of the incline, and stacks of dead bodies slick with blood. The Gollux made great leaps to attain each next step. Shadrach marveled at the strangeness of a sudden vision: that huge as the leviathan appeared to him, to the Gollux it must be as big as the world.

When they reached the lip of the leviathan's mouth, they stopped and looked around them. To right and left, intolerably close, the jaws rose like twinned cliffs. The teeth, as large as ships, glinted in their own white light; giant silver fish threaded their way through the teeth, intent on cleaning the pitted surfaces. Were the leviathan to close its mouth, snap shut like a trap, Quin's whole world would be gone. What did it mean that Quin had chosen to live within the jaws of so large and dangerous a beast?

But the jaws held his attention for only a second—he had seen them from afar; up close, it was merely more of the same. The sights within the mouth of the beast interested him far more, for it was here that Quin had built his underground empire.

Never had any beast so wide, so varied, so interesting

a throat. From where Shadrach stood, it was at least four thousand meters to the opposite jawline. Between, in the basin of the beast's gullet, a new world had been carved from nerveless flesh.

The teeth themselves lit the entire tableau—a deep yellow, so that the light had an erratic quality: some teeth had been pulled, others sunk into the gums, or teetered on the edge of falling, or had fallen down into the gullet. Parts of the gums had, like pieces of rotten fruit, sloughed off the mouth and lay now in puddles and piles down below, littering the entrance to the gullet, or having smashed into buildings. The hot wind that rose from the firmament, smelling of blood and rot, came from the gullet, and in this way the beast regulated its temperature, casting aside the coldness of being buried under thirty levels of stone.

Each side of the gullet represented an entirely different world. To the left lay a variety of vats (green and monstrous and dull) interspersed with a low, flat line of buildings. They hunched against the jawline as if carved from the flesh, a second set of irregular teeth, pressed up against the jaw out of fear of falling into the gullet. The dwellings and laboratories (Shadrach could not guess their function) boiled over with activity, as the skirmishes carried out on the leviathan's scales had blossomed into battles. Meerkats shot at one another and other creatures indiscriminately. From this distance, the miniature struggles had a curious slow-motion quality, the tactics as obvious and inexorable as some ritualistic game. One particularly tall tower crackled with flames, and the flesh of the leviathan curled and blackened when the tower touched it, a matchstick to paper. Inside and out, the leviathan was slowly being cooked, roasted as it idly hovered in the water and its eye sought a means of escape. Like giant discarded wine bottles, the vats lay open or cracked, their skins occluded with a fine green smoke. As Shadrach watched, a vat came free of its moorings, the gobbly flesh within screaming as the vat fell into the gullet, bouncing off one side and then the other, before disappearing into a pink and hungry darkness.

If the left half of the leviathan's mouth suggested a world gone mad, the right side had a preternatural calm to it. There, Quin had fashioned a forest of fir trees amongst which nothing moved, not even the trees themselves, despite the wind. Shadrach thought he could see a glint, as of a distant brook. The suggestion of a white bridge. The forest seemed strangely familiar to him.

Shadrach asked the Gollux, "Which way?"

"Into the forest. The Gollux has been there before."

"Why is the forest so calm?"

"Quin lives there. Not even now will they cross Quin, or tempt his anger. Quin is a Living Artist. Quin created the Gollux. He created all of us."

The path that led to the forest was a path of agony. To either side, creatures writhed on dozens of crucifixes.

Shadrach refused to look left or right, but merely took John the Baptist from his pocket and strapped him to his arm once again. It hardly mattered now what he did with John. The meerkat head looked around glassy-eyed at its surroundings. It sniffed the air, said something Shadrach could not understand.

"What did you say?"

"I smell crabs. I smell food."

"We're almost there."

"I know. We're both almost dead."

"Will you be defiant to the end?"

"What did you expect me to say?"

"Nothing. Do you see what's around us?"

"Yes. Chaos. Traitors to order. Waking dreams. Nightmares."

John's eyelids flickered and closed again. The meerkat had so little life in him that Shadrach almost laid him to rest by the side of the path, beneath the feet of the crucified, but he could not bring himself to do it. Somehow, John the Baptist had become more than his companion; he had become a talisman.

Besides, John still had a bomb in his ear.

Before they could reach the floor of the mouth, and from there the forest, they chanced upon a hundred Candles. The path veered sharply down and to the right, sidestepping one of the leviathan's teeth, which had fallen from the gums, probably many years ago. When it leveled out again, the forest was directly ahead of them. To either side, more crucifixes, this time uniformly hammered to them, a hundred creatures that looked just like Candle: more than half wolf or coyote, the elongation of the face revealed as muzzle, the eyes yellow and ancient. The legs ended in half paws, half feet. The tails were crusted in blood and hung limply down. Like vultures in their stance, but unnaturally so, the long arms and legs a burden to them. Behind them, the corona of fires amongst the buildings.

There was none of the moaning that had marked the other crucifixions. They made no sound at all. Nuts and bolts held them to the posts; there was no way to bring any of them down.

"Candle?" Shadrach shouted as they walked down the path. "Candle? Is one of you Candle?"

The one nearest to him raised its head, blinked through the blood in its eyes but said nothing.

"Why was this done to you?" Shadrach asked, while the Gollux skittered around impatiently and muttered under its breath.

"They always do this to traitors—it will be done to you," whispered John the Baptist. The meerkat whimpered, opened and closed its mouth.

The creature lowered its head as much as it was able, so it could look at Shadrach. "I am a priest of the Church of Quin. Quin no longer wants priests for his church."

"I can help you down. I can . . ."

"I'm dying. Kill me or leave me. That is all."

But Shadrach could not kill this Candle surrogate. He knew that if he killed this creature now, he would come all undone, would be worthless when he faced Quin. So he heeded the Gollux's pleading and continued down the path, promising himself . . . what? Nothing, really. He couldn't make such promises. His only allegiance was to the idea of the death of Quin, the life of Nicola.

When they reached the path of white pebbles that descended into the valley of dark fir trees—when he heard the sound of running water and saw the small bridge of red and white, half hidden by the trees—when he smelled the thickness of the fir trees . . . then he realized he had seen the forest in Nicola's head, in her mind.

And he wondered whether there really was such a place above level. What if he had entered a series of dreams in her mind—of things that actually happened, but that were distorted, unsound, mirror images. For a moment, this thought disoriented him (didn't it mean she might love him after all?). But the pebbles beneath his feet were real enough—and they scrunched against the Gollux's feet too . . .

Over the bridge they went, where the fiddler crabs stalked red and black butterflies. Just beyond stood a cottage with white walls and a thatched roof. Birds had built nests from the thatch, oblivious to Quin's workings. Or had Quin made them too?

"Is this it?"

"Yes," John the Baptist said, surprising Shadrach. "This is the place. Do not enter." He looked into Shadrach's eyes. "You will not come out."

"What is your real name?" Shadrach said. It suddenly seemed important, after all they had endured together. "Not John, not Affliction, not Salvador. What is it?"

The meerkat coughed blood, its tongue pale, and said a word that sounded like the chattering speech of beetles. "That is my name. My real name. It's nothing you could ever actually say yourself. It's nothing a human could ever say."

"You're right," Shadrach said.

He turned toward the Gollux and asked, "Is this the place?"

"Yes," the Gollux said.

"Then lead the way."

Inside, Shadrach found a long, empty corridor lined with blank glass cages occupied only by dust—and at the end, another remote of Quin, its sad face swaying on too long a neck. The glass cages embedded in its sallow flesh had been covered by a black panel. Surprised and unnerved by the emptiness, Shadrach kept close to the Gollux as they walked toward the Quin remote. He flipped the safety on his gun. The stillness of the empty room was more horrible than if it had been occupied by a hundred monstrosities. The Quin remote leered and bobbed at them.

When they stood before the remote, it said, "I am Quin. What do you want with me?"

The Gollux said nothing.

Shadrach said, "You're not Quin. You're a remote, a construct." He raised his gun and shot the construct through the head. The head flopped over its counter. A spackle of blood glittered on the wall behind it. It shivered. It shuddered. It slowly righted itself and rose again. "No," it said, staring at him with a smile as its head gushed blood, "this is not me."

The compartment in front of the facade slid open and there, on a small reclining chair, lay a puddle of pale flesh and scar tissue. Somewhere in the mass of perpetual double chins, the wriggly, maggot-like flesh, a dozen intense blue eyes shone out from jellied orbits. A lyrical laugh issued forth from some orifice hidden from Shadrach.

Like all creative beings, Quin, when compared to his work, failed to measure up. Shadrach felt as if he had just met a cretin who happened to be a brilliant holovid artist. If the situation had not been so tense, it would have been hilarious. He would have laughed out loud. This horrid gobbet of flesh, when he had expected a giant!

"Surprised?" the Quin remote asked.

"Just a little bit," Shadrach lied.

"What did you expect? A great head? A lovely lady? A terrible beast? A ball of fire?"

"None of the above. I'm just surprised that you seem more amorphous in the flesh than as an idea."

Shadrach thought he read disappointment in the glob of flesh that was Quin. Here and there, where the flesh was not translucent, Shadrach could see a nascent leg, an unborn arm.

"Were you always this way?" Shadrach asked. He felt no sense of urgency now that he had finally found Quin, simply a bone-aching fatigue and a need for answers.

"Not always. I was much more human. Once."

"What happened to you?"

The flesh formed a grim smile, but the eyes danced in the body.

"There is a point beyond which the human body cannot recover. I have passed that point. I have experimented on myself for too long, and I have put too much of my own tissue into my creations."

"You don't seem surprised to see me. Can you see the gun I'm aiming at you?"

"Why should I be surprised? I've expected you or someone like you for a long time. I've made enemies, sometimes by accident, sometimes on purpose. You just happen to be among the first to possess the combination of tenacity and insanity needed to find me. I assume you mean to kill me. By all means—kill me. It makes no difference. I've done what needs doing. There is no stopping it now."

"Do you mean the war going on outside?"

"No, no, no. Periodically, I set them upon each other. The ones who survive breed, creating an ever stronger strain. This time, though, it seems somewhat more permanent."

"Was it a game when you altered Nicholas and had Nicola taken for parts?"

"I'm not familiar with the names. I've done something to them, obviously, and you mean to seek revenge. Please, take your revenge. But I don't know what you're talking about. My empire is a vast and sprawling thing. I cannot keep track of every misfit, every transaction. It's buried somewhere in the records, I'm sure . . . I might have played with a human named Nicholas. I might not have. Besides, how do you know I didn't create them both? If so, wouldn't you say I have the right to do with them as I please? I can see from the look on your face that they were born in a vat. I was the city's birth engineer for a very long time. I may well have created them, you know. Certainly if so, I would be the one to take care of them. To nurture them. Listen to your creator, Gollux, and kill this man now."

It almost caught Shadrach off guard. The Gollux—which also seemed surprised—leapt at Shadrach. But Shadrach turned in time to cut its legs out from under it.

"The Gollux," the Gollux said, as it writhed on the ground, "is not designed specifically for combat. The Gollux is not designed for non-quadrupedal locomotion."

Shadrach fried its brains out the back of its neck stump, before aiming the gun once more at Quin.

"A pity," Quin said. "He was a good and true Gollux—he tried to obey me. He tried to kill you. He may not even have wanted to do it. It was worth a try. I think I even surprised myself by doing that—I must want to live after all . . . You know, it's amazing how relaxed we humans become if you just drone on and on about nothing in particular."

"Why?" Shadrach asked.

"Why what? Why am I a puddle of flesh? Why did I become a bioneer? Why what? You must be more specific."

"You cut up my lover and sold her for parts! You sent me to Lady Ellington's estate just so I would know about it!" Shadrach's shout reverberated around the room.

The Quin remote smiled while the eyes of the flesh beneath watched him intently.

"Maybe it was pleasurable, Shadrach. Maybe it was an interesting thing to do—at the time. Maybe I don't have the slightest idea what you are talking about . . . Do you honestly think that I have any reason to tell you anything? . . . Funny how easily humans lose control. My meerkats don't lose control. My meerkats make you humans look psychotic and frivolous at the same time. Perhaps I made them both—Nicola and Nicholas. Perhaps I deliberately didn't give Nicholas enough talent—so he'd have to come to me. Perhaps I watched Nicola all the years of her life, until she delivered unto me, at the right time, an unpredictable element: you. All so you would come down here and kill me. Wouldn't that be the most spectacular genetic experiment ever? To have that subtle a control? To know that much? I don't believe I have it in me . . . Perhaps none of this actually happened, and by dumb luck and persistence you reached this point entirely by your own—"

"Shut up," Shadrach said. "I don't believe you. You know who Nicholas was. You know who Nicola is."

"You can shut me up permanently by killing me, Shadrach. You can do that . . . but I might be lying about everything. You'd never know. I might be the biggest liar the world has ever seen. You're caught between the desire to kill and the desire to know *why*. What if you could have both?"

"The first might be enough."

"Ah, so you are interested. Then let's begin again: What do you want to know?"

"What is your plan? What is it you hope to accomplish with"—Shadrach gestured at their surroundings—"all of this?"

"Plans. Planning. At first I had no plan. At first the plan was to have no plan. But that got boring and as I came to hate humans more and more, a plan came to me. I thought to myself: the human race is obsolete. Why not make a new one? Or maybe not. Maybe I'm just crazy."

"Let's assume you have a plan. What is it?"

"Why should I tell you? I'll tell you why—because it can't be stopped, that's why. The humans who live aboveground haven't even *thought* about the implications of those 'toys' I've made for them. They're too busy *using* them for prestige and to make their lives easier. They never stop to think what it all *means*. They could never believe in a giant fish that holds a whole world. They'd laugh. They'd scoff. Even if they saw it, they wouldn't believe it. That is why the human race is dying—too limited an imagination. No thought for the consequences."

"Arrogance," Shadrach said. "*You* are dying."

"No, the human race is dying. It's had its time, and yet has done nothing but squander it, each age a fainter echo of the last. Enough, I say. Be done, I say! Let some other species have its turn."

"You're crazy. The world will be a better place with you dead."

"I happen to agree with you, Shadrach. My creations need a martyr. They need a God who art in Heaven. They need a myth of human intervention to make them whole. There is only so much you can breed into them, only so much you can do with their genes—look at me: I know. The rest is environment. The rest is *religion*. If you kill me, the slow unraveling of the human race begins, for this death will be the first sign, the first symbol, from which all the others derive, until one day the humans find their servants have become their masters. And if you don't kill me, be assured: I will erase all trace of you and your beloved from this city. I will find Nicola—assuming I don't already know where she is—and I will kill her.

"I think this is a great test for you as a human being: Will you buy more time for humanity by not killing me, or will you buy more time for a single individual? I'm fascinated to see what you choose. What would Nicola think if you saved her life but sacrificed the species?"

"Assuming you are telling the truth. Assuming that if you tell the truth, your predictions are accurate." The pressure in Shadrach's head had grown intense. He felt as if he'd been listening to a hypnotist.

"And think of this: If I've truly programmed Nicola, then even if you kill me and return to the surface, could you ever really trust her again? Wouldn't you always be waiting for her to betray you? . . . What are you doing?"

"You'll see."

Shadrach had set his gun for a two-inch laser beam. He began to burn a hole in the glass that housed Quin.

Ice water coursed through his veins. He had decided on a plan of action. No further thought was necessary.

"Kidnapping me won't help you—those creatures out there will tear you limb from limb."

He was almost finished cutting the circle.

"If you're going to kill me, this seems a very awkward way to do it."

The circle fell out and shattered against the floor. The Quin remote took a swipe at him from above, while Quin himself cowered in a corner.

"I've changed my mind—I don't want to die. Not just yet. Perhaps we can reach some kind of arrangement?"

Shadrach adjusted the beam once again, severed the remote's neck, so its head flopped impotently on the counter. So much for Quin's voice.

Then he snatched Quin from his sanctuary, placed him on the countertop, and proceeded to beat him with the butt of the gun until the weapon was slick with blood.

From his arm, John the Baptist shuddered uncontrollably at the sight. "I wished I'd died in the closet," he said over and over.

Quin said nothing at all. Quin was dead.

Shadrach pulled the meerkat off his arm. He flicked the switch on the bomb in the meerkat's ear. He placed the head next to Quin.

"Goodbye, John," he said. "I'm sorry. Your kind may

take over the world, but it won't be easy. It won't happen in my lifetime. It might never happen."

As he ran for the door, before the explosion propelled him forward and out into the forest, burning his back, he thought he heard one last muttered curse from the meerkat.

9

Afterwards was simple enough. Afterwards didn't require any thought either. He picked himself up from the bomb blast, assured himself that nothing inside the cottage could have survived it, and began to head upward along the edge of the creature's mouth. He cursed the would-be thieves from which he had taken the bomb for his deafness. What had they expected? To sell tiny pieces of him and themselves to the organ bank?

Meerkats ran past him, intent on reaching the cottage. He ignored them, and they, in their concern and panic, ignored him. He didn't even bother showing them his badge.

At the docks, he found a saylber loitering in the water

nearby and swam out to it. It began to glide away from the leviathan at a good rate of speed. As the leviathan faded into the distance, it faded from his mind as well. Of more immediate concern was the moodiness of the saylber, which, after several false alarms, finally decided to submerge itself. It left Shadrach floundering about in his trench coat with the shore only barely visible on the horizon. For a few anxious minutes he thought he would drown because of his coat. Thrashing as he tried to get it off, he floated several feet below the surface. But, kicking off his shoes and contorting his arms, he managed to rid himself of the coat—and pop, breathless, to the surface.

Luckily, any current was minimal, and he was a good swimmer. Eventually, he felt land beneath his feet. He rose from the water sodden and dripping, a sudden ghost, an echo, a shadow of who he had been. He imagined no one could see him. Who would want to see him?

The shore had become a graveyard for the abandoned cathedral-rafts of the meerkats: black and incomprehensible and toppled over on their sides. He shot the two flesh dogs he saw sniffing around the cathedrals before they even saw him. He was not sorry at all for such premeditated violence. Rather he slaughter every living thing in his path than never see the light again. He used his gun to char one of the flesh dogs on a spit, and he ate some of the meat.

After he had eaten, he stood up and looked around. He was alone for the first time since he had picked up John the Baptist; the absence of the meerkat on his arm made him feel as if he were missing a limb. There was no one to help him. There was no easy way to get back to the surface. There might be no way at all. But this did not deter him. His mouth was dry. He felt hollow. He felt as if he were dead. He decided that this was a good way to feel, after all of the hate, all of the love, that had passed through him. He wanted to be empty for a while.

Above him, the red light from the passing train mocked him with its thin, forced smile of motion. He would have to reach the tracks and find a way out. It did not strike him as an impossible task.

He began to climb. Boulders and outcroppings of rock barred his way. Giant purple lichen covered the rock. Tiny, stunted trees grew between there. Strange creatures slurped and wetly plopped over the rocks, their cilia gliding in synchronized motion to serve as their eyes. They startled Shadrach, but ignored him, and after a time, he forgot about them. The rhythms of the climb became automatic, the blistering of his hands a dull throb, the mechanics of his breathing as he gulped the air harsh but irrelevant. His physical body was no longer his concern.

◨

By the time he at last reached Rafter's door, Shadrach had passed through exhaustion into some other realm entirely. His arms were cut, his back still burned, his left ear bled from a bullet wound, his legs had been bruised from the punishing climbs. He shivered like Lady Ellington's fine crystal rung with a spoon.

Once on the train tracks, it had proven just as difficult to walk to the train station, the train barreling by with alarming frequency, Shadrach reduced to molding himself into alcoves on either side to avoid being killed, shivering with the aftermath of the train's tumultuous passage. News of Quin's death had not made it to the train station—or had bypassed it entirely—and everything seemed as normal as before. At the train station, he had waited for a few hours, recovering his strength, using his Quin badge to bully a cube of food out of a vendor. The hideous figures that walked past him as he ate—these seemed as normal as anything he had seen aboveground. He had almost choked with laughter. What he took for granted now was beyond anyone's expectations.

When he felt strong enough, he had continued to make his way, level by level, to Rafter's offices. The entire time, he could feel the light above him like an irresistible force—and below the light, standing in its rays, Nicola. Or so he hoped. He hadn't bothered to conceal his gun, holding it out in front of him instead. But even when he had used his gun, there was at the heart of him only someone who wanted desperately to reach the light.

He knocked on Rafter's door.

A hesitation, and then the door opened, and Rafter

stood there. She stared at him with a mixture of horror and awe.

"Is she—is she still here?" he asked.

Rafter frowned. "You're just in time to ruin her life again. She's conscious and walking."

"Walking?"

"Yes," Rafter said. "Come in."

Rafter led him into her waiting room. Nicola sat on a couch. Her face was haggard; she stared at the floor. Her legs were a ghoulish white, but intact. Her hair fell in straggles across her face. Rafter had dressed her in black pants and a plain white shirt. She looked like a person newly born.

Shadrach tottered, almost fell, but managed to sit down beside her. For him, that moment would define the rest of his life. He let his gaze linger. He drank her in. He stared at that which he had never thought to see again.

Rafter left them alone together, the look on her face unreadable.

"You look terrible," Nicola said in a raw voice. "Are you okay?"

He fumbled for her hand, took it in his. She felt warm to his touch, and her warmth invaded him. He didn't feel capable of speech, his sentences all unraveled and incomplete.

"Rafter says," Nicola rasped, then coughed, started again. "Rafter says you've seen into me. You've read my mind—you've been me."

Didn't you feel me there? he thought. *Was I no comfort to you?* But all he said was, "I thought it was necessary to protect you."

"What did you see there?" She stared into his eyes.

"Beauty. Courage. Intelligence."

She looked away. "And ugly things, too, I'm sure."

Shadrach shrugged. "No. Not really."

"But you saw, Shadrach. You saw? You know?"

Shadrach nodded. "I know." Pain, yet that bittersweet relief in acknowledging it.

"I'm sorry, Shadrach. I'm sorry if I've hurt you. Rafter says you've saved my life. Rafter says I would have died without you."

"She exaggerates," Shadrach said. He had a sudden flash of seeing her again, buried within a mountain of limbs, and shuddered. "How do you feel?"

Nicola blinked twice, closed her eyes. "I feel very tired. I ache all over. I'm thirsty all the time."

"Can you walk?"

"Yes."

"Then we should walk. We need to get to the surface. We need to get you into a hospital."

"I can try," she said. They stood up. Nicola almost fell. Shadrach grabbed her shoulders with both hands. They swayed there together.

"Careful," he said.

She hugged him. Her hair still smelled of the organ bank.

"Don't leave me," she said.

Shadrach laughed bitterly. "I won't. Don't worry, I won't."

Rafter had returned, stood by the door. She glared at Shadrach, said, "You must be careful. She'll be disoriented for a while. She may not make sense. She'll be weak. She'll need care. Afterwards, she'll be close to herself again."

Nicola said, "Nothing will ever be the same."

"It will be completely different," Shadrach said. "That's not a bad thing."

After Shadrach had paid for Rafter's work and Nicola had said her goodbyes, they began to walk toward the terminus for the next level. Rafter had given them a map. Nothing so beautiful as a Quin map—just scribbled lines and words on a scrap of paper.

Only a few minutes into their journey, Nicola said, "I'm tired, so tired," and staggered against the wall.

"Sleep then, Nicola," Shadrach said. He lifted her off her feet and began to carry her.

When they were safely in an elevator that would take them to a higher level, her breath on his shoulder soft and even, he allowed himself to relax a little. It began to seem that they would make it.

Later, as they continued their slow progress upward, she woke, her breath shallow, her grip on his shoulder sharper.

"Thank you," she said dreamily as she got to her feet.

The second level beckoned from beyond the elevator. Here, people didn't flinch away from them. Stores were open. Women walked with their children. The pale light did not hide monstrosities. It seemed that the real city, the city of sun and horizon, must be close by.

"Thank you for what?" he said.

"For saving my life."

"I didn't have a choice."

"I don't believe that, Shadrach."

"But it's true. I love you," he said hopelessly, the back of his throat sore.

"I know you do," she said. And then: "Nicholas is dead."

"Yes. And Salvador. And Quin. They're all dead."

"I knew my brother was dead," she said. "I couldn't sense him anymore."

She shuddered while Shadrach held her close, still amazed by her presence, there, in his arms.

Even after she had woken up, Shadrach supported her weight at first, held her up, let her lean on him. From the second level, they still had to walk to the disembarkation point, which was really above the city, rising out of the city's wall so that those who came through would get a full view of Veniss. They would have to hope the guards along the way would honor Shadrach's badge.

As she grew stronger, he grew weaker. After they had successfully passed the next checkpoint and neared the ramp leading to the surface, he began to feel faint. He leaned on her and she held him up. She stroked his hair. "It's okay," she said, "it's okay."

The final checkpoint before the ramp consisted of a dull gray wall of some hard metal. Embedded in the wall was a guard protected by three layers of glass. The guard, they could see even from far away, was a meerkat. Shadrach stiffened, reached into his pocket for his gun, even as he readied his badge and identification card. His alarm proved unfounded. What had looked menacing from a distance was less so in the flesh—fur mangy, a lost look on its face, its voice low and dull. It waved them through with just the slightest of glances at the badge. The stiff metal doors released, a space opened in front of them. Shadrach could smell fresh air coming from the darkness ahead. They walked through and stood on the ramp. Behind them, the wall became solid again.

As they struggled up through the shadows of the ramp, some part of Shadrach still doubted they would reach the outside world. He thought he heard the sound of something at his back, stalking them. "Don't look back," he whispered to Nicola as she now leaned on him again. "Don't look back." Their steps were so slow, weighted down with a terrible anticipation. The steep ramp seemed to have no end. Shadrach imagined he could see bits of glowing graffiti on the walls to either side: A *child in the dark, a kiss in the dark; remakes the world in his own image; the weave and warp of flesh*. But when he blinked, rubbed his eyes, the walls were bare.

Shadrach's thoughts became wide and deep. Walking upward, even if only, it seemed, from one darkness to another, reminded him of when he had first come above level—the first time he had seen Nicola. The look on her face in that moment—had it been happy, sad, reserved? He tried to remember, even as he seemed to hear more footsteps behind them. Perhaps it was wistful or melancholy, or a bland smile that indicated a blank attention to duty.

As Shadrach had emerged from below level, from the darkness of which a lack of love was only part, he had wanted only the light, not love. Nor did he allow people to stand for symbols—how could he, living in a darkness where people were often just a touch, a scent, a voice? Abstract symbols could never comfort him in his despair, in the aching of his body for something better. His loves before Nicola had sometimes just been a voice and a gray-tinged body in the dusk of before-death that comprised the hovels and split-levels of the poor. And everyone below had been poor.

Perhaps, he thought, as tiny lights broke the darkness of the ramp ahead of them, it had been the sadness on her face. How much in common would he have had with a woman whose life also appeared to be a tragedy? No, it was not sadness that drew him to her. He'd known more sad and ruined people in the mines than he cared to remember. He had known love as a voice and touch, surely, but also a desperate coupling in the dark for a moment of release, of freedom from below level. A rare thing. A precious thing. It could transport you out of time, so that the world had no hold on you.

A hint of fresh air. Nicola's body leaning against his.

So perhaps he had believed in symbols after all—perhaps the frame of light as he ascended that first time drew him to her as it touched her body: blind moth to blinding flame. And maybe it was just this: when he came up into the light, the light shone upon her and she was not perfect. She had a face a trifle too narrow, a dull red birthmark between her thumb and forefinger, hair framing her face in tangled black strands. Such perfect imperfection, and he fell into her eyes because now, and only now, could he believe in this new world into which he had been reborn. It was populated with imperfect, beautifully imperfect, strangers, and how it had broken his heart that first time—to know that after so much darkness, the light could be so real, so alive. Not perfect, but real—all of it, the world, the woman, his life.

He felt the wind on his face and heard Nicola say, "It's the stars . . ." and realized that she, too, had not known until that moment that they were looking out at the night sky, slowly working its way toward dawn. He had not seen the sky for so long that the stars were each and every one a revelation to him, a new way of seeing the world, like the first time.

They stood at the top of the ramp, which overlooked the city. It glistened with lights.

"It's beautiful," she said.

And deadly, he thought. The city was a strange, hidden place with a white bridge and a gravel path. The city was a place of intermingled species, of minds. Was this evolution? He recalled the intricate beauty of the caterpillar map. He recalled John the Baptist's stoicism.

Down below, he could see the thick, cool aqueducts of the Canal District, the sides of the canals lined with lights. The world was silent. It seemed to him that the silence hid, and would forever hide, a living, breathing mystery. No matter that the city would eventually build a protective skin over this riddle, so that it would be but the dim red of a beating heart seen through milky tissue. No matter that, if Nicholas was right, the city was filled with a thousand unturned keys, ready in the lock, always just a gesture, a color, a sound away from clicking into place. The particular hue of a chemical sunset. The guttural command of a private policeman. The farewell kiss of lovers on a canalside beach. Of all the signs and symbols in such a chaotic city, which would be the one to unleash Quin's circus upon the world? Or would they stand forever at the ready, awaiting a command from a ghostly hand.

Ahead of them, stairs led down into Veniss. Behind them, Shadrach heard the footsteps, the rustling, getting louder. What had come up with them from below level?

He pulled Nicola behind him, whirled around, hand on his gun, and saw . . . nothing. No one was standing in the mouth of the ramp. Just shadows. *A kiss in the dark.* He had imagined it. *The man living in the belly of a giant fish.* The real and the unreal had finally traded places.

Then and only then did he allow himself to cry: silent tears that ran down his face, dripped off his chin, fell to the pavement. He wept for the pain of his ordeal and for what he had had to do to rescue Nicola. He wept for his parents, who surely must be dead and for Nicholas, stupid, a fool, led astray and discarded. He wept for his former self now that he had changed in so many ways and could not yet comprehend the half of them. But most of all, he wept with relief—that Nicola was alive, and that he was alive with her.

But even though he hurt, and even though it was such sorrow to look upon Nicola's bruised face, and even though most things would not, as Nicola had said, ever again be the same, it was joy, not pain, that finally buckled his knees and brought him to the end of his endurance. He lay down against the rough stone of the ramp, staring up at the stars, wordless. Nicola sat beside him, together but alone, her hand in his as she looked out over Veniss.

At dawn, he knew that they would walk down into the city, not sure what they would find there, but knowing it must be better than what they had left behind. He knew that memory would make the past easy, by blurring the details and distorting time. He would grow old to this. He would become sentimental. He would forget he had become a murderer. He would forget many things. But he would never forget that he loved her, despite that niggling thought, which he would never be free of: Had he done enough? Could he have done better?

Still fighting it, still not sure, Shadrach closed his eyes and slept for the first time in seven days.

AFTERWORD TO THE FIRST EDITION

Note: This afterword contains spoilers.

The first thing Bunadeo saw was the ceiling of the laboratory: the grain of rough, dark stone smoothed by human technologies. The first thing he heard was the rushing surge of the sea, which he mistook for the sound of his own pumping blood. The first face he saw was that of Madrid Sybel, smiling. No memories haunted Bunadeo's head. Although an adult, he did not even know his name until Madrid told him.

"Who am I?" he asked, his throat dry.

"Bunadeo," the smiling face told him.

"Where am I?"

"In a kingdom by the sea," the smiling face said.

The room smelled of plastic and of brine.

He fell into darkness for a while. When he woke, he knew little more, but he had held on to his name: Bunadeo. He was Bunadeo . . .

Madrid Sybel, the first bioneer to create a semisentient species, lived in a labyrinth of caves that opened out onto a beach of black rocks. The caves lay at the bottom of barren cliffs. Dayton Central, a city that would someday be known as Veniss, sat atop the cliffs. The AIs that ran Dayton Central bankrolled Madrid. He spent all day creating and extinguishing life in his cave laboratories, accompanied only by his assistant Bunadeo and a little girl named Nicola. Madrid had a long white beard that framed a long face from which peered startling blue eyes. Those eyes made his face look like a disguise to Bunadeo, because they belonged to someone much younger. Nicola had blonde hair she tied up in braids and eyes that stared into the middle distance. She rarely said anything.

Bunadeo did not know that Nicola was actually his mother, in a sense. Madrid had told him that his parents were dead, that his lack of memories meant he had suffered a terrible trauma before the AIs had given him over into Madrid's hands. This was not true. Madrid had created both Bunadeo and Nicola. Madrid had created Nicola from the DNA of Bunadeo's birth mother. Bunadeo had been created, nurtured, and birthed in a vat, using an ovum from the original Nicola. Madrid had no idea how they had died; he knew only that the AIs had provided him with a fresh source of DNA. As he had stared down at his creation as it woke for the first time, Madrid hadn't known whether he would keep it or discard it and start afresh. Something about the look of innocence on Bunadeo's face, the way he asked his questions, made Madrid keep him.

Bunadeo never found out about this hesitation, but many years later, he did suffer a hint of his connection to Nicola. As he stared down at a woman preserved beneath a protective sheath, buried beneath a mound of severed legs, he had a flicker of awareness that had no scientific basis. This sudden piercing pain in his head, his heart, almost led to a reversal of his fate. For a moment, he was back by the sea, by the rocks, and he could see the little girl Nicola standing beside him. But the image disintegrated, the thought fled, the erosion continued . . .

Madrid taught Bunadeo his Living Art, but did not let him into his life. It took many years before he could think of his creation as more than an assistant. The role he played, that of an inattentive father, hurt Bunadeo, for too often he thought of Madrid as more than his mentor. His relationship with Nicola was more mysterious. Sometimes she would behave toward him in a motherly fashion;

at other times, she lived so completely inside her own head that no one could reach her. But he was grateful to both of them; he had no other family.

It took Bunadeo as long to understand the secrecy of their mission as to understand his family. Madrid had told Bunadeo from the very beginning that neither he nor Nicola could ever leave the caves or the seashore. Although he became used to this fact, he never liked it; sometimes watching holovids of the city above them helped assuage his curiosity, sometimes it just made him angry.

The work itself he found fascinating. They captured pseudowhales and married their genes to those of apes and kangaroos. They unfroze DNA from the extinct elephant and wedded it to that of mice, rats, birds, and frogs. Sometimes, it seemed as if they were very close to making a sentient life-form. Sometimes, the excesses of their failures would send a tide of blood washing down one edge of the lab floor to the other, mimicking the wildness of the sea at their backs. The smell at such times made Bunadeo tremble, but it also excited him. It was the smell of life, tangy and rich. The screams, the shrieks, however, terrified him, as some malformed creature became a secondhand memory.

Most days, the lab work fell between the two extremes. Bunadeo wrote about it in his holographic diary. He kept the diary because he had the constant fear that he would one day wake up and his mind would be as blank of experience as the first time he had seen Madrid's smiling face. Sometimes, he would wake up in the middle of the night, screaming, and would find himself compelled to record even his nightmares. Better nightmares than nothing. Once, Bunadeo wrote this in his diary:

> Today we tried lizards. When I came into the laboratory, Madrid was staring at a lizard on a tray. It had two tails and three heads. It was golden brown, scaly, and almost dead. The eyes stared up at me, the glassiness telling me it had had enough, that it was weary, that this would never work. It smelled like burnt grass. I think it was trying to talk. I don't know what it wanted to tell us. To stop? To give up? I'm still not sure.

But Madrid never gave up. Every day, year after year, he worked at the task the AIs had assigned to him, Bunadeo helping him. Every few months, the AIs would visit to discuss Madrid's progress. They ignored Bunadeo and Nicola. They used holographic manifestations to show themselves: giant manta rays, winged rhinos, minotaurs, chimeras. Their presence scared Bunadeo, who felt more like a ghost with their ghostlike presence all around him. The electric discharge of their avatars tasted like lime on his tongue. Madrid talked to the hulking shapes as if they were old friends who had stopped by to chat. Bunadeo never understood why the AIs wanted Madrid to create a new intelligent biological life-form.

"Why do they let us do this?" he asked his mentor once as they sat looking out at the sea.

Madrid winked and replied, "Because they're curious."

"Just because they're curious?"

"Maybe they want to see what happens to humans because of it. Maybe they even think . . ."

But Madrid never completed the sentence. Instead, a distant look on his face, he got up and walked back into the caves. Bunadeo didn't see him for three days, and Madrid never said where he'd gone.

Over time, Bunadeo realized that Madrid hid things from him. For a while, he thought Madrid was trying to protect him, that Madrid's distance came from a love so strong that it had the discipline to remain removed from that which it loved. Much later, when he turned this thought over and over in his mind like a coin between his fingers, he wasn't so sure.

Did their work have a hidden purpose? *Had* Madrid hidden something from the AIs? Bunadeo already knew that Madrid kept a boat concealed by the rocks and would sometimes use it to visit an island just visible on the horizon.

He only knew about the boat because he had stumbled across it one day when his research took him to the tidal pools in the rocks. Thousands of creatures lived in these pools. Staring down into the miniature ecosystems— the sky a lathe of boiling blue above the waves that, foaming white, crushed themselves against the blackened rock—made Bunadeo feel less isolated, less removed. At times, the brine stench overwhelmed him, and he would crouch for an hour beside one pool, soaking up the smell and the rush-withdrawal of the water. He would watch a starfish move across a bed of seaweed, a tiny translucent shrimp pick crumbs of food from the tentacles of a sea anemone.

Usually Nicola came along with him, to help carry the specimen containers. She would stand at the edge of the tidal pools, weighed down with containers, while Bunadeo waded into the pools. If Nicola spoke to Bunadeo, it would usually be during these expeditions; the sea seemed to bring her out of her thoughts, into the world.

Other mysteries besides the boat became revealed to him through the tidal pools. Once, he caught a tiny fish and kept it in a tank in his room. Over time, he experimented with increasing its size and numbing its reactions to pain. Many decades later, he would live inside this fish and be reminded of the place in which he had found it. Another time, Nicola gave a little gasp and pointed to a stinking bed of washed-up kelp. A man's head had become enmeshed in the kelp, the body hidden by the deep green fronds. The surprise of it left Bunadeo dislocated for a moment, in search of context. A sudden thought came to him, later recorded in his diary: "The kelp looked like skin to me, like the dark, oily skin of some beast. And the man's head, so pale, looked as if it had been set into the side of that beast."

Bunadeo stood there for a long time, Nicola beside him, staring at the man. Later, the image would reenter his memory like an air bubble struggling to rise to the surface, and he would use it to create the first flesh dog. In a sense, everything Bunadeo would later become he found first in the tidal pools beyond the caves.

For more than twenty years, Bunadeo, Madrid, and Nicola lived in the caves, always a few steps away from success. Every morning, Bunadeo would rise from the cot in his small room and join Madrid and Nicola in the laboratory, where a new subject might already be squirming on the examination table. Every few months, the AIs would manifest themselves, talk to Madrid, and dematerialize again.

Every year, Nicola's agelessness became more and more apparent. She never changed, and as the years passed, Bunadeo felt more and more estranged from her, imagining a closeness between them in previous years that had never existed in reality. He felt as if he was being flung along by the undertow of a powerful current, while she had found a rock to cling to; soon, he would be so far from shore that he would be unable to see her. This fact began to obsess him more than his fear of losing his memory. Even Madrid aged, if slowly. Madrid, meanwhile, laughed at Bunadeo's hints that Madrid should also transform him into a creature that never aged.

"Everything in its time, Bunadeo," Madrid would say. "You should be in less of a hurry to become young again and in more of a hurry to *learn*. I won't always be here."

Madrid knew that the AIs had become impatient with him. New research using modified meerkats had been promising, but success might still be many years off. He also knew that when Bunadeo could slow his own aging process, his apprenticeship would be over.

For Bunadeo's part, he told himself he resented Nicola, when he actually already missed her.

The end came suddenly. One day Madrid took him aside and told him to visit the most remote area of the caves to capture a particular type of bat. When he returned two days later, the laboratory had been destroyed by men sent by the AIs. He had only to consult the surveillance holograms to find out who had been responsible. The equipment had been dismantled or crushed into little pieces. The test animals had been slaughtered or were missing. Madrid and Nicola had been butchered: they lay in a crumpled heap on the floor, surrounded by dried spatters of blood. Nicola had died in the middle of a scream. Madrid looked peaceful, a characteristic smile upon his lips. From the wounds, Bunadeo knew that they had died slowly. The loss overwhelmed him. He would have been moved to weep, if he hadn't seen beside them a perfect replica of his own body, also dispatched in bloody fashion. Seeing this, his grief became transformed into a different kind of shock.

Bunadeo circled the body several times, mouth agape. He prodded it with his finger. He lay down beside it. He rolled it over. It looked more like him than he did. It was perfect in every detail. Except that Bunadeo's eyes were blue, and when he pulled back the eyelids on the body, he found that his doppelganger's eyes were brown.

A thought occurred to him. In the grip of a secret emotion, Bunadeo crouched over Madrid's body and opened its eyes. They, too, were brown, not blue. Only Nicola's eyes were the same color as before.

He lay there beside the Nicola body, under the intermittent flickering of the ceiling lights, and wondered if he had gone insane. But in the morning, when he woke, the bodies still lay there, stiffening. Including his own. The discovery that Madrid's hidden boat had disappeared from its mooring near the rocks prompted him to write in his diary.

> I cannot be sure of anything, but I believe that Madrid
> is alive somewhere. That he knew this would happen.
> That he purposefully sent me away so I would not
> be killed. That he may or may not have fashioned a
> double for Nicola too. That she may also be alive,

somewhere. That I do not know why they would not take me with them, why he would send me away instead, why he would want me to find those bodies like that, and why he would want me to doubt not only him but my own thoughts, because how can I ever be sure? About any of this?

Although the AIs' men and the AI avatars had left long before his arrival, Bunadeo did not feel safe in the caves, among the ruined equipment. He took the bodies out to the sea and let the current take them. The strangeness of watching his own likeness slide away into the waves would never leave him. It lent a chill to the air, a sharpness to the contours of the sky. He stood on the rocks until the bodies had disappeared and then stared out at the island. If Madrid had sought refuge there, it meant he did not want Bunadeo by his side. So be it.

Before leaving his home, he went into his room one last time. There, he found the fish he had taken from the tidal pool still alive. He also found one of his creatures, a large ball of pregnant flesh with no eyes, no brain, and no legs. He took both the fish and the creature with him. He also gathered together the few unbroken pieces of equipment. Finally, he took vials of both Madrid's and Nicola's DNA from previously stored samples.

Then, numb, he found his way out of the caves and into Veniss Underground. There was nothing for him aboveground. He could never live there as long as the AIs ruled; he could never be sure they wouldn't want him killed, or worse.

Bunadeo never saw Madrid or Nicola again, or at least not in their original forms. He hid himself in Veniss Underground, going as deep as he could, taking any job to survive, often cold, often beaten, often hungry. Wherever he went, he could not drive the thoughts from his head: that, ultimately, Madrid hadn't wanted him, or, worse, that it had been Madrid's body on the floor of the laboratory and Bunadeo had betrayed his memory by not trusting him. This second possibility hurt more than the first. As time put more distance between him and the event, Bunadeo even had days when he imagined that the dead Madrid's eyes had been blue, not brown. The brine of the sea was always in his mouth.

When he did begin to experiment again, a year later, within the confines of his tiny apartment, it was as much to distract himself as from any interest in the research. He was working for a psychewitch at that point, looking into people's minds with crude equipment. It paid enough for him to begin to buy what he needed, and gave him experience he would later find useful.

The pregnant ball gave birth in that month. It gave birth and died, but what it gave birth to was a miracle: a modified meerkat that could reason, could talk after a fashion. Bunadeo had placed the embryo of a dog-lemur inside the creature, not that of a meerkat. Only Madrid could have performed the operation to switch them.

The meerkat did not last long—only two months—but that was enough for Bunadeo to begin to understand where Madrid had made a mistake. And to realize that by leaving the creature in his room, Madrid had sent him a message. At least, this was Bunadeo's reasoning. He could not tell for sure. But he preserved the meerkat's DNA.

Over the next few years, he worked hard to duplicate Madrid's success, and to improve upon it, despite several interruptions. The first period of civil unrest, during which the human population of Dayton Central tried to overthrow its AI overlords, led to horrible suffering for Bunadeo. His paranoia about his memory returned, he lost his position with the psychewitch, and he had to take a series of illegal, demeaning, and often morally repugnant jobs. He also fell into the habit of having surgeries performed that appended limbs or just sections of flesh from other creatures onto his own form. This intrusion of foreign flesh gave him great pleasure.

He wrote in his diary:

There's nothing to stop me from taking my own life, or taking the lives of as many others as I like. There's no one in my life that could tell me to do otherwise. I might as well still be in those caves by the sea. I am a god in this apartment; how the creatures I create try to please me, try to escape their own extinction. But it's hardwired into them. Once born, their deaths are already set, while I have discovered how to slow my aging. How lonely can a man be before such an option no longer seems inviting?

The unrest led to Bunadeo changing his name, to escape people who were now pursuing him. He remembered a character in an old holovid he'd watched once, based on an ancient book, and changed his name to "Quin."

By this time, he had begun to take liberal tissue samples from his own body and introduce them into his test subjects.

This practice would continue when Quin, for a brief time, served as an anonymous assistant in the production of artificially created children for the now-failing AIs. However, his main focus remained perfecting the experiments Madrid Sybel had first performed using meerkats . . .

◻

And that is the story of Quin, gleaned from a few fragments of short story I never finished (and which may or may not match the reality of the novel). In a sense, what makes it to the printed page is always a fragment of something larger, whether because you wrote character studies in aid of character development, or because inspiration left you at a critical time, or because a scene didn't really belong in the novel after all—even though somewhere out there, in a universe where everything literary is real, that scene actually occurred, because life (unlike fiction) isn't all about dramatic potential.

I suppose I could have worked more about Quin into *Veniss Underground*, but I always felt that the narrative was more about Quin's influence on the main characters than about Quin himself. Quin should remain an enigma, mysterious yet purposeful, whose will was expressed through his agents in the world: the meerkats who did his bidding. In *Veniss Underground*, Quin becomes a three-faced avatar created by the perceptions of, in turn, Nicholas, Nicola, and Shadrach.

Quin's influence shows up indirectly in the short stories set in the same milieu, including "The Sea, Mendeho, and Moonlight," "Detectives and Cadavers," "Balzac's War," and "A Heart for Lucretia." These stories describe the gradual domination of the Earth by Quin's creatures. But there are more fragments than completed stories, and I find it unlikely that I will complete most of them. It's more likely that their stillbirths were necessary to bring the finished stories to life—much as Madrid's failed experiments eventually brought a sentient meerkat to life, for a little while anyway.

Veniss Underground almost became one of those stillbirths, those fragments. I started with the short outline of a man going to buy a meerkat, sort of a futuristic magic shop story, and then conceived of the overall narrative arc. However, at the time I didn't really have the skills to implement such a complex narrative. I was still learning my craft and acquiring technique, not to mention life experience. It took me over a year to find the right voice for Nicola, and to discover the pleasures (and dangers) of second person. It was easier to figure out how to portray Shadrach because he had such a direct and straightforward mission during the time when the reader would know him. (Nicholas's vain, whining arrogance was easiest—I just channeled and intensified the worst aspects of my own personality.)

But when Shadrach reached the organ bank, I found myself stuck for a different reason: I couldn't visualize the place. For some reason, without visualizing the organ bank, I couldn't visualize the rest of the novel.

Some months into this writer's block, my future wife, Ann, and I visited England, where I discovered York Minster (with help from friends Chris Reed and Manda Thompson). York Minster became my grand epiphany, perhaps the most visionary experience I have ever had while writing a story or novel. As soon as we entered the cathedral—a place older than Westminster—and I traced the path of the columns up to the stunningly high ceiling, the little hairs on my arms lifted, and I shivered.

The columns, looking like multiple tubes tied together, were utterly alien to me. I'd seen nothing like them. My scalp was tingling. I could feel something rising up inside of me. The organ bank was becoming a reality right in front of my eyes. But it wasn't until I walked around a corner and saw steps leading down to a door and a window set into the wall, wooden bars across it, that the back of my head exploded and I found myself hardly able to breathe. I could clearly see Shadrach walking around the corner as I had . . . and being confronted by a scene out of Dante's *Inferno* in that room with the little steps leading down to it. In my vision, that room stretched out and opened up into a much larger space filled with body parts in various stages of decay. As I saw this spreading out before me, so too the rest of the cathedral changed, until the columns became conduits for blood and the sculptures of saints on the columns were bodies set into the columns and the design on the ceiling of the cathedral was instead a series of floating cameras and there, coming down the walkway, were two old women with purses; no, two old people carrying the body of a young girl between them, and behind them, Dr. Ferguson in his bloody smock, and although I'm not religious, this was a religious experience, the world transformed, the world's surface peeled back to reveal the flesh beneath the skin. I stood there scribbling away like a slack-jawed idiot for long minutes, writing down what was being written into me. I couldn't keep up with the images and ideas cutting into my head. I had to find more paper. I had to keep writing. It was all spilling out. It was all becoming real. In every possible way, I experienced exactly what Shadrach experienced up to that moment when he saw his love buried beneath the mound of legs. Then it was past and gone and I was in the world again, and it was just a cathedral, and I was exhausted and speechless—spent.

If you're lucky, you have three or four experiences like this in a lifetime. I can't describe it as anything other than a vision, a transformation. Such a happening does not mean that the writing that occurs because of it will be any better or any worse than writing achieved through discipline and a slow grind forward. Anything I put down on paper could only be a shadow, an echo, a ghost of what I had experienced in the flesh.

But, on a grand scale, it does remind you why you write: for those everyday epiphanies, the little moments of sudden knowledge that occur when you are *written*. In my case, that half hour in the York cathedral saved *Veniss Underground*. It got me past the point of most resistance. A lot of hard work remained ahead of me, but I could see my way to the end.

Whenever I think of the novel, I think of that moment in the cathedral. But I also think of the relationship between *Veniss Underground* and my Ambergris stories, with their own, much more enigmatic, underground. While I was writing *Veniss Underground*, Ambergris began to colonize my imagination. In a way, this happened at just the right time. For very sound reasons—frustrating to the more direct part of my nature—I could not describe the subterranean passageways of Ambergris in anything other than fragments and conflicting glimpses. The integrity of the stories I was writing at the time would have been threatened by a clear view. But for the third part of *Veniss Underground*, I needed to strip away the darkness of a subterranean land and show, unflinchingly, what hid in that darkness. In a strange way, *Veniss Underground* allowed me to show readers—metaphorically, at the level at which images resonate—the nether parts of Ambergris. At the same time, the milieu of Veniss, in the novel and the other stories, showed me a way to write future Ambergris stories.

Veniss Underground is an unabashedly decadent, phantasmagorical novel. Like the Gollux, it may be a flawed location, not a flawed creature, if read as science fiction. Fed by fragments the reader cannot see but can sense, by visions and transformations, by cross-pollination with other story cycles, it is a mutt, a mongrel, but, to me, oddly beautiful nonetheless. When I reread it now, it reminds me of Bunadeo/Quin, working toward his master's ends: creating an entire world out of a tiny fish, revealing a man's pale face in the grip of some other beast's flesh. I like that sense of it. I think it's fitting.

—*Jeff VanderMeer*
March 9, 2003, Tallahassee

BALZAC'S WAR

1

Balzac and Jamie stumbled upon the flesh dog on a day when the sky, seared white as bleached bone, split open the world and allowed any possibility. Sixteen and free of the crèche, two as one, they ran across the desert floor to the ruined city of Balthakazar. Balzac sucked air as he tried to match her long strides, his tunic and trousers caught by the wind as if he were a human sail. Just ahead of him he could see Jamie's tangles of black hair snarling out behind her, her calves pumping beneath the flurry of white dress plaited at the knee and drawn up between her legs. Within hours his older brother and self-proclaimed guardian, Jeffer, would track them down and, returning them to the crèche, force them to complete their lesson with the boring old water dowser Con Fegman. No doubt Con

Fegman was, at that very moment, recounting for the thousandth time how he had discovered the oasis lakes with a mere twitch-twitch of his fingers.

Ahead, the ruins shimmered in the heat, the dark metallic glints beginning to resolve into cracked causeways, broken-down battlements, and crooked buildings fifty stories high. The city had in its demeanor, the sand ever in motion across its carapace, a sense of watchfulness, a restlessness.

At the fringe, where buildings slept worn smooth, they found an ancient highway; it shook itself free from the sand, from a dream of drowning. Once, it might have been eighteen lanes wide, but now, choking on sand, it could fit only four abreast.

Breathing hard, Balzac slowed to a walk. Sweat dripped down his face. A delicious nervousness pierced his stomach.

Jamie, hardly winded, turned her face out of the sun. "Why did you stop?"

"Because," Balzac wheezed, "*this* is the city . . ."

Husks and shells, as dead as the mummified corpses of tortoises and jackals after drought: the idea of "city" stripped down to its most fundamental elements, the superfluous flourishes of paint, writing, road signs, windows, scoured away in an effort to reveal a beautifully harsh truth. Gutted weapons embankments pointed toward the sky, but could not defend the city from the enemy.

Jamie interrupted his reverie. "C'mon—we've got to hurry. Your brother will find us soon."

He held out his hand.

She stared at it for a moment, then took it. Her palm felt flushed and warm.

"I'll deal with Jeffer," he said with newfound confidence, although as he led her forward he didn't dare to see if she was impressed or just amused.

Beneath their feet, four-o'clocks, cactus blossoms, and sedge weeds thrust up through cracks in the highway pavement. Scuttling through these miniature oases, anonymous gray lizards waged a war with coppery metal scorpions that pursued with mechanical implacability, their electric stingers singing static to the wind. Con Fegman had shown them one cracked open: beneath the metal exterior lay the red meat of flesh and blood.

Balzac loved even this most deadly part of the mystery that was Balthakazar. All the crèche machines— heirlooms from centuries past—broke down regularly and had to be cannibalized to repair other machines, and yet the Con members did nothing. Even practical Jeffer must realize that someday there would be no machines at all. Someday only the dormant technologies of the city would save them.

"Look at the bones," Jamie said. Scattered across the highway were whitish-gray shards. It made Balzac shiver to think about it. Bones did not fit his pristine, cold-metal vision of Balthakazar in its prime.

"How do you know it's bone? It could be plastic or mortar, or almost anything."

"It's bone. Why else do you think the Con members don't move us back into the city? Why they don't even want us to visit?"

"Because at night, *creatures* come out of the underground levels, *things* with sharp teeth, and they *eat* you."

Jamie threw her head back and laughed; Balzac could see the smooth skin of her neck and marveled at its perfection even as he blushed and said, "It's not funny." Yet even her laughter pleased him.

"You," she said, wiping tears from her eyes. "I stopped believing in that old tale a long time ago."

Something in his expression must have given him away, because she shocked him by saying, gently, "I'm sorry about your parents—really, I am—but the only truth is this," and she bent to pick up a shard that might have been bone. "My father says no one knows what did this. If these are just old graves opened by the sands or if something killed them all off." She paused, looked at him odd, as if weighing her options, then said, "My father brought me here when I was much younger, and I just liked the texture of the bones. I didn't know what they were. All I knew was that they felt good to touch—lightweight and with those porous grooves—and that my father was there with me after so many nights away from the crèche, showing me something that filled him with awe." She tossed the shard aside. "It's only bits of bone, anyhow. Whatever happened, happened a long time ago. There's nothing to be done for them."

True enough, and it was reassuring to know he could look at them as curious reminders of another age. How many times had Con Fegman, or even Jeffer, retold the old legends from before the collapse of the cities, as if the mere repetition would fend off the spirits of the dead?

The pavement became hot, cool, then hot again as the sun sliced through the spaces between structures. The landscape changed, become both rougher and smoother until buildings were all edges or had no edges at all. Others gleamed with an odd hint of self-repair, their skins smooth and shiny.

They encountered the hull of a rusted hovercraft over which, looking like a weathered lizard, lay the leathery, discarded skin of a dirigible. Balzac did not recognize the faded crèche insignia on the wrinkled cloth. Near the hovercraft lay a misshapen rock, as tall as two or three autodocs. The top of the rock was black and shiny.

"Let's sit down for a moment," Balzac said.

"If you must."

"I must. And besides, it's not just to rest. I've got leechee fruit."

They climbed up onto the rock and lay down on its

smooth surface. He handed her a leechee and bit into his own, the juice dribbling down his chin. The fruit tasted good, and he soon became acutely aware of her rising and falling chest, the sharp lines of her legs, the faint musk of sweat. She ate the leechee in huge bites, wiping away the juice before it could trickle down her neck and stain her dress.

The rock was warm and it relaxed him to lie there with her, so close together. Confidence rising, he tried to explain why the city intrigued him so. He spoke of its rich history, how it must be considered the home of their ancestors, how it used structural designs and technologies unknown to the crèche.

Propped up on one shoulder, Jamie gave him no encouragement. He stuttered, groping for the words that might unlock a true sense of mystery, of scale.

Stymied, he started all over again, afraid that when he opened his mouth, the words would come out jumbled and senseless.

"The city is alive."

"But it isn't," she said. "It's dead."

"But you're so wrong. I mean, you *are* wrong." He squinted at the city's outline until his eyes burned. "I see these buildings and they're like dozens of individual keys, and if I can turn enough of the keys, the city resurrects itself. Take that thing there." He pointed to a rectangular patch of sand dotted with eroded stone basins and bounded by the nubs of walls. "That's not just a box of sand. That used to be a garden or a park. And take that strip." He pointed to a slab of concrete running down the middle of the highway. "That wasn't just a divider for traffic lanes—that was a plot of plants and grass."

"You mean that you see the city as if it were organic."

"Yes! Exactly! And if I can rebuild the city, you could bring back the plants and the trees, flesh out the skeleton. There's a water source here—there must be—how else could the land support a city? In the old books, if you look, you'll see they used plants for decoration."

"Plants for decoration," she said slowly. Then she lay back down against the rock.

His heart pounded against his rib cage. He had made her see it, if only for a moment.

A silence settled over them, the sun making Balzac lazy, the leechee fruit a coolness in his stomach.

After a time, Jamie said, "No rain for at least a month."

"How do you know?"

"The water dowser's last lesson—don't you remember, stupid?" She punched his shoulder. "Look at the clouds. They're all thin and stretched out, and no two are grouped together."

Balzac shielded his eyes against the sun and examined the clouds. At the edge of his vision, he thought he saw a series of black slashes.

"What are those?"

Jamie sat up. "I see them. They look like zynagill."

The scavenger birds circled an area east of the highway. Balzac shivered and stood quickly.

"Maybe we should go back now. Maybe if we find Jeffer before he finds us he won't be as angry."

But a narrow intensity had crept over Jamie's features—a stubborn look Balzac had seen before. It was the look she wore in class when she disagreed with her teacher. It was the look she wore with her friends when they wanted to do something she didn't want to do.

"No," she said. "No. We should go see what they've found." She shimmied down the side of the rock, folded her arms, and stared up at him. "Well?"

Balzac stood atop the rock for several seconds, his pulse rapid, the weal of sky and sun burning above while all around lay the highway, littered with bones. Only when he looked into Jamie's eyes and realized she doubted him did he move; even then he hesitated, until she said, "If you don't go, I'm going alone."

She held out her hand. Her palm was calloused from hard work. He grasped it awkwardly, leaning against her compact weight as he jumped down off the rock. As they came together, her lips brushed his cheek; where she had kissed him the skin tingled and flushed bright red. He could smell her hair, was caught between its coolness and the heat of her lips.

But she was already moving away from him, and before he could react, she shouted, "Catch me if you can!"

and sprinted down the highway, smiling as she looked back over her shoulder.

He stood there for a moment, drunk with the smell and feel of her. When he did begin to run, she had a lead of more than a city block. Even worse, she didn't so much thread her way through the fields of broken stone as charge through them, leaping curved girders as blithely as if playing coddleskatch back at the crèche. To see her run for the joy of it, careless of danger, made him reckless, too, and as much as his nature allowed he copied her movements, forgetting the zynagill and their destination; watching only her.

Balzac had gained so much ground that he bumped into her when she finally stopped running.

A mountain of sand rose above them. Vaguely pyramid-shaped, it buttressed the sides of a massive amphitheater. Balzac could just see, at the top of the sand pile, winged phalanges curling out from the circular lip. Above, the zynagill wheeled, eyeing them suspiciously.

Jamie moved away from Balzac. She pointed at the sand and bent to one knee. Balzac knelt beside her, saw what she saw: an outline in the sand, seven times larger than his own palm, so large that at first he didn't realize it was a paw print. A greenish-purple fluid had congealed inside the paw print. Several more indentations followed the first, leading up the side of the amphitheater, gradually obscured by a huge swath of sand where a heavy body had dragged itself forward.

Jamie traced the paw's outline and sand fell inward.

"Whatever it is, it's hurt," Balzac said. "Probably dangerous. We should wait for Jeffer."

"No. Let's at least walk up to the top and see if we can find it." Jamie softened the rebuke with another dazzling smile that made his ears buzz.

Helpless, Balzac let her lead him as they trudged up the slanted wall of sand, parallel to the purple trail until, his sense of balance nearly betraying him, his muscles aching, they stood at the lip, blasted by the sudden wind.

He looked out across the city. Now, finally, it revealed the mystery of its structure: a broken pattern of radial spikes piercing toward a center to the southeast, obscured by the sun and the distance. The sight confounded him, and he almost lost his balance for a second time. No longer did he have to fill in the gaps with his imagination. The buildings at the center of the spokes, those would have to be governmental in purpose; this would explain their archaic shapes, the arches and the domes. The remains of one- to three-story buildings immediately north of the center had to be the former homes of the city's leaders. Each revelation led to another until he forgot his chapped lips, the grumblings of his stomach, and the beast. He could have stood there forever, linking the city's streets in his mind, but Jamie tugged on his arm and pointed down, into the amphitheater.

"Look," she said.

The amphitheater had concentric circles of seats, most nubs of plastic and metal. Railings trailed off into open space while a series of gap-toothed entranceways spiraled down into the circle of what had at one time been a stage but now could only be called a hundred-meter-wide depression. At its center a large, black hole spiraled farther downward. Halfway between the edge of the stage and the hole lay a dark shape, onto which the zynagill, leathery wings aflap, would land and then relaunch themselves. Not a single zynagill used its double-edged beak to saw at the flesh.

"It's some kind of animal," Balzac said. "And it's dead. Satisfied?"

Jamie stared at him, then peered into the amphitheater again, as if weighing his unease against the mystery of the beast.

"Jeffer needs to see this," she said. "It might be important to the crèche."

"He'll just get mad at us."

"You worry too much," Jamie said. "Stay here—I'm going down."

"Wait," he said, but he was already climbing down into the amphitheater because he knew he couldn't stop her.

By the time they reached the stage, Balzac noted with satisfaction that Jamie was breathing hard. A thin layer of sand covered the stage, broken only by the animal's purple-tinged drag marks. Jamie plunged forward. Balzac followed cautiously behind. The zynagill loitered, their leathery hooded heads bobbing nervously, then rose as one, the rasp of their wings, the cry of alarm, making Balzac think he saw movement from the body itself.

The body lay on its side, heavy flanks rising to the height of Balzac's chest. A dog. Coarse, black fur covered the body and the legs, sparser only at the paws, which ended in dulled double-edged hooks. The jowly, horrific head ran into a muscular, thick neck that disappeared into the torso without delineation between the two. The head lay against the ground and from the open mouth the purple tongue lolled, running over fangs longer and more numerous than Balzac's fingers. A pool of green and purple liquid had congealed near the mouth. The dog's eyes, staring blankly into the far wall of the amphitheater, shared the purple tint of the tongue, although they were partially hidden by loose flaps of skin; these same flaps camouflaged a bulbous knot of tissue, twice as large as a clenched fist, that jutted from the forehead. The beast could not have died more than an hour previous and yet it had an unnatural, almost mechanical, stiffness. The curled, taut quality of the limbs made him wonder how it could have walked or run. A chilling image came to Balzac of the creature dragging itself across the desert floor. The thought of the creature injured disturbed him more than the thought of it whole.

Jamie knelt beside the forepaws. She took one paw in her hands.

"It's raw."

Five pads formed the underside of the paw. The pads had been worn to redness and the sides of the paw were as smooth as wind-washed stone.

"This beast traveled a long way just to die here. I wonder where it came from—another city or maybe even from beyond the desert. How could anything with such thick fur come from the desert?"

"It looks dangerous to me."

"It's dead, Balzac."

"Even so."

Balzac's gaze traveled the length of the creature and beyond until, lightheaded with dread, he realized the beast's destination: the hole. The hole that must spiral down into level beneath level, threading its way through catacombs without number, musty and old, where lived the creatures from nightmare.

"Jamie. Jamie, we should go. We should find Jeffer."

"Too late now. He'll find us." She did not bother to look up, but held the paw gently in her hand. "Such a distance to travel."

The sun beat down, hot and withering. It stung Balzac's eyes. But, despite the sun, the creature had no smell, no stench of decay. This creature had padded across the desert, the mountains, perhaps, and seen things Balzac could only imagine, and it had had the singleness of purpose to head for the darkest hole it could find when its legs had begun to give out . . . and it had no smell.

He wanted to run, to finally leave Jamie behind if

she insisted on being so foolish. But, foolish or not, she was right: it was too late, for at that moment Jeffer appeared above them, staring down from the lip of the amphitheater.

2

Ten years after the amphitheater, on the forty-eighth night of the war for Balthakazar, Jeffer saw Jamie for the last time and his mind wobbled strangely. He stood on the third-story balcony of the crumbling, baroque building he had chosen as a resting place for his men, but seeing her he was suddenly adrift, the stone beneath his feet shockingly porous, apt to fall apart and spill him onto the street below. Almost in self-defense, his thoughts circled back to the one ritual that had proven impervious to change: When he slept in those years before and after the amphitheater, he would dream of the oasis lakes reflecting the stars. In his dreams, the lakes transformed themselves to light-choking, frictionless surfaces, as motionless as, as smooth as, lacquered black obsidian, the stars that fell upon the lakes screaming down like shards of broken, blue-tinted glass. Other times, the lakes became the land and the surrounding desert metamorphosed into thick, churning oceans through which swam fish flipped inside out so that their organs slithered and jiggled beside them.

Once, he had found Balzac at the oasis lakes, alone, his bony, frail body naked from a midnight swim, skin flushed blue with cold. Balzac's smile of greeting had suddenly shifted to doubt when Jeffer told him the news; and then Jeffer could see the darkness invading his brother, that luminous, expressive face blank with self-annihilation.

The images, the content, of the memory maintained a blurry constancy, across the years, so that Jeffer could always conjure up the pale blue gloss of Balzac's face, lit from within, and the awful curling of his lips, through which he sucked air as if he were a deep lake fish, slow and lethargic in the cold, dying out of water.

What had he told Balzac at the time? The exact words had been erased from his memory; they lingered only as ghosts and he knew them only by their absence, the holes they left behind. The event itself he remembered with perfect clarity. He had been in a service tunnel with his parents, all three struggling to fix a clogged wastewater conduit sensitively located next to a main support beam. Polluted water streamed onto the tunnel floor. They all knew the dangers of compression, how that stream could become a flood. Their portable light flickered an intense green, staining the white tunnel walls as they toiled silently. The air, recycled too many times, tasted stale. Above them groaned the weight of five underground levels, enough rock, sand, and metal to bury them forever.

When it began to look as if the patch on the conduit

would hold, Jeffer took a break, turning away to sip from a water canteen. He was sweaty and covered with grit. He faced the blinking red light that beckoned from the exit and wondered idly whether there would still be time to get in a quick drink or a game of cards before the night shift.

Behind him, like a door slamming shut, the supporting wall collapsed. Deafened, he heard nothing, *felt* the weight of sand and rock suddenly smother the tunnel.

He knew.

Before he spun around.

His parents were dead.

The foreknowledge strangled the scream rising in his throat, sent it imploding into his capillaries.

Kill the messenger, Jeffer thought. *Then maybe the message will die too.*

Seeing Jamie on the street below, Jeffer knew of no way to protect his brother from the image of her.

It was two hours before dawn, and as Jeffer stood on the third-story balcony the wind blew out of the southwest, cold and oddly comforting against his face. He hadn't showered or shaved for three weeks and there were holes in both his shoes. Sleep had become a memory.

Also from the southwest came the smell of gunpowder and the acidic stench of flesh burned by laser. Gouts of flame revealed dirigibles on fire, their barrel bodies cracking like rotten orange melons. There, amid the fiercest fighting, the crèche leaders had decided to use most of their remaining laser weapons. Spikes of light cut through the jumbled horizon of rooftops. The enemy hated light. It could not use light. Every spike of light extinguished was a human life snuffed out.

Jeffer's men, sequestered inside the building, numbered four. He could no longer lie to himself and call them a unit, or pretend they had any mission other than survival. Sixteen men had been killed in less than three nights. Of the rest, Con Fegman, wounded, had become delirious; Mindle counted as no more than a dangerous child; and Balzac . . . Balzac he could no longer read, for his brother hid beneath his handsome features and revealed himself to no one. Even their sole remaining autodoc—a portable, two-meter-high model with wheels and treads—had become increasingly eccentric, as if, deep in its circuitry, it had succumbed to battle fatigue.

Their predicament had become so dire that Jeffer found himself giggling at the most unexpected times. For over a week they had been cut off from communications with their superiors. The four of them had fought and fled from the enemy through tunnels, aqueducts, the ruins of old homes, and across the cracked asphalt of a thirty-six-lane highway.

Through it all—the deadly lulls and the frenzies of violence—Jeffer had survived by fashioning a new identity for himself and his brother; they were refugees fleeing the past, and their best strategy had proved to be the simplest: in the unraveling of their lives to forget, to disremember, to exist purely in the *now*. They had successfully eluded the past for two nights running and yet, somehow, she had found them again.

The war had extended into the heart of the desert winter, the buildings that crowded the street etched in sharp, defining lines by the cold. But how to define her? She walked in the shadow of her own skin, lit by the intermittent flash of laser fire. Was she human? She loped along the chill pavement of the street below, nimble and dainty and muscular as she navigated the long-abandoned barricades.

Jeffer stared, his body stiff. His breath caught in his throat. Centuries slow, he picked up his rifle from the balcony railing.

"Who is it?" Balzac's tired voice, muffled, came from the room at Jeffer's back. They had barricaded themselves in and had booby-trapped the stairwells. Inside the room, the autodoc produced a thin, blue-tinted light that couldn't be seen from the street.

The pale, moon-faced boy Mindle, a refugee from a northern crèche already destroyed by the invaders, sidled along the wall until he was close enough to whisper, "Is it her again?" Mindle's voice held no fear, no surprise. Only Mindle's body registered such nerve-end pricklings; at his spiritual core he had been frozen solid for a hundred years. Jeffer had seen too many like him in recent months as the crèche sent younger and younger men into battle.

"Keep Balzac quiet," Jeffer whispered back. "If she hears him . . . get Con Fegman, if he's able, to watch the door."

Mindle nodded and, wraithlike, disappeared into the darkness.

Below, Jamie began to cry out Balzac's name in the plaintive timbre of one who is lost and alone and afraid.

Balzac muttered a few words and Jeffer heard Mindle's soft voice, calm and reasonable, coo a soothing reply.

The shape on the street below stiffened, sneezed, and said, "Balzac, my love?"

Balzac's voice in reply: "Is it—could it?"

Mindle cursed. Jeffer heard a scuffle, a strangled cry, and silence, his gaze never straying from her. Lost and afraid. How could he ever consider her someone he had known? The sounds of her aloneness, her confusion, struck him as faintly pitiable, that she should, in any manner, try to re-create her former life. Such a curious double image: to see her on the street below and yet to remember all the times when Balzac had invited him over for dinner, Balzac and Jamie both exhausted from twelve hours of overseeing their reclamation projects in Balthakazar. She had never seemed vulnerable while arguing with him over the Con's latest decisions or about how to adapt the hydroponics hangars to open-air conditions. The lack of hardness in her now, the weaning away of any but the most dependent attributes, made him wary.

The stone wall behind him bruised his back. He didn't play the statue very well; he was sweating despite the cold and he imagined his breath as a vast, unmoving field of ice particles.

Perhaps, as on the two previous nights, she would miss them, would pass by, rasping out her song.

Jeffer raised his rifle to his shoulder. *Pass by*, he wished desperately. *Pass by and be gone.* He did not want to risk the sound of a shot. Come dawn, they would move elsewhere, maybe come across another unit and cobble up enough numbers to mount a counteroffensive.

Pass by. Even better, remake history. Let Balzac come to me swimming at night at the oasis. Let Balzac tell me of our parents' death. Let him be the eldest and follow me to Balthakazar.

She stopped directly beneath his balcony, at an extreme line of fire. She sniffed the air. She growled deep in her throat.

"Balzac, are you there?" Such a reedy, ghostly voice.

She paced in a circle, still sniffing.

Jeffer allowed himself to be seduced by the fluid grace, the single-minded purpose behind the strides, the preternatural balance, for she was still beautiful.

She stopped pacing. She stared right up at him with her dead violet eyes, the snarl of fangs below the mouth.

"Jeffer," she said.

His finger closed on the trigger. The red tracer light lit up the pavement. The bullet hit the pavement, sent up a rain of debris.

But she was not there.

He could already hear her—*inside* the building. Battling through their booby traps. Barricades ripped apart, flung to the side.

"She's coming up!" Jeffer shouted, running back into the room. "She's coming up!"

Mindle and Con Fegman stood against the wall farthest from the door. Balzac sobbed, curled in a corner, guarded by the autodoc. It was clear Mindle had propped Con Fegman up and that the old man would fall down given the opportunity. Which left Mindle and him to stop her. Mindle had their last two laser weapons, a rifle and a hand-held beam. He aimed the rifle at the door. They both knew it had only two or three more charges left.

"Give me the rifle," Jeffer said. "Keep the other one—a crossfire."

Mindle nodded, threw the weapon to him. Jeffer caught it. His heart pounded. His hands shook. He flicked the safety.

Mindle said, "Soon now. Soon now." He rocked back and forth on his heels. His eyes were dilated. He licked his lips.

They heard the scrabble of claws upon the stairs. Heard the rasping of her breath.

The terror left Jeffer in that instant, as if he had become as cold as Mindle. He wanted her to come through that door. He wanted to kill her.

The sound of claws faded. Silence settled over the room.

Jeffer looked at Mindle in puzzlement.

Mindle smiled and winked. "Just wait. Just wait."

Then she hit the door with such force that the metal shrieked with fatigue.

"Balzac! Open the door!"

Another blow to the door. An indentation the size of her paw. A growl that would have ripped up Jeffer's insides a minute before.

"Go away," yelled Con Fegman, who fell, thrashing, in the fever haze of his infection.

"Balzac! Open the door!"

Balzac looked up from his corner. Jeffer could see the anguish in his eyes.

"Don't," Jeffer said.

The door tore open as if it were paper.

□

Metal and stone exploded into the room. Jeffer was yelling but Balzac couldn't hear the words. She stood there— huge, black, half seen in the autodoc's blue glare. She shook herself, debris fluming out from her body. Mindle dove into Balzac's corner and caught him in the ribs with an elbow. It drove the air out of Balzac's lungs. Before he could get to his feet—to warn her? to protect Jeffer?—she leapt at Jeffer. Jeffer's laser rifle flashed and burned her hindquarters off. Jamie screamed and, trajectory altered, landed in a bloody, crumpled heap beside him, brought to a stop by the wall.

The body thrashed, the claws whipping out from the pistoning legs. Balzac ducked, covering his head with his hands. Con Fegman, struggling to his feet, was ripped by a claw and sent reeling by the impact. The front legs sought traction, flailed, and the great jaws beneath Jamie's head gnashed together, opening reflexively only inches from Balzac's throat. Fangs the size of fingers. Breath like an antiseptic wind. Blood spattered over the blunt muzzle. He could see the tiny pink tongue muscles tensing and relaxing spasmodically.

Jeffer shouted an order to the autodoc. The autodoc lurched over on its treads, extended a tube, and stuck a needle into what remained of the flesh dog's left flank. The flailing died away. The great jaws lost their rigidity and rested against the floor. Blood seeped out from beneath the body, licking at Balzac's drawn-up feet. Con Fegman moaned.

Balzac sat up against the wall, unable to look at his beloved. An endless singsong ran through his head: if only, if only. If only Jeffer had let him talk to her while she was still on the street, perhaps he could have persuaded her to go away—and perhaps he didn't want her to go away. He let out a deep, shuddering sigh and stood on trembling legs.

Mindle blocked his path, so close he could smell the boy's rotten breath.

"Kill it," Mindle hissed, his face white with hatred. "Kill it now!"

Mindle's eyes had narrowed to knifepoints. Balzac looked away—toward Jeffer, toward Con Fegman.

Con Fegman, in a misty, faraway voice, said, "I can't see anymore. I can't bear to see anymore," and covered his eyes and began to weep.

Balzac pushed past Mindle, turning his shoulder into the boy so he stumbled backward. He went over to Con Fegman and knelt beside him, looked into his ancient face. Such sadness, such shame, that one of the crèche's elders should be dying here, like this.

Balzac took one of Con Fegman's hands, held it tightly in his own.

Con Fegman grinned with broken teeth and said, "I need water. I'm so thirsty."

"I'll get you water. Autodoc—Con Fegman. Full medical."

Balzac stood and allowed the autodoc to do its job. It injected tranquilizers, enveloped Con Fegman in a sterile white shield and, away from meddling eyes, went to work on him.

"Don't waste ammunition," Jeffer said. "It's dying anyhow. It can't hurt us."

"No, she can't hurt us," Balzac said.

Mindle's hand wavered on his laser. Balzac stared at him until he lowered it.

"Jeffer," Balzac said. "Please, get him out of here. The traps. Have him redo the traps."

"I'm here," Mindle said. "I'm in the room."

Mindle's hot gaze bore down on him, and he tensed, prepared to defend himself.

Jeffer nodded to Mindle. "Go downstairs and fix the barricades. Put up more traps. I'll keep watch on the balcony. At dawn, we move out."

"And will we take that thing with us?" Mindle asked, in a voice sweet as poison.

"No," Jeffer said, and stared pointedly at Balzac. "I promise you we won't take her with us."

"Compassion!" Mindle spat, but he headed for the door.

Balzac watched him—a man-child, both ancient and newly born, gaunt but innocent of hunger. Balzac couldn't blame him for his rage, or for the madness that came with it. He could only fear the boy. He had always feared the boy, ever since he had come to the crèche: an albino with frazzled, burnt white hair sticking up at odd angles, and eyes that made Balzac want to recoil from and embrace Mindle all at once. The eyes hardly ever blinked, and even when he talked to you, he was staring through you, to a place far away. Mindle had laughed at their reclamation project, had not seen the point in the face of war. Why did they persist when they knew what they knew? Perhaps, Balzac thought, they had simply refused to believe in the proof Mindle brought with him.

It had been Mindle, a refugee from the north, who had first given a name and a face to the enemy, fed the growing unease of the Con members. Before him, there had only been disturbing phenomena: strange, ungainly creatures lurking at the edge of campfire and oasis; dismembered human corpses not of the crèche; then little gobbets of divorced flesh with cyclopean eyes that twitched like epileptic rats as they walked and, when dissected, proved to be organic cameras, *click-click-clicking* pictures with each blink of the single liquid-blue eye.

Mindle had brought them a present, unwrapping the corpse of one of the enemy at a Con meeting. It was the only body yet recovered, badly burned and curled up into a fetal position like a dead black cricket, but still recognizably mammalian. Weasel-like. Two meters tall. Fangs snarled out from the fire-peeled muzzle.

"At first they walked around in plain view, directing their troops," Mindle had told the Con members. "Darting here and there, sometimes on four legs, sometimes on two legs. A meerkat hybrid, no doubt a leftover from biotech experiments before the Collapse, with a much bigger skull and an opposable thumb. *Made* creatures. When we captured this one, they went into hiding, and now they only send their servants, the flesh dogs . . ."

Watching the grimace of Mindle's features, the hatred embedded there, Balzac had felt a prickle of unease, as if Mindle were not the messenger, but the presence of death itself.

◻

With Mindle gone, Balzac turned to Jamie, her face set like a jewel in a ring, nearly buried by the folds of tissue on the flesh dog's head. Clinically, he forced himself to recall the little he knew about such symbiosis: Jamie's head had been cut from her body and placed in the cavity usually reserved for the flesh dog's nutrient sac; the nutrient sac allowed the beast to run for days without food or water. Her brain stem had been hardwired into the flesh dog's nervous system and bloodstream, but motor functions remained under the flesh dog's control. She could not shut her eyes without the flesh dog's approval, and although she kept her own eyes, they had been surgically enhanced for night vision, so that now her pupils resembled tiny dead violets. Sometimes the wiring went wrong and the symbiote would fight for muscle control with the flesh dog—a condition that ended with uncontrollable thrashing and a slow death by self-disembowelment.

Jeffer stumbled over a chair and Balzac became aware that his brother still shared the room with him.

"Why don't you leave, too," Balzac said, anger rising inside him.

"You shouldn't be alone. And what if there were others? I need to watch from the balcony."

"There's no one with her."

"I'm staying. You'll hardly know I'm here."

Balzac waited until Jeffer had stepped out to the balcony. Then, thoughts a jumble of love and loathing, he forced himself to stare at his lover's face. The face registered shock in the dim light, stunned as it began to recover itself. As he watched, the eyes, pupils stained purple, blinked rapidly, the full mouth forming a puzzled smile. Balzac shuddered. She looked enough like the Jamie he remembered for love to win out over loathing. He had known it would; deep down, in places he would never reveal to anyone, he had hoped Jamie would track him here. He had assumed that once she had found him again he could bring her back from the dead.

Looking at her now, he had no idea what to do.

"Balzac? Balzac?" That voice, no longer demanding and sexy.

He was so used to her being the stronger one, the one who had an answer for everything, that he couldn't reply. He couldn't even look at her. Throat tight and dry, legs wobbly, he took a step toward Jeffer. Jeffer was only a silhouette, behind which rose the night: a ridge of black broken by faint streaks of laser fire.

"Help me, Jeffer."

"I can't help you."

"What should I do?"

"I would have shot her in the street."

"But you didn't."

"I missed."

"Balzac," Jamie said. The disorientation in her voice frightened Balzac. He ground his teeth together to stop his tears.

"She can still hurt you," Jeffer said.

"I know," Balzac said. He slumped down against the wall, his shoes almost touching Jamie's head. The floor was strewn with dirt, pieces of stone, and empty autodoc syringes. Beside Balzac, the flesh dog's entrails congealed in a sloppy pile.

"Balzac?" Jamie said a third time.

Her eyes blinked once, twice, a miracle for one who had been dead. She focused on him, the flesh dog's head moving with a crackly sound.

"I can see you," she said. "I can really see you."

You're dead, he wanted to say, as if it were her fault. *Why aren't you dead?*

"Do you know where you are?" Balzac asked. "Do you know who you are?"

"I'm with you," she said. "I'm here, and it's cold here."

The effort too much, too soon, with the flesh dying all around her, Jamie's eyes closed to slits.

Balzac wondered if what he saw was not just a carnie trick, if beneath the flesh lived nothing more than an endless spliced loop, a circuit that said his name and tried to seduce him with the lie that Jamie lived, long enough for it to drive him mad. Jamie had died. He knew that; if he saw her now, she was ghost cloaked in flesh, as dead as the city of powdering bones. The same war that had given the city a false heart—a burning, soul-consuming furnace of a heart—had resurrected Jamie. Yet he must assume that she was more than a shadowy wisp of memory, because he could not prove her ghostliness, her *otherness*. What cruelty for him to abandon her should she be aware. And trapped.

Jamie had died on the front lines a month before, *then* and *now* separated by a second and a century. His recollections were filtered through a veil of smoke and screams, the dark pulsating with frantic commands. Particular moments stood out: the irritation of sand grit in his shoes; a lone blade of grass caught *just so* between yellow and green; an ant crawling across an empty boot, its red body translucent in the laser glow; the reflection of an explosion, the burnt umber flames melting across the muzzle of his rifle; the slick feel of Jamie's grime-smeared hand in his, her pulse beating against him through the tips of her fingers.

Crowded together in long trenches, they had been only two among several thousand, waiting. They did not talk, but only touched.

The flesh dogs appeared promptly at twilight, bringing silence with them in a black wave. They wore the masks of friends, the guise of family. They jogged and cantered across the fires: fueled by a singleness of purpose, pounding on shadow muscles, ripping swathes of darkness from the night so as to reimagine themselves in night's image. Eyes like tiny dead violets. An almost-silent ballet of death.

Then, on cue, they halted, forming a solid, uniform line. They stood so still it would have been easy to think they were a row of ancient statues built on the order of a brilliantly deranged despot.

In the lull, Balzac hugged Jamie, taking comfort in the feel and scent of her body.

Above, dirigibles coughed and grunted with the effort of discharging missiles, flashes of light catching ground combatants in freeze frame.

As the flesh dogs came into range, in such numbers that the ground reverberated with the thunder of their passage, the defenders of the trench opened fire: the spitting sparks of lasers and the rhythmic *phutt-phutt* of rifles entwined in an orgasm of recoil and recharge. It took immense discipline to stand in the teeth of such a charge. The rifle in Balzac's hands seemed heavy, difficult—it wanted its head, and in the heat of battle it was all he could do to keep it aimed and firing, his finger awkward on the trigger.

In reply to the defenders' barrage: a chorus of bone-thin voices attached to alien bodies, a thousand ghosts wailing across the ruins in the timbre of old friends pleading for their lives, calling out to the living by name.

It brought madness bubbling to the surface, so that the defenders shot and recharged with incredible speed, shouting back their own hatred to block out the voices, obliterating the present that it might not obliterate the past.

As the wave broke over them, the tableau dissolved in confusion. Mostly, Balzac remembered the stench of gunpowder as he loaded and reloaded—but more slowly now, mesmerized by the carnage—and the fleeting images through the smoke . . . Huge bodies flung without reason or care . . . a dark blue-black wall of flesh . . . the swiftness of them, almost as fast as a dirigible, so that a blink could cost a life . . . Sinuous muscles, caricatures of human faces as wincing passengers . . . The bright black slickness of spilled oil . . . Throats ripped from bodies . . . bodies fallen, whirling and dancing in the jaws of the flesh dogs . . . flesh dogs toppling, sawed in half or legs cut off, crawling forward . . . others, shot in the head, falling over on their backs.

Through the black-white-black of dirigible flashes, Balzac saw Jamie fall in stop-gap motion *and his heart stopped beating* away from him into the darkness *he couldn't see her anywhere.* As he put out his hand to pull her up, she was no longer there.

"Jamie!"

A flesh dog galloped toward the breach in the line left by Jamie's absence. He spun, shot it, and jumped to the side, the fangs snapping inches from his throat. It slammed into the trench, dead. He got up . . . and when he looked back toward the gap in the line of defenders, she still hadn't filled it, hadn't regained her feet as he'd expected, even when the dirigibles scorched the night into day.

In his panic, he couldn't breathe, he couldn't think.

"Jamie!" he shouted over the screams and detonations. "Jamie!"

And the echo passed along the line to him: "Retreat! Fall back! Breached! Breached!"

A death sentence for Jamie. A section of the trench had been overrun and to avoid being flanked they must fall back. The retreat, a haphazard, broken-backed affair, piled confusion on confusion, some soldiers running away while others commenced a vigilant rearguard action to allow stragglers to cross back over what was now enemy territory.

A dirigible exploded directly overhead, the impact knocking Balzac to the ground. Swathes of burning canvas floated down on the combatants. Molten puddles crackled and hissed around Balzac as he got up. Mechanically, he haunted the burning ground, searching for his beloved with his infrared goggles. He dove into ditches, crawled through the most dangerous of firefights, lending his rifle only long enough to clear a path to the next embattled outpost. Each minute of failure added to the heaviness in his chest, the rising sense of helplessness.

Later, he would recall the black-and-red battlefield as if he had been aboard a dirigible; he would even remember watching himself run across the treacherous ground:

a tiny figure leaping recklessly between trenches, scurrying through flames without hesitation. Other times, he would remember it only as a series of starts and stops. He would be running and then fellow soldiers or flesh dogs would be all around him like a sudden rain, and then he would be alone again, his thoughts poisoning his skull.

Only the sight of the creature saved Balzac from the endless searching, for it was only then that he realized Jamie must be dead.

He sat down heavily, as if shot, and stared at it as it bustled about its business some thirty-five meters away. It was so sleek and functional and not of this world—so much more *perfect* than anything perfect could be—that for a moment Balzac could not imagine its function: it was merely a beautiful piece of artwork, a thing to be admired for its own clockwork self. How could humankind compete with such a creature? He watched it with mounting dread and guilty fascination.

It scuttled along on cilia-like feet, almost centipedal, and yet it was clothed in dense, dark fur—long and low to the ground so that it seemed to *flow*, a species composed of the most elemental combination of flesh and bone. The head, which swiveled three hundred sixty degrees, reminded Balzac of a cross between cat and badger, the bright, luminous eyes and curious smile of muzzle conspiring to make the beast almost jolly. Thin, Balzac thought at first. Thinner than thin, the spine caved in on itself so that its back appeared to have been scooped out with a shovel, leaving a long, low compartment walled in by shoulders and flanks. The smooth-squishy sound it made with its thousand limbs he had heard before, on the battlefield, as a low, underlying counterpoint to the screams and explosions.

But although the beast stunned him with its perfect strangeness, the function it performed stunned him more.

As he watched, the beast threaded its way through the scattered corpses. Finally, at the body of a young man with open, vacant eyes, and a thin line of blood trickling from the mouth, the beast came to a halt. Then, with a discernable *pop*, spinning wildly, the expression on its face insanely cheerful, the beast's head unscrewed itself from its body and, with the aid of cilia positioned beneath its now autonomous head, lifted itself over the edge of its own shoulders. Once it had sidled up to the head of its victim, the beast grunted twice and two appendages emerged from the thick fur: a powerful blade of bone and a two-thumbed hand. The blade came down, slicing through the man's neck. Almost simultaneously, the hand grasped the dead soldier's head and placed it over the hole left by the departure of the beast's head. It waited for a moment, then pulled the man's head, which had been "capped" with a pulsing purple slab of flesh, back out of the hole. Balzac watched with horrified fascination as the hand then tossed the capped head into the scooped-out cavity of the beast's body. Both blade and hand disappeared into the beast's grinning head, which then rolled and huffed its way back onto its own neck and twirled twice, before the whole nightmare contraption scuttled on, out of sight.

Leaving Balzac alone, with the dead.

◻

After the battle, behind the lines, they assigned him to Jeffer's guerilla unit. Jeffer would watch over him as he always had in the past.

Jeffer placed his hand on Balzac's shoulder. Balzac flinched. Jeffer realized that the gesture was unappreciated, but he tried by an act of will to put all of his love and fear for Balzac into that simple touch of hand on shoulder. Love. He might not have admitted to love a few years ago, beyond the love expected by blood, but Jeffer had seen an unlikely transformation come over Balzac.

Balzac, with his piercing green eyes and firm chin, had always been handsome to the point of callowness. But slowly, as he and Jamie became closer, and especially in the year after their marriage, Jeffer had seen the callowness stripped away. A certain *weight* and *depth* had entered the perfect lines of his brother's mouth, a seriousness and mischievousness that illuminated the eyes. It was as if a fear had conquered Balzac simultaneous with his love for Jamie—fear for the death of his beloved, that their love could not last forever—and that these entangled twins of fear and love had peeled away his shallow qualities like a molting lizard skin.

Jamie had remarked on it during a tour of the Balthakazar reclamation projects, as they sat and watched Balzac out in the sun, badgering the engineers.

"I used to love him for his mouth and his eyes and his awkwardness, and I wanted to protect him. Now he's grown up and become real."

The memory haunted Jeffer as he said to Balzac, "It will be okay. You don't have to do anything. It won't be long . . ." Jeffer suddenly felt weary. Why must he comfort others at those times he most needed comfort? The muscles in his throat tightened. Ever since he had been left with an eleven-year-old boy who could never again quite be just his little brother it had been this way.

"I should have rolled in the dirt and disguised my scent," Balzac said. "I should have become someone else. Then she couldn't have found me. Ever. I shouldn't have let her find me. *But where's the kindness in that?*"

Jeffer smiled at the mimicry of Mindle's favorite phrase.

"Kindness?" Mindle said, surprising them both. Eyes bright and reptilian, he stood in the doorway. "Kindness? How can you speak of kindness? There's no room for it. We've no need of it."

Jeffer half expected Mindle to crouch down and lap up the blood pooling around the flesh dog's body. Who could predict the actions of a child who had never been a child?

"Are you finished with the barricades, Mindle?" Jeffer asked.

"With the barricades? Yes."

"Then wait outside until dawn. Stand watch from the second-story window."

Mindle stepped inside the room. He licked his lips. "Yes, sir. But first I thought we might interrogate the prisoner."

"The prisoner will be dead soon."

"Then we must be quick—quicker, even," he said, and took another step into the room.

"Take up your post on the second floor," Jeffer ordered.

Mindle took a third step into the room.

Before Jeffer could react, Balzac snatched up Con Fegman's rifle from the floor. He aimed it at Mindle.

Balzac said: "Go. Away."

Mindle smiled sweetly and turned to Jeffer, one eyebrow raised.

"Do as he says, Mindle," Jeffer said. "And Balzac— put down the rifle!"

Mindle shrugged and turned away.

Balzac tossed the weapon aside and hunkered over the flesh dog's body. His brother's gauntness, the way the autodoc's light seemed to shine through him, unnerved Jeffer. Such an odd tableau: his brother crouched with such love and such gentleness over the massive body of the flesh dog, as if it were his own creation.

Jeffer tottered forward under the spell of that image, his intentions masked even from himself, but Balzac waved him away.

"Please, let me be," Balzac said. "Watch the window. Watch Mindle."

Even as he nodded yes, Jeffer hesitated, wondering for the first time if he could aim a rifle at his own brother. He walked over to the balcony and watched Balzac and Jamie from the darkness. Jamie's face was pale, her lips gray. The beast's flesh surrounded her like a rubbery cowl.

He marveled at the affection in Balzac's voice as his brother touched the creature's face and asked, "How do you feel?"

"Cold. Very cold. I can't feel my legs. I think I'm dying. I think I'm already dead, Balzac. Why else should I feel so cold?"

Balzac flinched, and Jeffer thought: *Think? Feel? Can it do either?*

"It's a cold night," Balzac told her. "You need a blanket. I wish I had a blanket for you, my love."

"Cold. Very cold," she said, in a dreamy, far-off voice.

"I'll find something for you," Balzac said, his voice cracking with grief. "Jeffer, I'm going to look through the supplies downstairs—maybe there's a blanket. Watch her for me?"

"She's almost . . . I mean, I don't think we have a blanket."

"I know! I know that. Just watch her."

Balzac scrambled to his feet and fled through the ruined doorway, leaving Jeffer with the enemy. As he circled her, he wondered if he should kill her.

"Who is there?" Jamie said. "Are you cold too?"

At the sound of that voice, Jeffer stepped away from her, made sure she couldn't see him. What if she recognized him? What if she spoke his name again? What then?

In the corner, Con Fegman stirred and said, in a singsong voice, "The sand toad told the sand itself and the sand told the toads and the toads told the sand and . . . and . . . and . . ." He faded back into unconsciousness, the myth trapped between his withered lips.

Jeffer tried to ignore Con Fegman. He had so resigned himself to the old man's death that he sometimes started in surprise during Con Fegman's moments of lucidity, as if a ghost had drawn breath.

"I want to get up," Jamie said, face tightening as she strained to move the flesh dog's leg muscles. "I can't seem to get up."

Jeffer knew better than to interrogate her. If he couldn't shoot her, he would have to content himself with watching her.

In the early days, before the full-fledged invasion, he had volunteered to help capture and interrogate such surgically altered specimens. They never had much to say and, anyhow, who could tell if what the prisoners said was authentic or preprogrammed? The heads when separated from the bodies would live on unimpaired for two or three hours, and perhaps there was a hint of miracles in this delayed mortality, but surely nothing more.

Locklin, the subject of Jeffer's final interrogation, had believed in miracles, and as Jeffer stared at Jamie he could not help but see Locklin's face superimposed over hers.

Locklin had laughed at him even during those moments of the interrogation that most resembled torture. When asked a question, the creature would say its name and make a low, bubbling laugh through its flesh dog and human mouths. The violet eyes would widen, his craggy, heavily tanned and scarred face sprawled across the flesh dog's forehead. "I am Locklin today, but tomorrow? You will all be me."

Locklin claimed to come from a crèche located in the far north, nestled against a frozen sea. Cliffs four hundred meters high sheltered them from the cruel winds, and from these same cliffs came the enemy in great numbers, on a winter's day when many of the crèche were dying from cold; the heaters had failed and the crèche's leadership had wavered on whether to wait out the weather or to abandon the crèche.

"But the m'kat," Locklin offered near the end, contempt for Jeffer poisoning his voice, "they fixed us up! Ho! They surely did. Immortality in return for service—a fine, fine body that will run forever, and we said *yes*! We said *yes*, all of us shivering in that frozen place . . . as most of you will say yes in your turn."

Always it was flesh dogs fashioned from members of this particular crèche that Jeffer found least like a poorly animated holovid. If some responded like sand through a sieve to his questioning, then these hardened types were steel traps. For they had not just pledged allegiance to the "m'kat" but worshipped them, giving up their children to immortality and abandoning their old religions. This betrayal of species terrified Jeffer. Among the Con members it was the greatest of all fears: to be captured by an enemy that did not know mercy as humans knew it, an enemy unparalleled in the art of psychological warfare. To be sent back in the guise of a flesh dog, mouthing your own name or the name of your beloved as the creature fought you.

Only now did Jeffer realize he had talked to Locklin too much, for as he watched Jamie, Locklin's hypnotic words drifted in and out of his thoughts: *"You could live forever this way, if you would only submit . . ."* A great sadness welled up inside Jeffer, for he and his brother had become estranged; it was there in Balzac's words, in his face: that the love he had for Jamie had become monstrous, had taken him over and eaten him from the inside out. Did Balzac sense a truth to Locklin's words that escaped him? A chill crept into Jeffer's skin. He could already foresee an outcome monstrous beyond imagination and he told himself he would not help *in that way*—he could not—and he tried to convince himself this was because he loved his brother, not because he stood alone in the same room with a creature so familiar to him and yet so alien.

◼

Mindle had been Balzac's hateful shadow as he rummaged through their meager cache of supplies for a blanket. The boy had said nothing, had followed almost without sound, but Balzac could feel that gaze blasting the back of his head, scorching his scalp. He didn't mind; better to know where Mindle was than not. At times on his miniquest, he even tried talking to Mindle, and took a perverse pleasure in his facade of cheeriness, knowing it must make the boy burn even brighter. Burn, then. Burn up.

But there was no blanket, and with each step back up the stairs, the facade faded a little more until he could barely walk for the weariness that pulled at him. On the third-floor landing, Balzac heard Mindle's retreating footsteps and was glad of it, not wasting time with a taunt, but ducking into the room where Jamie still lay in the autodoc's blue light. Jeffer stood to one side.

"I couldn't find a blanket. You can go back to the window."

Jeffer gave Balzac a wan smile, but Balzac only slumped down beside Jamie.

"Jamie," he said when Jeffer had gone back out onto the balcony.

"I'm cold." A voice like an echo, rich with phlegm or blood.

"Cold like the oasis lakes—do you remember the oasis lakes?"

He thought he saw her mouth curl upward. She gave a little hiccuping laugh.

"I remember. I remember the cold. It makes me sneeze." Then, doubtful: "That was a long time ago . . ."

The water had been cold. They'd dived in together, into the hardness of the water, swum through it, their muscles aching. They'd snorted water, gurgled it, luxuriating in the decadence of so much water, and surfaced to kiss, breathlessly, under the stars. Her lips had tasted of passion fruit and he had pressed her into the shallows where they could stand, then moved away from her shyly, only to find her pulling him back toward her and putting his hand between her legs; making sharp, quiet sounds of pleasure as his hands moved lightly on her.

But, faced with her in the flesh, he could not hold on to the memory of the emotion. It dissipated into the grime and darkness: a dimly glittering jewel against whose sharp edges he could only bleed.

"We made love there," he said.

Silence.

Dawn would come soon and they would have to move on while they had the chance.

Jamie whimpered and moaned and cried out in her

half death, half sleep. He was cruel (wasn't he?) to prolong her pain.

He could feel Jeffer staring at him. If not Jeffer then Mindle. Mindle hated him. Jeffer loved him. But they both wanted the same thing.

Balzac let his gaze linger over Jamie's face, the thickness of it that had overtaken the grace, as if the architects that had put her back together could not quite re-create their source material. This was the woman who had worked side by side with him to rebuild the city, she planting trees as he excavated and drew plans. He had even grown to enjoy the planting—long hours, yes, and the work made his fingers bleed and blister, but he had liked the smell of dirt, enjoyed the rhythms of the work and the comfort of her presence at his side.

He thought of the times they had been intimate on the cool desert sand under the stars, and how they would sneak back to the crèche in the years before they were married, there to lie in bed for hours afterwards, talking or telling stories. The smell of her, the taste of her tongue in his mouth, these were *real*, as was the peace that came over him when he was so very close to her, as close to her as he could, looking into her eyes.

He owed it to her. If he loved her.

In agony, he ran to the balcony, pushing Jeffer aside, and beat his fists against the stone railing.

"Listen to me: it's better this way," Jeffer whispered.

"Come morning, there's a good chance we can come under the protection of a larger unit. If we can only survive—"

"Shut up!" Balzac hissed. "Shut up or I'll yell and *they'll* all hear us."

"Should I leave?"

"Leave? No . . . but I don't want to talk. I just want to stand here for a moment."

"That's fine. That's fine. I'm your brother, Balzac, *your brother*. I don't want to hurt you."

Balzac tried to slow his breathing. He leaned on the railing and looked out across the city. Dawn soon, and still the dirigibles burned and still the darkness closed in around them. A hundred shades of darkness for a hundred different tasks—darkness to cover buildings; darkness to cover pain; darkness to cover thoughts; darkness to cover the light, and the light, when it came, only emphasized the darkness all the more. He could no longer hear the faint, ghostly shouts from the front lines; the darkness had swallowed the voices too.

For the first time, looking out over not only the ruined city but also the ruins of his own ambition, Balzac felt the pull of that darkness, felt overpowered by it. He was tired. He was so tired. He began to weep. He could not bear it. He must bear it. He could not. He must.

Where into that darkness had she been taken? Where had the scuttling creature dragged her? Had it dragged her into the hole at the center of the amphitheater? Some place underground where the darkness grew thick and unfettered—in the tunnels under the city, wherever *they* had their headquarters, where the creatures from nightmare used to live before the enemy displaced them. It hurt to think of such places. They scared him more than anything. All he could imagine was suffocating dirt, the tunnel imploding and burying him alive.

What sort of immortality had she found there? When they'd reawakened her, had she pleaded with them? Did she know, even now, exactly what had been done to her?

And if he took her back there, could they live together, in the darkness, all alone with only each other for company amongst the ghouls and ghosts . . .

"Help me to imagine it, Jeffer."

"Imagine what?"

"Never mind."

A red wound bled across the horizon. Balzac stared at Jeffer. Jeffer looked away.

"I know I have to do it," Balzac said.

"You don't. I'll do it for you."

"No. I have to do it."

"Then do it."

Balzac nodded and walked back to Jamie. He leaned over her, touched her face once again, smoothed back a strand of hair. Strange, the calm that settled over him.

"Balzac?" she said in such a questioning tone that he almost laughed with grief.

"Jamie. Jamie, I have to ask you something. Do you hurt, Jamie? Jamie, do you hurt a lot?"

"I'm so cold," she said. Then something clicked behind her eyes and he thought he saw the old confidence.

"Close your eyes then, Jamie. I swear, Jamie. This won't hurt. Jamie, it won't hurt. I wouldn't lie. Not to you, Jamie."

"I know, my love."

He exchanged weapons with Jeffer: his rifle for Jeffer's laser. Then, hugging the flesh dog's head to him, he adjusted the setting on the laser for a needle-thin, ten-centimeter-long blade. If he cut the throat, she might last for a few minutes, in pain. But if he could spear her through the head . . . His hand wavered and for a moment every atom, every particle that made him Balzac streaked in opposite, splintered directions. If only she wouldn't stare at him . . .

His hand steadied, and with it his resolve. Two smooth strokes and he had separated the node of tissue that contained Jamie. There was no blood; the laser cauterized the wound instantly. Her eyes still stared up at him though her lips did not move. He held her against him, closed her eyes, kept the rifle in his right hand, reactivated the normal settings.

He looked up at Jeffer, who was staring at him in horror.

Balzac's shoulders sagged, the weight of darkness too great, and then he righted himself, found his legs.

Jeffer took a step forward, as if to block the door.

"Don't. Don't do that," Balzac said.

"Balzac! Leave her be."

Tears blurred Balzac's vision; he wiped them away viciously with his forearm. Seconds were as precious as water now; he could not waste them.

"I can't do it, Jeffer. I. Just. Can't."

"You can! You know you can. You remember how I was after . . . after our parents died? You remember how I was? You brought me back. *You did that.* I can do that for you. I know I can."

"And if you do? I couldn't bear it. I couldn't bear it. *I can't lose her too.*"

"It's too late. You'll lose her anyway."

"Not if I find them in time. I've got an hour. Two, maybe."

Silent as an executioner, Mindle appeared at the door, his handheld laser aimed at Balzac.

"*Mindle, get out of here!*" Jeffer screamed, raising his own rifle. The barrel wavered between Balzac and Mindle.

Mindle's eyes had the fatal density of dead stars.

"Shut up, Jeffer," he said. "If he moves, I'll shoot him."

Into the deadly silence crept the first light of the sun. Grainy yellow rays revealed them all as tired, grime-smeared, gaunt figures frozen in time, while Con Fegman stared with sightless eyes directly into the sun. Balzac could hear his brother's muttered prayers, could sense the tension in Mindle's trigger finger. He looked first at one and then the other, their shadows flung against the far wall.

Looking down into her sleeping face, Balzac knew he was impervious to the other voices, the voices that were not hers. For her sake, he had to get past Mindle, make it to the doorway, and onto the street below. The odds were bad, and yet he felt at peace: the darkness was still with him, cloaking and protecting him.

Vaguely, he heard Jeffer tell him to put down his rifle and Mindle scream that if he took a single step he was a dead man, but their words came from very far away. They could not touch him—not Mindle, not his brother. No one but Jamie. The darkness covered his face like a veil. He caressed Jamie's cold cheek with one trembling hand.

"Goodbye," he said. He threw his rifle in Mindle's face. He ran toward the door. Behind him he heard Jeffer's slow, drawn-out shriek of loss, and then the ice-heat of Mindle's star exploded against his back. The force drove him forward, knocked the breath from his body, and he was falling through the doorway, falling into the darkness of the stairwell—and kept falling, a numbness enveloping his body, until the darkness was complete and it was no longer the stairwell but the black oasis lakes, and he was diving into and through them, the wet wave and wash licking blackly at his limbs, and just when he thought he might fall forever, he caught himself.

Sand, bright sand, beneath his feet, the grains like

glittering jewels. He looked up—into the glare of late afternoon—and saw Jeffer staring down at him from the lip of the amphitheater. Jamie saw Jeffer a moment later and gasped in surprise.

Jeffer stalked down to them, cold-shouldered and stiff, sand spraying out around his boots. Balzac had risen from his position near the beast, thinking Jeffer would give them both a thrashing.

But instead, Jeffer became very quiet and asked them if they were all right. Balzac said yes and Jamie asked how he had found them.

"The zynagill," Jeffer said, still staring at the beast. "I thought you might be dead."

Before Balzac could speak, Jamie laughed and said, "No. *It* is. What do you think of it?"

"I think you should get away from it." Jeffer walked closer.

"It came from underground," Balzac said.

"It came from far away," Jamie said. "Look at its paws."

"It's like something from the old books," Jeffer whispered, skirting the edge of the beast as if it were poison. "We should burn it."

"Burn it?" Balzac said. "It's dead."

"Burn it," Jeffer said.

But it was too late. They heard a leathery, cracking sound and the flesh dog's bulbous forehead split open and out struggled a creature the size of a man's heart. It glistened with moisture and, seeming to grow larger, spread its blue-black wings over the ruins of the flesh. It had all the delicate and alien allure of a damselfly.

"It's beautiful," Jamie said.

The creature gazed at them from one red-ringed eye (luminous amber, with a vertical black slit). The bone-thin legs ended in razor claws. The wings rose and fell with its breathing, which was steady and unruffled. The wings were those of a fallen angel, miraculous in that the black, shiny surface reflected greens and purples and blues. They were monstrously oversized for the body and the beast flapped them to keep its balance.

Jeffer moved first, fumbling for his gun. The creature, alarmed by the motion, moved its wings more vigorously.

Balzac put himself between Jamie and the creature, his swift embrace so tight she could not move, though she struggled against him.

Before Jeffer could aim, the creature launched itself into the air and spiraled up through the flock of hovering zynagill, scattering them in all directions. It made a swift pass over the amphitheater, still gaining altitude, then veered abruptly toward the west and began to pick up speed, soon out of sight.

Jamie wrenched herself from his grasp. "Why did you do that?"

"I didn't want it to hurt you."

"I don't need your help," she said, but when he looked into her eyes, he saw a sudden awareness of him that had not been there before. It sent a shiver through his body.

"What does it mean?" Balzac asked Jeffer, whose face was still clouded with thought.

"I don't know. We will have to tell the Con members."

"Where do you think it went?" Jamie asked.

"I think . . . I think it was a messenger. A beacon. I don't know."

"It was incredible," Jamie said.

The afternoon shadows so emphasized the brazen lines of her eyes, nose, cheekbones, that her image burned its way into Balzac's heart. He would have willingly lost himself in her, if only for the mystery he could not unravel—that her beauty was as luminous and sharp-edged as that of the winged creature. He experienced a rush of vertigo, fought for his balance on the edge of a darkly glittering future that would bind her to him beyond any hope of untangling.

Then he was falling again, willingly, gripped by sudden happiness, laughing as he saw the adventure of their lives together spreading out before him.

❑

Jeffer and Mindle stood side by side at the top of the stairs, looking down through the early morning gloom of dust motes. Mindle shook with spasms of tears, undoing all the savagery of his face. Below, on the landing, Balzac's body lay sprawled, a wide, black hole burned through his back. His hands were tightly clasped around the flame-distorted head of Jamie, whose lidless eyes stared sightless at them. Even in the shadows, Jeffer could see the thin, pale line of his brother's mouth fixed in a smile.

An emptiness Jeffer could not quantify or describe opened up inside of him. For a moment, he could not contain it, and he looked over at Mindle, intending to kill the boy should he discern even a trace of mockery upon that ancient face. But the tears had washed away the predatory sarcasm, the bloodlust, and he was almost vulnerable again, almost boyish again.

Jeffer slung the laser rifle over his shoulder and motioned to Mindle.

"Come on—if it's safe, we can bury them in the amphitheater," he said.

Horror, yes, and pain, and sadness—and yet, this relief: *It was over.* It was finished. And this final thought, which overcame the guilt: *I'm alive. I survived it.*

Mindle looked disoriented for a moment, as if he had been dreaming or listening to a distant and terrible music. Then the mask slid back over his face and he sneered, muttered a hollow "Yes," and followed as Jeffer walked down the steps to the body of his brother, the sun warm on his back.